FORGOTTEN
FLOWERS

For additional stimulating reading by fine authors please check out:

www.publishauthority.com

Scan this image with a Smart Phone app that reads QR Codes.

FORGOTTEN
FLOWERS

A Novel of Redemption and Second Love

Michael J. Sullivan

Publish Authority

Newport Beach, CA - Roswell, GA

www.PublishAuthority.com

Forgotten Flowers A Novel of Redemption and Second Love

This book is a work of fiction. Names, characters, places, and incidents are products of the author's imagination or are used fictitiously. Any resemblance to actual events or locales or persons, living or dead, are entirely coincidental.

Publish Authority – Offices in
Newport Beach, CA and Roswell, GA USA
PO Box 4015
Newport Beach, CA 92661

Cover design: Raeghan Rebstock
Editor: Gordon Jackson
Production Editor: Frank Eastland
Interior design: Daria Lacy
www.PublishAuthority.com

Dedication

There more than 28,000 assisted living residences in the United States caring for more than one million people. To those residents who have no one willing to visit them, no one willing to talk to them, and recall memories from the depths of oblivion, let them not be forgotten

Acknowledgments

There are many people I want to thank for their help in bringing this story to print. To my wife, Ginny, for her patience over the last ten months as I wrote and rewrote the story. To my daughter, Kelly Andrews, and to Chris Bitonti for their editing efforts. To Jerry Gritz for his help in guiding me in story organization. To Rob Gordon, for his editing efforts and never-ending emphasis to add description to scenes and characters. And lastly, to Jane Kotowski for her explanation and inspiration at the Palazzo Vecchio in Florence, Italy, to come with the title "Diaphanous Minds" for the story inside this story.

Other published works available on Amazon are: The Letters II, Letters to You? The Stolen Heart, Broken Chains, The Bench, and Newman's Wave authored by Mike Sullivan. With Secrets, I used my full name, Michael Sullivan, as author.

Donations from the sale of this novel will be given to Bright Focus Foundation, a nonprofit that supports research and education on brain and eye diseases such as Alzheimer's and macular degeneration.

Introduction

It was a beautiful late summer morning in rural Charleston, South Carolina, as Daniel Kilgore made his way to his now familiar destination. He had made his first trip to Magnolia Gardens a little over one year ago, just weeks before the start of school. He hadn't worried about his classroom and being ready or about his lesson plans because it had been his first year of retirement. He had taught elementary school for over thirty years—he had started right out of college and retired early.

Last summer he and his wife, Vivian, had seen a documentary on TV on the pros and cons of long-term health care insurance and facilities. Vivian, the consummate CPA, had announced that given their ages, they should research long-term facilities in the greater Charleston area. Daniel and Vivian had begun to research and evaluate the facilities. Magnolia Gardens was the only one which came close to meeting their exacting standards—at least on paper. Kilgore had gone to see if the facts reported online were accurate.

A year ago, the sign announcing, "Magnolia Gardens: A Caring Facility—five miles ahead on the right" had produced quite a different response from that elicited now. Then, the slogan seemed a bit "too cute," as if it were taken from a Dignity Health or Kaiser commercial. Now after a year of volunteering at the facility, he often thought the sign should read, "Magnolia Gardens: Home of the Forgotten."

Today, however, he was not in such a pessimistic frame of mind since lately his "friends" had made such great progress, thus making his volunteering efforts seem very much worthwhile. He had heard several staff members refer to Magnolia Gardens as "the dump," comparing it to an urban waste disposal system where people place their recycled items in one bin and trash in another. Kilgore had rejected the comparison but was willing to concede that for most patients, this was a terminal destination. The "dump analogy," however, had made a great impact on his thinking and reinforced his inherent optimism that "caring" should be the major focus, not "maintenance."

On his first trip, Kilgore had met the Executive Director, Madeline Orsini, who had given him a tour. Magnolia Gardens was nestled on nearly five beautifully landscaped acres, with the entrance to the main building set off by twin marble columns. It had one hundred one-bedroom suites and a forty-room wing devoted exclusively to those patients suffering from various degrees of dementia. In the latter, each room was furnished with many of the residents' personal furniture, mementos, and belongings because it was Orsini's belief that familiarity with the environment would help promote positive mental health. The positive environment was further promoted by the large communal dining room with tables set for four. There were also rooms for arts and craft, music, and socialization. The outside veranda was nicely arranged with space set aside for several conversation groups—residents, staff, and visitors.

After the tour, Orsini had led Kilgore to one of the tables and ordered tea. During the conversation which followed, he had discovered that Orsini was responsible for the entire operation and that she also had a Director of Volunteers who provided much of the needed manpower. She had explained that the volunteers were necessary because quite often the residents' family members, for whatever reasons, did not visit. Orsini believed that family visits, or volunteer substitutes, were necessary to the resident's well-being. Conversations with them were a bridge to the past. The lack of personal contact was especially hard on the dementia patients because they had trouble making sense of the present and past under the best of circumstances.

Since Vivian was still working, Kilgore needed some activity to occupy his time until they could do the "retirement stuff" together; but he would first need to be accepted as a volunteer, and secondly, he would need to find several patients who needed his help. While not impulsive by nature, Kilgore decided to become a volunteer— to become a bridge to the memories of those residents forgotten by their families.

Orsini had readily agreed to add him to the volunteer workforce once he had cleared a routine background check. He soon felt at home in the care environment. He gained access to the patient records, the staff room, and Orsini's ear. Before long, he found three women whom he was sure he could help. Over the previous year, he had worked diligently with these three "friends," as he called them, and had prepared complete records of his approaches, his successes, and his failures. He now had sufficient data to write a book, a chronicle of his bridging efforts.

Environment was further promoted by the large communal dining room with tables set for four. There were also rooms for arts and crafts, music, and socialization. The outside veranda was nicely landscaped and had space set aside for several conversation groups—residents, staff, and visitors.

Kilgore, at Orsini's urging, had collaborated with a dementia researcher and university professor to gain additional insight into his bridging efforts. Because of this initial contact, Kilgore obtained the help of the expert to help him with his own wife, who had suddenly developed the dreaded dementia symptoms. This collaboration would take a different path with the sudden death of Vivian. Having lost both his son and wife within the last two plus years, Kilgore was left needing more than grief to occupy his time. He had found it in his volunteer work; a way to get these events off his mind. His "friends" would save his sanity.

Part One

The flower sits among others whose time has come.

Once radiant and regal in appearance, emitting a heavenly sweet fragrance.

Chapter 1

MAGNOLIA GARDENS

ll of his adult life, Daniel Kilgore had held doors open for others—others being the thousands of children who filed through the doors of Summerville Elementary School where he had served for nearly thirty years as teacher and principal. Today he was grateful for the automatic opening front doors of Magnolia Gardens as he was holding four bouquets of summer flowers in his arms. He was glad to see Madeline Orsini was at the front desk. She was the kindest of all the staff who worked at Magnolia Gardens. Her compassion and kindness for both residents and staff made Magnolia Gardens more than a residential care facility. Madeline Orsini made it like home. She was also the Executive Director.

As a fully tenured professor at The College of Charleston, it had taken a lucrative package to lure Madeline Orsini away to become the Executive Director, but that's exactly what the Board of Directors had offered, and she had accepted. In addition to impeccable academic credentials, Orsini's physical presence added to her charm. Nearly 5' 7" in heels, she had the looks of a Hollywood starlet in professional attire. Her auburn hair hung in ringlets reaching her shoulders. Gold rimmed glasses accentuated her hazel eyes, and when she smiled, her face illuminated a sense of warmth and sincerity. She had finely formed lips with a hint of tinted gloss covering them.

"This one is for you," Daniel Kilgore said, handing her one of the bouquets. "The others are for my friends," he said with a smile.

Madeline thanked him and wondered why after Kilgore and his wife had visited the facility over a year ago, he continued to come and visit certain residents.

"Do you mind if I ask you something, Mr. Kilgore? It's something of a personal nature."

Kilgore set the remaining three bouquets on the counter. "Ask away."

His open nature had always appealed to Madeline.

"You've been coming here every week for well over a year, visiting the same three residents. Sometimes you even come three times a week. It is the kindest and most selfless thing I've ever seen. But you do realize that the moment you leave their rooms, they don't remember who you were or why you were there. Why do you do it?"

Though her remarks were sincere, they were tinged with an objective realism. She sounded professorial in tone as if she was probing his motive, so she could make some sort of value judgment. Kilgore was not accustomed to such a pointed question. He was somewhat shocked and taken aback.

"Let's sit outside, shall we?" Kilgore said, surprised by her question.

Madeline stepped out from behind the counter and followed Kilgore outside to a large veranda. Magnolia Gardens was nestled on nearly five lush green acres outside of Charleston, South Carolina. Besides the towering Magnolia tree in front of the facility, the property was liberally sprinkled with the iconic and omnipresent symbol of South Carolina estates—the Sabal Palmetto.

The outside veranda was covered by a huge pergola that extended nearly sixty feet in length and thirty feet wide. Flower pots filled with

Indian Pink, Northern Sea, Helen's flowers and Swamp Lilies, hung along the perimeter beams of the pergola. A four-foot high decorative wrought iron fence surrounded the veranda. There were a dozen spacious tables of teak wood with matching chairs available for residents, visitors, and staff. Kilgore and Madeline sat at one of the tables. Kilgore stared off into the distance as it was hard for him to formulate his thoughts. He turned to Madeline.

His face was darkened, brooding as he blurted, "You know, I don't come to see what they'll remember. I come because someone needs to listen and remember. To make it seem, at least for a time, that what they did mattered."

"Listen to what?" Madeline asked, a bit confused by Kilgore's obtuse answer.

When he looked at her, Madeline noticed a dampness in his eyes.

"Their loves, their heartaches, their successes and their failures; those small, sometimes inconsequential events that made up the sum of their lives. Someone should listen and remember."

Madeline thought *some woman would be very lucky to be loved by this man.* She was having difficulty maintaining her professionalism, and it was evidenced by her expression.

"You're amused by what I said?" Kilgore asked, reacting to the smile on Madeline's face.

"Oh no," Madeline said. "I was thinking how grateful their families would be knowing that you visit their loved ones so regularly."

She was clearly conciliatory in her tone.

"Wouldn't you think that's what they should be doing?" Kilgore responded. His voice seemed to carry the weight of all who lived there.

"Perhaps, yes," Madeline answered. "But the excuses to not meet that responsibility are numerous and justified in their minds," she answered. She had returned to her former objective, rational self.

Daniel Kilgore drew unwanted attention wherever he went. He was 6'2' and still carried the body of a cross-country runner he was in college. His jet-black hair was liberally sprinkled with gray around the temples. The dark horn-rimmed glasses he wore gave him the appearance of Clark Kent. But Daniel had at least one outstanding feature. His smile was infectious. He had the ability to make people laugh. He also knew how to listen. He applied these small gifts to audiences with the least reason to laugh and the most likely not to listen.

He would be their bridge to their past, the connection between their memories and the present. He hadn't been completely honest with Orsini when he told her why he was visiting the residents so regularly. He had another reason for not being straightforward with Orsini.

Magnolia Gardens was hardly the all too familiar residential facility for warehousing the elderly until they passed on to the next world. Its large dining room with tables set for four provided three well-prepared meals a day, and well above the institutional style most similar facilities provided. Bouquets of Hibiscus, Crested Iris, and Bee Balm adorned each table. The chairs, stuffed and covered with crimson fabric, were on small rollers to facilitate the residents seating themselves. Two large crystal water pitchers were on each table. Place settings were smartly rolled in large white napkins embroidered with a Magnolia tree. The floor was elegantly carpeted with a cut pile fabric of gold and red colors.

Across the hall from the dining room was a well-stocked reading room. The room was bright with recessed lighting and table lamps next to each of the over-sized chairs. The long rectangular room painted in a soft beige hue was particularly relaxing and inviting. Crown molding accented the ceiling. One wall featured floor to ceiling windows with plantation shutters, overlooking a well-manicured lawn bordered by a trellis of Honeysuckle vines.

Against the interior wall, a dozen rolling wooden bookcases made of Carolina pine were stationed. Residents could choose materials from them, or the bookcases could be easily rolled to their chairs over the level loop seafoam green carpet. There were twenty over-sized leather chairs, each with its own end table and lamp. A few even had audio plug-ins with headsets for residents who preferred to listen to CDs.

Thanks to Orsini's connection with The College of Charleston, a student majoring in Library Science worked three hours a day cataloging books, magazines, and newspapers for the residents.

The music room was the sanctuary where melodious sounds of the past met with the frail memories attached to them. TJ Harris, a smallish man in stature who wore thick coke bottle type glasses was the part-time staff who oversaw the music room. TJ was studying broadcasting at a local junior college. He had an unusually deep voice for his age and would practice his radio voice to the delight of the residents whenever they entered. "Good Morning and welcome to the melodious sounds of old with your host, TJ Harris." He never failed to get a smile in return.

TJ had cataloged a large collection of CDs consisting of songs from famous Broadway shows. Glen Miller, Artie Shaw, and the Dorsey Brothers were among the favorites in the Big Band section. Singers such as Tony Martin, Doris Day, Gordon McRae, Bing Crosby, Frank Sinatra and Dinah Shore, among others, were also available for their listening pleasure, as TJ would say. Every CD was on display along the wall to the left as the residents entered. TJ had thoughtfully arranged them in rows so those in wheelchairs could easily see them.

Twenty or so cushioned chairs were strategically spaced facing the wall to the right. Each had its own small CD player with earphones. The wall was adorned with the Cinema size pictures of many of the musical stars from the past. For those who could operate the CD player, TJ could give them whatever they wanted to listen to and if they couldn't remember, TJ had been developing a memory of what they liked to hear. If needed, he would personally get the resident to a chair and place the CD into the player for them.

For a young man so far apart in years from the residents he served, Harris took immense pleasure in watching the residents keep the beat by the tapping of their feet or the swaying of their heads. No one was ever disturbed by the occasional resident who broke into singing along with their favorite song. The far end of the room formed a small arc and was used by the music therapist for group activities.

Daniel Kilgore's presence at Magnolia Gardens was no accident, nor did he spend time there because he had nothing else to do. He and his wife, Vivian, had enrolled in long-term health care insurance for each other. It had been Vivian's idea to investigate some of the long-term care facilities in the area, with the full knowledge that living in such a pace was virtually inevitable, especially as they had no family to fall back on.

"You never know, Dan, someday one of us could drop from a stroke or be in an accident and have to go to a care facility. We should at least have an idea of what they're like and what's in store for us," she said.

If there was one thing Daniel Kilgore knew about his Vivian, it was this: if there was something, anything, she could worry about, she did. Within a few days after calling the insurance agent, Daniel Kilgore had the names and addresses of four of the best long-term care facilities in the greater Charleston area. They visited each one. Vivian Kilgore had a successful career as an accountant and was accustomed to taking meticulous notes. Each facility had its own separate notebook.

Daniel Kilgore had been an elementary school teacher then principal for over 30 years. For him, the hallmark of a well-run, well-taught school was simple: the laughter of children. Daniel applied this logic to his search. Did their staff make the residents smile and laugh or at least try? To his abject disappointment, only one of the facilities came close to meeting his criteria—Magnolia Gardens.

It was while going through this evaluation process that Daniel Kilgore realized he had missed a very critical element. Staff members can't do it all by themselves. They need help from caring, compassionate, and devoted volunteers, but especially loving family members. In combination, they could maximize the degree of happiness and joy in the lives of the residents.

During their tour of the Gardens, Kilgore had a chance to speak privately with the Executive Director, Madeline Orsini, when Vivian went off with a staff member to look at the recreational facilities.

"How do you manage it, Madeline? You've got staff members, volunteers and visitors all over the place," Kilgore asked

Not normally one to partake in comedic repartee, she responded with a chuckle, "In another lifetime, I was a juggler in the circus."

"No. Seriously, how do you do it?" Kilgore asked, somewhat annoyed at her flippant response.

From the tone of his voice, Madeline realized he was serious. Her reply took a different direction.

"Well, for one, we have a very stable workforce. There is little turnover because we pay our staff very well. Unfortunately, that's a negative for the families with loved ones here. Secondly, our Director of Volunteers does a terrific job of getting and keeping people who are interested in serving this type of population, especially when family members fade away."

"That's the last thing I would have expected," Kilgore said, "family members not coming."

His furrowed brow reflected his perplexed state of mind.

"Don't be too critical, Daniel," Orsini said. "The effects of dementia turn a person's mind into a giant jigsaw puzzle. After a while, they can't remember what pieces fit where, what face belongs to who and to what memory. It becomes so painful for some; they stop coming. And then there are the others."

"The others?"

"Yes," responded Orsini, as the frustration rose in her voice. "Those families who put a loved one here and think we can provide everything they need. We are not the familiar faces they long to see or the voices they need to hear. We can't share precious family memories because we are not their family. We can only be present when they choose not to be. We can't be the bridge to the memories of birthdays, anniversaries, graduations, weddings, the birth of grandchildren, memories of all that. All those events constitute the sum of their lives."

Madeline's telling words had a profound impact on Kilgore. He would be that bridge. Daniel was not impulsive, but once the facts presented themselves, he was capable of making quick decisions.

A week or so after his conversation with Orsini, Daniel Kilgore finished his morning coffee and left a half-finished crossword puzzle on the kitchen table. He walked down the hallway and opened his bedroom door. His wife was still sleeping. He picked up his leather man bag, as his wife called it, and headed off to the Gardens.

As he drove along the highway toward the Crestline exit, he thought about how easy it had been to gather information about his, "friends," as he called them, despite being a serious violation of the HIPPA law. All he had to do was listen to the conversations around him. That's how he learned about Sandra Cotton's family, her son, Jim, his wife, Carrie, and their two children. He was buying coffee one day in the lounge, and he overheard two recreational therapists talking about Sandra.

Ellen Taggart, a Recreational Therapist intern in her senior year at the University of South Carolina and Joan Wallace, the Senior Recreational Therapist, were having lunch together. Kilgore was sitting at a table nearby. Each wore nurses' scrubs which Kilgore found amusing since neither of the girls was a registered nurse. It was as though the apparel somehow lent legitimacy to their work.

"I asked her if she wanted to play checkers," Taggart said. "Sandra looked at me and said, 'Jim, that's my favorite game. You remembered?' I set the board up, and when I asked her if she wanted to go first, she looked at me and said, 'Carrie, where's Jim? I want to play with Jim, not you!' I got the feeling she didn't like this person, Carrie."

Wallace made a jaded laugh. "Carrie is her daughter-in-law, but I can go you one better. Last week I came to take her for a walk. Sandra asked me if I was up to it. I told her sure I was. She reached out and grasped my hand in the gentlest way. The poor dear looked at me and said in her sweetest grandmotherly fashion, 'Samantha, I know the baby's a surprise, but life has a way of taking care of such things.' She must've thought I was her granddaughter."

The two therapists got up to leave and walked past Kilgore's table.

"Hi, Daniel," Joan said. "How's your day going?"

"Like yesterday and the day before. It's another day," he replied. He didn't intend to sound so gloomy, but that's how it came out.

The fatalism in his voice suddenly made Joan feel depressed.

"At least you're on the green side of the grass," she replied.

Kilgore did not respond, at least perceptibly. To Daniel, who had a level of maturity far beyond the young woman, her remark was not amusing.

So are the residents here, he thought. *Being on the green side of the grass isn't all it's cracked up to be. Merely existing isn't enough. They are still deserving of a measure of a full life. There must be more. Someone must do more!*

*I*f staff continued talking about the residents, Madeline was going to have a huge confidentiality issue with her staff, Kilgore thought, as he was finishing his lunch in the staff break room. Hannah McCoy, a nurse with ten years' experience at the Gardens and Melody Hoover, the charge RN who was nearing the end of a thirty-year career in health care, had just sat down with their trays.

"I just finished the saddest intake I've done in months," Hannah said.

"How so?" Melody inquired, thinking that every intake was sad. After all, these are people nearing the end of their time.

"Dolores Samuels was admitted last month. I emphasized to her son and his wife how important it was in the beginning to decide on specific visiting days and who was coming. The trauma of being left with no one seeing you, going cold turkey, so to speak, can exacerbate dementia."

Hannah took a sip of coffee and continued her description of events.

"For nearly fifteen minutes, the son and his wife checked out my calendar. Every time he asked his wife if a certain date was good she'd say 'I guess so.' Finally, they settled on the first of three visits, but said they'd have to decide on who was coming and they would get back to me. No one showed up for any of the visits. Guess no one could decide," McCoy said.

Across the aisle, finishing his lunch, Kilgore made notes. His level of concern and desire to help was only accentuated by what he had heard—so much so that he failed to finish the last of his favorite variety of chips, something he seldom did. With a new-found sense of eagerness, he began to formulate a plan of action.

On his next visit, Kilgore was signing the volunteer check-in binder when Madeline approached the counter. The expression on her face was pained. She swallowed hard, her eye brows lowered and pinched together. She crumpled the piece of paper in her hand.

Stating the obvious, Kilgore asked, "Something wrong?"

Orsini placed the crumpled paper on the counter, attempting to smooth out the wrinkles.

"Another attempt to ease his conscience," Orsini said. "George Hillman's check for his wife, Mary."

The cynicism in her voice was unmistakable. She turned to Kilgore to give him her full attention.

"Too bad he doesn't visit her as regularly as he sends these checks." The disdain in her voice had not lessened.

"You're suggesting that I get involved? Sounds like this lady could use a visitor," Kilgore responded.

"Oh Daniel, you'd be a lifesaver if you would add Mary to your list of friends," Orsini said. It was comforting for her to see the compassion that one person can have for another manifest itself in action.

"Consider it done," Kilgore said, not realizing the enormity of his answer for Orsini. The coming weeks would be a testament to that.

His trio was complete: Dolores Samuels, Sandra Cotton, and Mary Hillman. They were three souls forsaken by those who should have cared the most. The sons of Dolores Samuels and Sandra Cotton came into this world and survived with the nurturing love of their mothers. Mothers never too busy to listen to their son's problems. Mothers who seemed to have mystical powers of understanding and the tenderness to smooth the pains and disappointments of growing up. Now they were but a passing memory to the ones they loved. Present, yet absent at the same time.

George Hillman once had a wife, a soulmate, who shared his dreams and abated his fears of failure as he ascended to success in the financial world. Yet when she needed him the most, when her life's dream was about to come true, overwhelming greed caused her husband to forget all she had done and eventually extinguish her memory as well.

Fully understanding that he lacked the professional credentials to proceed, Daniel Kilgore would endeavor to be their bridge to everything that had previously made their lives complete and thus worth living. He was about to embark on a strange journey. His quest was to find a way to be a connection between the present and past, to retrieve the long-forgotten moments of happiness that could be shared once again. For his own private reason, Kilgore was thankful for this opportunity, but he also wondered why he was the only one visiting.

Chapter 2

THE BEGINNINGS OF GUILT

*J*im Cotton looked at the calendar and was suddenly overcome with the guilt that settled on his shoulders. He placed his hands on the bathroom sink as his head slumped forward.

"Jim, are you coming?" His wife called impatiently from the other room. "We don't want to be late."

Resuming control of his emotions, James Cotton straightened up and stared into the mirror. He stood just over six feet tall, a trim one hundred and seventy pounds, with striking blue eyes and ebony hair sprinkled with traces of gray. *I'm a good man, he thought. I'm a Colonel in the United States Air Force. I oversee a $15 million procurement budget. I have a lovely wife, my son, William, a sophomore at Rice University in Texas, and my daughter, Samantha, a Cotillion Princess, who has finished her sophomore year at Vanderbilt University. I'm a good, decent man. I* *have no reason to feel guilty.* Despite his best efforts to the contrary, guilt was what he felt.

Caroline Cotton stood in front of the full-length mirror in their bedroom, admiring her gown. At forty-five, she caught the eye of every male when she glided into a room. Brunette hair flowed to shoulder length. Rich brown eyes sparkled in the light. Carrie, as she was called by family and friends, had an hourglass figure thanks to years of trying every diet known to mankind. She reveled in the attention her breast augmentation brought her. She glanced at her watch. *Damn, if he doesn't hurry up we'll be late,* she thought. Patience of any kind was often absent.

The Air Force Birthday Ball was the social event of the year for Carrie. She could care less about the military tradition involved. This was her opportunity to massage the inner circle of General's wives which she could be in if her husband made the next promotional board, and a position far more suited to her sense of self-aggrandizement.

James came into the bedroom. She loved to see him in his dress blues. She'd love him even more if there were a general's star on the epaulets. Carrie walked over to him, stopping a few feet away, "You look very handsome, Jim," she said, as she adjusted his tie.

"You know what today is, don't you?" He asked.

"Of course, darling," she said. "It's the birthday of the United States Air Force."

Jim moved around her to stand in front of the full-length mirror. He was hoping not to see the sense of shame that overwhelmed him. He was wrong, as he looked at his reflection. "It's my mother's birthday," he said, conscious that his wife would view his emotion as a character flaw.

Carrie opened her gem-studded jewelry box, took out a double strand of ivory pearls, oblivious to her husband's emotional torment. She slammed the top of the jewelry box closed. She walked in front of her husband and turned around, holding up each end of the necklace, It was as though she hadn't heard a word he had said.

"Be a darling and connect this," she cooed.

Jim snapped the clasp. He would have gladly climbed Mount Everest in the nude if he could avoid the conversation which he was about to initiate. He didn't have to as Carrie started it for him.

"Jim, let's not have another conversation about visiting your mother. Her mind is gone. She doesn't know you from that half-wit janitor at the Officer's Club. If we did visit her, she wouldn't remember what was said or who said it. You might as well have a conversation with a perfect stranger." She picked up her evening purse and said, "Let's go, my love," obviously completely satisfied with her objective analysis and entirely emotionally detached. None of this did the slightest bit to alleviate his growing anxiety.

Fred Samuels flopped backward on the bed, *"God, I hate this,"* he thought. Fred Samuels was a nationally renowned expert in the mechanics of fiber-optic communication and its relationship to surgical procedures. His company, Biometrics, Inc. sent him all over the world to make presentations. After three days in Australia, he was finally headed home to Dallas, Texas. Seventeen hours later his flight landed at Dallas-Fort Worth International. His five o'clock shadow and tired eyes signaled his fatigue. An hour and a half later, the limo dropped him off at his home in Bluff View, Texas.

When his company had relocated to the Dallas-Fort Worth area years earlier, he and his wife, Sheila, had sat down with a real estate agent to discuss neighborhoods. He could still remember the frustration on the face of the agent after touring neighborhood after neighborhood.

"Sheila, you're the wife. What are you looking for in a neighborhood? Good schools, close to shopping, you tell me," asked the agent, barely able to control her impulse to throw her MLS book out the window of the car.

Exasperated, Sheila Samuels kept her eyes on the mansions they were passing by and responded, "I really don't know. Ask my husband."

Glancing in her rearview mirror, the agent noticed the husband engrossed with something on his iPad.

"Well, Fred? What are you looking for in a neighborhood?"

There was no response. The agent repeated the question with greater intensity.

"Huh?" He asked as he looked up from his iPad, "What was that?"

The agent focused her frustration on the steering wheel on which she now held a death grip.

"A neighborhood. What are you looking for in an ideal neighborhood? The proverbial golf course, lake frontage, close to work, what?"

The agent's displeasure grew with each failed response to her professional inquiries.

"I really don't care that much. Ask Sheila," he said, rapidly returning to his iPad.

To this day, he couldn't tell you how or who had made the decision, but eventually a decision had been made and eventually a home was found. It appealed to Carrie's sense of entitlement: four bedrooms, a three-car garage, a gourmet kitchen, formal dining room and a swimming pool/spa combination in the backyard.

Fred set his bags down and closed the door. The quiet in the room was somehow disturbing.

"I'm home," he called out.

"Be right there," his wife called from the kitchen. She emerged with a freshly chilled bottle of Chardonnay and two glasses. She knew he preferred Pino Grigio, but the last bottle had long been consumed. She made a mental note that she should get some more soon.

"For my Prince," she said, as she extended her arms to allow him to put his arms around her waist.

He pulled her close to him, kissing her gently on the lips. "For my Princess," he whispered.

These keywords once uttered in all sincerity, had begun to sound rote. Their affection for each other had waned in recent years.

She already knew the answer, but somehow, she still had to ask, "Long trip?" as they rested on the leather L-shaped sofa.

"Seventeen hours, but who's counting?" Fred replied, the sigh in his voice a reflection of his frustration. He let his head rest on the back of the sofa. He felt the presence of a still small but mounting tension headache.

"I hate this job," he groaned. With his eyes closed, he recited a litany of complaints. He never enjoyed working for others, but this perception of the joys of self-employment was not in line with the reality of living that life.

"I have to explain procedures to a bunch of supposed technical experts who don't have the collective IQ to change a lightbulb. When I got there, Biotech didn't have the feed to the computer display hooked up properly. When I called them to fix it, I got a song and dance about not having a technician available, so I did it myself."

"Honey, if you hate the job that much, sell the damn company," she said determinedly. "You can always find another job," she said.

Really! Fred thought, *and who's going to pay the mortgage, buy you the car you want, take you on the vacations you want, and put the kids through college.* He loved his wife but trying to get her to understand the complexities of their financial situation was hopeless. He looked at the end table next to the couch and saw the small picture of his mother. Perhaps it was the frustration of his current situation, but he welcomed the change of subject.

"How long has it been since I've seen my mom?"

"I'm not sure," she replied, as she refilled her wine glass, now distracted by her Facebook posting.

Fred picked up the picture and studied it.

"This was taken when Jimmy graduated from high school, and that was almost three years ago."

"If you say so," she commented absently, becoming more detached and absorbed in her Facebook posting.

"We need to see her!" His words almost defiant.

Fred's determination to make this happen was apparent even to Sheila, who now clearly understood it was important to him. He seldom was this forceful with her, but when he was, she knew it was time to take notice.

"Okay," Sheila answered, putting her iPhone down for the moment. "When do you want to go?"

"What's on your calendar for the next month?" Fred asked with mild annoyance. He knew he was fighting an uphill battle with her on this.

"I don't know," Sheila said, as she continued to scroll down her Facebook page, her emotional detachment resurfacing.

"Could you check please?" He answered, his irritation growing.

Slightly miffed that he needed to know right now, but inclined to placate him, Sheila set her glass on the coffee table. Her iPhone was synced to her iPad where she stored everything. Half a dozen dates were available.

"Okay, when do you want to go?" she asked

"How about the week of the third?" He suggested.

"I guess so," Sheila replied. "I'll have to reschedule an appointment. How about you." She immediately went back to her iPhone.

Fred opened his iPad. "Damn, I'm scheduled to go to the Mayo Clinic that week. How about the week of the eleventh for you?"

Without even looking at her calendar, Sheila said, "I guess so," with absolute indecisiveness.

"No way!" he said, with a ton of exasperation, "We're committed to going to the lake with Jim and Donna on their houseboat that weekend."

Good, he saw it, she thought. Sheila Samuels had gotten everything she wanted in life by not deciding herself, but letting Fred or time make that decision - or so it seemed.

"**N**ice round, George," said Leo Ainsworth, George's oldest friend, and his personal attorney.

His smallish stature betrayed his huge ego, and Leo Ainsworth had just that. After all, he was one of the most successful attorneys in Southern California, specializing in tax law. His bald head, rimmed by a fringe of brown hair, horn-rimmed glasses and a perpetual cigar in his mouth would never land him on the cover of GQ magazine. At the other end of the good looks spectrum was George Hillman. At 6' 2" and blessed with good genes, even at fifty-five years old, Hillman could have been a professional model. His hazel eyes, tan complexion, and alluring smile attracted more attention from his clients' wives than he wanted.

"And you didn't do badly either, Gilda," Leo added, as the three sat in the clubhouse at the 19th hole of Torrey Pines Country Club in San Diego, California. The three looked out the expansive glass window to the 18th green at a foursome approaching the water hazard that lay before them. Each was enjoying their preferred beverage as they watched all four golfers put their balls in the water.

Gilda Ellis would be viewed by the uninformed as George Hillman's trophy wife—that is, if he weren't already married. George's marriage was not a topic to be brought up in front of Gilda Ellis, and Leo had already learned that lesson. Once when the three of them were out for dinner, Leo let it slip out, and in a most innocent manner, how much George's wife Mary loved the seaside restaurant where they were dining. "Jesus! not another Mary story!" Gilda snapped. Leo Ainsworth never mentioned Mary's name again in Gilda's presence. Though an experienced attorney, he was never quite able to steady himself against her feminine vehemence.

Gilda finished her glass of white wine and excused herself to go to the ladies' room. George and Leo politely stood up and couldn't help but notice several necks twisting, part of the male radar response network, to catch a glimpse of Gilda as she passed by.

"She's got a figure, doesn't she?" Leo remarked.

A barely perceptible and disinterested shrug of George's shoulders was all the answer Leo would get. Leo Ainsworth had been George's best man at George and Mary's wedding. Maybe George had forgotten that fact, but Leo had not. Now that they had a moment free from Gilda, he asked, "George, your wedding anniversary is coming up soon. How's Mary doing?"

George quickly turned in the direction of the ladies' room to make sure Gilda didn't catch any of the conversation, and once he was confident that she was beyond hearing range, he turned back to Leo. Clearly, Gilda's ability to intimidate was not confined to Leo.

"As well as can be expected. I get a letter each quarter with the medical update."

"And?"

"Same as always, Leo, a steady degradation of cognitive functioning is the way they express it."

Leo pressed the point. "When was the last time you saw her?"

"Christ, Leo! What are you doing, writing a book?" he groused.

The subject was clearly more emotionally charged than Leo realized.

"Hey, let's not forget Mary was a friend of Lois and mine too."

There was an awkward moment before George finally responded to Leo's question.

"The day I put her in Magnolia Gardens."

"My God, it's been almost two years," Leo said.

"That's right," George replied, as he signaled a nearby waiter to bring him another double scotch, neat. "She barely recognized me then. I can't imagine how she is now."

Though brief, his response was not devoid of emotion.

Why do you have to imagine, you thoughtless son-of-a-bitch! Why don't you know? Leo thought, but then he knew the answer to that—Gilda Ellis.

Returning from her trip to the powder room, Gilda sat down with George and Leo. George sat staring at his glass which he was slowly turning with his fingers. Leo stared out the expansive glass windows overlooking the 18th green. The verdant expanse below him would have been a delight to any avid golfer. There was an evident change in the atmosphere since she left.

"What?" Gilda asked, "not a spat over the score?"

She knew that George and Leo were both highly competitive. They often came to loggerheads over their reported scores. Though exchanges were sometimes testy, they were always couched in their mutual understanding of a time-tested friendship.

George remained silent. Clearly, he was annoyed by her for delving into a matter that did not concern her.

"No, not the score," answered Leo.

"Then what?" Gilda asked as she dug down into her clutch purse. She quickly obtained and lit a cigarette. She puffed distractedly for a moment on her Virginia Slim, then abandoned it to a glass ashtray.

It was George that fell on his sword, sensing the futility of the silence.

"It was Mary. Leo asked about Mary. I tried to get him to understand why I don't visit, but he is not buying it."

Retrieving her cigarette, Gilda took a long and deliberate drag. In a failed attempt to disguise her anger, she slowly exhaled until all the smoke was gone from her lungs. She gently tapped the cigarette on the edge of the ashtray. She was not adept at concealing her displeasure.

"I've explained to George countless times that Mary is probably not much more than a breathing body, hardly a wife by any definition. Certainly, a divorce would not be a disgrace. Oh, and I have never quibbled over the expense of her care."

She made a point of appearing to be quite humble in the manner she delivered her remarks.

Suddenly Leo Ainsworth felt very sorry for his friend not only because of Mary's condition but also because of Gilda Ellis. His friend had attempted to escape from the guilt of what he had done only to imprison himself in a relationship with an unfeeling woman.

Chapter 3

DANIEL'S PLAN

*T*he monthly staff meeting was just about over; there was just one more item Madeline Orsini needed to cover.

"There's going to be a conference in a couple of weeks at The College of Charleston, which some of you may want to attend. The overall theme is the reconnection of neurological pathways as it relates to traumatic brain injuries; however, there are some sessions more directly related to dementia. For any of you who choose to attend, I will pick up the enrollment expenses and authorize the time off," Madeline said, as she passed around a handful of flyers.

"You know, Madeline, this is exactly the kind of thing some of our regular volunteer staff need to attend. I'm thinking in particular of Daniel Kilgore," said Evelyn Stevens, Director of Volunteer Services. A matronly woman in her early sixties, Stevens was only months away from retirement and saw a certain potential in Daniel Kilgore as a possible replacement. Daniel Kilgore had not wanted to appear unappreciative when Orsini had approached him about attending the conference. He had told her that of course, he'd be glad to attend. After all, his friends had already started exhibiting certain symptoms of dementia. It wasn't until he had gotten home and reviewed the pamphlet more closely, that he saw the session he wanted to attend—Degeneration of Neurological Pathways because of TBI (Traumatic Brain Injury). Orsini didn't need to know why.

On arriving home, Kilgore set the pamphlet on the coffee table, already littered with day-old mail, and walked down the hallway to the master bedroom. He opened the door slowly. The hospital bed was raised at a slight angle. His wife was in a deep sleep, exhausted from an intensive physical therapy session earlier in the day. Aluminum braces held both hands in a curved position. The reality of her physical decline caused his heart to ache—a once vibrant and active Vivian reduced to this. Because of the car accident nearly a year ago, nothing seemed to hold together the memories in her mind. Kilgore wanted desperately to talk with her of those precious times. He slowly closed the bedroom door and returned to the living room. Picking up the pamphlet, he thought, perhaps naively, he could open the doors to memories passed. If hope were his only chance, he would take it.

Apparently, this conference was much more popular than Kilgore had been led to believe. Though it was a Saturday, the parking lot adjacent to the Graduate School of Education/Mental Health was packed. Founded in 1770, the buildings on the campus of The College of Charleston reflected the revolutionary times of its birth. The colonial motif of the red brick education building with its marble columns, ivy-covered walls, and obligatory statues of southern revolutionary war and civil war heroes, brought Kilgore back to his collegiate days at Clemson University.

There was a large sign on the steps of the building directing those attending the conference to the registration table inside. Kilgore had mailed in his preregistration form for the conference so he could avoid the long line at the registration table. His eyes ran down the list of a dozen specific sessions that were offered and the classroom number next to it. There it was, the one he wanted, Room 201.

He made his way up to the second floor and down the hallway to Room 201 and went inside. The room had been originally set up for graduate seminars, so rather than individual desks, there was a large oval conference table. There were a couple of people already sitting at the table exchanging viewpoints on the state of mental health in America. Kilgore intentionally sat far away from them. Within thirty minutes, the table was full. By his count, about twenty people were attending the session. Promptly at nine o'clock a.m., the presenter came into the room.

"My sincere apologies for being late," she said," but excuse the expression, parking's a bitch!"

Her apology brought outright laughter from many at the table.

"My name is Doctor Jane Lincoln. My expertise is in the field of regeneration of neurological pathways damaged by traumatic brain injury. Our focus today will be the current trends in this field of research. Doctor is an academic title; please feel free to call me Jane. I've been on the faculty of The College of Charleston for nearly ten years and have done extensive research in the field of traumatic brain injury and memory restoration. I would like to know something about each of you. Let's go around the room, starting on my right. Please tell everyone your name and what drew you to this conference and, in particular, this session."

Around the table it went; some were graduate students enrolled in the master's program in Mental Health, others were professionals working in various rehabilitation facilities dealing with traumatic brain injuries. Kilgore realized he was in over his head when compared to the experience of the others sitting around the table, but then he had a special reason for being there that had nothing to do with work experience.

"My name is Daniel Kilgore, and I work as a volunteer at Magnolia Gardens. I thought this session might help me be more effective in dealing with the residents who are suffering from memory loss as the result of dementia or traumatic brain injury."

His work at Magnolia Gardens veiled his true intention, the opportunity to have his old Vivian back, at least in part. His straightforward and concise response did nothing to alleviate any feelings that he might be somewhat out of his element.

Doctor Lincoln pondered Kilgore's response carefully, responding, "Without question, Mr. Kilgore, there are many similarities between dementia cases and traumatic brain injury cases in terms of restorative capabilities of neurological pathways. Perhaps we can talk one-on-one after today's session?" she asked.

Kilgore smiled. *This might work after all*, he thought. All thought and concern of not belonging in the session vanished. It was evident in the instructor's response that she saw a legitimacy in his presence at the seminar. His new-found comfort level made him more receptive to what followed.

For the next three hours, Kilgore remained mostly silent, taking notes on what was said by Doctor Lincoln, especially when she spoke of something called "temporal relationships between auditory or visual stimuli and physiological response." She answered questions without belittling the questioner. Though the subject language was somewhat technical, Doctor Lincoln lectured in a way that made it understandable even to a layman.

At some point during the lecture, Kilgore began to take notice of the speaker herself. She dressed professionally, but that did not completely hide her figure. Emerald green eyes accentuated her tan complexion. She wore her brown hair almost shoulder length, with the ends flipped slightly upward. Her deep dimples emphasized the smile on her face. The gloss lipstick she wore framed the most perfect white teeth Kilgore had ever seen. Soon Kilgore found himself more attracted to her than to her lecture. That's when it struck him. An overwhelming sense of guilt over the illicit feelings gripping him. It was as if he had been caught in a tryst. He forced himself to look away from her. However, when she brought up the topic of associative stimuli and degraded memory recovery, he refocused his attention. After a time, it was evident that Lincoln was drawing to a conclusion.

"Ladies and gentlemen, if there are no further questions, I want to thank all of you for attending and commend you on your decision to pursue work in the area of traumatic brain injury."

As she gathered up her materials, Lincoln noticed that Daniel Kilgore had yet to stand up. *Good,* she thought, *there's something I wanted to talk to him about.* Kilgore had purposely stalled as those who had attended the session were leaving the classroom. He was uncomfortable asking his final question. Lincoln surprised him by approaching him first and asking him to discuss a recent research project. The fact that she was interested in his input thrilled him.

This might be my opportunity, Kilgore thought.

Well, I'm retired, Doctor Lincoln, so my time is your time," he replied with a grin.

His infectious smile made her laugh and feel a little embarrassed at the same time. She had noticed the wedding ring on his left hand. Though she had not expected it, this observation somehow disappointed her.

"There's a small sandwich shop just around the corner. Perhaps we could get a bite to eat, and you could call your wife and see if she would be interested in coming also?" Lincoln asked.

As professional as she tried to be, a slight blush spread over her face. Kilgore liked that. Already impressed with her appearance, professionalism, and knowledge, he was beginning to appreciate her personality. Though Lincoln's offer to have Kilgore's wife come along was intended to neutralize any appearance of impropriety, it drove Kilgore into a confluence of emotions he was ill-prepared to deal with at that moment.

"I'm afraid my wife will not be able to come. She was in an accident nearly a year ago, and recovery has been slow."

Uncomfortable with her offer to have lunch with Kilgore, Lincoln offered to postpone it.

"That won't be necessary, Doctor. I have a friend sitting with her today. I would ask you this small favor - if you'll talk human speak and not that scientific jargon I spent the last three hours listening to, lunch would be my pleasure. I'm afraid most of those folks speak a language I don't understand."

"Then, allow me to translate anything you don't understand over a chicken salad sandwich," Lincoln said.

"Lead the way," Kilgore said, as he held the seminar room door open.

"Two chicken salad sandwiches, one sweet tea, one iced tea, for here," Lincoln told the young teenager behind the counter.

Kilgore reached around her and slipped the counter-boy a twenty. From the smile on the clerk's face, he might as well have worn a sign saying 'high school kid needs tips.'

"My treat."

Sam's Deli was a favorite eating place for those in the neighborhood to grab a bite to eat on the run. Sam had a small meat counter with a variety of Italian meats, cheeses, home-made rolls, and a small number of tables as he did mostly take-out orders.

As they settled at a corner table, Kilgore asked, "So what exactly is this research project you mentioned?" He took a sip of his sweet tea, taken aback somewhat by how quickly he had become comfortable with her.

Jane Lincoln leaned forward, eager to present her idea.

"Simply stated, my particular area of research specializes in neurological degeneration due to traumatic brain injury. However, I believe there could be significant similarities between those who have suffered traumatic brain injury and those in various stages of dementia as it relates to memory regeneration."

Kilgore took a bite of his sandwich and followed that with another sip of his tea. He was transfixed by the subject matter. His features appeared serious and committed to her every word. Finishing his sandwich suddenly seemed unimportant.

As he thought about the description of her research work, he queried, "Ok, but how exactly does my volunteering at Magnolia Gardens fit into that scheme? I am just a volunteer. What could I possibly add to a sophisticated research project like yours?"

"I'd be asking you to do the same thing with the people you visit that I'm having my own research assistants do with the people they are visiting at several rehabilitation facilities here in Charleston," Lincoln said. "It's possible that you, as a volunteer, might have some insights the research staff do not."

"And that is what?"

"I believe it is possible to reestablish damaged neurological pathways through a combination of something I call 'Repetitive Stimuli Application' and the use of personalized background information," she said.

The expression of Kilgore's face caused Lincoln to apologize for using scientific jargon.

"Let me put it this way. You're familiar with the term muscle memory?"

Kilgore nodded as he had just taken a bite of his sandwich.

"It's the same concept. My thesis is if you stimulate the brain with sufficient repetitive information, eventually the damaged neurological pathways will cause a response without the brain trying."

"There's got to be more to it than that."

"Yes, there is," Lincoln continued. "Some of the variables I'm interested in require that when my research assistants are working with a client, they must track the time of the visit and the exact activity they used with the client. Repetitive stimuli application means they must track the exact number of times a specific question is asked, or a personalized object or past event is used to strengthen a disassociated memory. Most importantly, they must notate to the second, the time between stimuli application and response, or in some cases, stimuli application and a fading of awareness."

Kilgore smiled. "That's quite a lot for what you say are a few variables. Are there more?" He had the look of someone slightly bemused, but still invested in the conversation.

"If you know anything about neurological research, Mr. Kilgore, you know the more variables that are addressed, the more significant the results. Most of my research assistants are pursuing advanced degrees. They need to get used to this type of research scrutiny."

"Obviously, you haven't told them about the daunting task of being published," Kilgore said.

Lincoln titled her head slightly, as an impish grin appeared indicating her surprise at his comment, "What do you know about publishing?"

"When I was working on my master's at Clemson, I remember from my college professors complaining about the pressure to publish or perish."

Lincoln allowed herself to feel a little excited, but only her professional side. She wanted to reinforce the value Kilgore could provide.

"As a volunteer at Magnolia Gardens, do you visit on a regular basis?"

"Yes."

"Do you see the same residents when you visit?"

"Yes again."

"With your education background, data collection data should not be a problem. I'll give you precise parameters of what to ask and how to document it, and if it matters, there might be a small stipend involved. It wouldn't be much, but it could put gas in your car."

She realized at once what a small token this was in comparison to her requested investment.

Kilgore leaned back in his chair and eyed Lincoln as if they were in a Texas Hold'em tournament. He sat expressionless, focusing on her eyes, looking for some sign or tell, as poker players refer to it, that she would be receptive to his plan. He carefully delivered his response in measured tones.

"Ms. Lincoln, let me make you a counter-proposal, and if you accept, I believe we will have a basis for an understanding."

After listening to Kilgore's proposal, Lincoln recognized there was more than a basis for an understanding. She was nothing less than dumbfounded by Kilgore's proposal. She was being offered an opportunity to work one-on-one with Kilgore's wife. With unfettered access to medical records, it was a researcher's dream come true; but it came at a price—no longer would traumatic brain injury be an antiseptic academic pursuit. She would study the frustration and the depression of those suffering from traumatic brain injury and the helplessness their loved ones endure in a real, live subject.

Chapter 4

DOLORES SAMUELS' PATH TO MAGNOLIA GARDENS

There was no love lost between Brenda Samuels and her brother-in-law, Fred, and his wife, Sheila. For years, Brenda stifled her true feelings as Mitchell took on more and more of the burden of looking after his mother.

"I don't get it, Mitch. With a smidgen of help from your brother or his wife, checking on Dolores would be so much easier."

The tone in her voice echoed what his conscience had already told him. Mitchell knew his wife was right. He tried talking to Fred and Sheila on separate occasions, but nothing worked. Fred was sympathetic to Mitchell's plight and promised to do better. Sheila was equally sympathetic and promised nothing.

The brothers were enjoying a rare game of golf together. Mitch had much more time to attend to his game, and it showed in his score.

"I don't know why they call it the rough the way its manicured," Fred said. "Or maybe I have just spent so much time in it, I can't tell the difference.

They sat in their cart awaiting their turn on the elevated tee of the third hole at Coastal Pines golf course. Mitchell nodded in agreement as he gazed out over the fairway. The foursome ahead of them had just teed off and were half-way down the steep fairway headed to the green.

Towering pines bordered both sides of the fairway. Not a single pine needle or pinecone was anywhere to be seen. The rough, if you could call it that, had been freshly mowed and looked as smooth as the fairway they'd be driving down. The smell of freshly cut grass and the fragrance of the pines rode the gentle coastal breeze up the hill to the tee area.

"Nothing like it," Mitch said, as he inhaled deeply, enjoying every particle of the fragrant breeze.

"Amen to that, brother," replied Fred.

The foursome on the green had just started to putt. With a foursome already ahead of them waiting to drive, Mitchell thought there was plenty of time to ask him now.

"Fred, I know you travel a lot, but how far out in advance do you know when you'll be gone?"

"Quarterly, why?" His brother asked.

"It's mom. As it stands right now, Brenda and I do everything for her, and I'm sorry to say this my brother, but Sheila is no help at all. I was thinking if we could get together and go over your schedule we could divide up the visits among the four of us."

Fred took a swig of water, now wishing he had added several ounces of rye whiskey to it. He was already laden with guilt regarding his mother, and his brother was unintentionally intensifying that feeling.

"Between you and me, Mitch, I don't get any help from Sheila either. I can't remember the last time her hands touched a vacuum cleaner, much less picked up clothes, hamburger wrappers, and God knows what else that's lying on the floor. She treats the kitchen sink like it's the terminal destination for dirty dishes."

Mitchell was sorry he had brought up the subject. He loved his brother and was fully aware of Sheila's shortcomings, probably more than Fred.

"I've tried talking to her about Mom and everything else, but Sheila's idea of communication is to sit there until she's tired of hearing me talk. Then she walks away, throws her hands up in the air and groans, 'Tell me what you want me to do!' I tell her, and nothing happens."

The foursome ahead of them finally teed off and headed down the cart path. One of the groups' shots careened wildly to the left causing the others to laugh wildly. Mitchell and Fred both grabbed seven irons and approached the tee area. A short par three, they could clearly see the flag lazily flapping in the wind.

"Maybe if you talk to her, Mitchell, you'd have better luck," Fred said.

The blank stare on his brother's face did not bode well for that conversation.

"I'll try, Fred."

Both of them knew that Mitch would influence Sheila like a chipmunk challenging a forest fire.

Watching Fred distractedly swing his seven iron with one hand, Mitchell asked him, "Fred, are you happy with that woman?"

"What do you mean happy?" What does it mean to be happy?"

"You know. Are you truly happy in your marriage?" Mitchell replied, more than a little annoyed that he had to explain his question.

Fred rested the head of his club on the ground. The verdant scene of tranquility around him could not conceal the growing tension.

"What part of for better or worse is supposed to mean happy, Mitch? Better than worse is only not as bad."

With that, the two men absently pursued their game, each to his own thoughts.

To be successful selling health supplements, you had to do more than just sell it; you had to demonstrate the benefits via your own persona. Sheila Samuels was certainly healthy looking. Too bad she didn't pay the same degree of attention to her housework. Thanks to weekly sessions at a tanning salon, she had a perpetual bronzed complexion. Daily workouts at her Pilates gym and an absurd devotion to the "Buns of Steel" exercise regimen had produced a model's figure.

However, it took a year of constantly nagging her husband to get her what she really wanted: breast augmentation. Sheila Samuels not only wanted to make a sale whenever she walked into a fitness center, but she also craved the ogling stares of any male in the place.

Fred had emailed Mitchell his travel schedule following their golf game. Mitchell took advantage of Fred being out of town to schedule a lunch appointment with Sheila.

"With your devotion to good health, I'm surprised you picked a place like this for lunch," Mitchell said, as his eyes scanned the menu at the local Waffle House.

"A little cheating now and then doesn't hurt," Sheila said, as she waved to the waitress.

Mitchell Samuels was about to discover that Shelia's diet regimen wasn't the only thing she cheated on.

"I've been meaning to talk to you and Fred about Mom. Since he's out of town, I thought I'd start with you."

"What about her?" Sheila said, her eyes never wavering from the menu.

It was evident that her list of priorities, whatever they might be, didn't include that subject.

"Twice a week, either Brenda or I stop in to see Mom," Mitchell said. "Fred and I talked, and we thought if you could take a week it would ease the burden on Brenda and me. When Fred's not traveling, he could take your place on the schedule."

Sheila put her menu down and picked up her iPhone. What had begun as a distraction now was multiplying into genuine irritation.

"Mitch, I'm all over the greater Charleston area every day."

"Well, let's make it easy," Mitchell replied with a smile, as he took out a copy of Fred's schedule.

"Here's Fred's schedule when he'll be traveling and when he's home for the next three months. We can pencil you in right now."

As if on cue, Shelia's iPhone began to vibrate, and she looked at the screen.

"It's a client, Mitch. I've got to go, sorry."

His interest in high carb food vanished immediately. Undaunted, Mitch pressed his point.

"Would you at least take the schedule and email me back with whatever dates you can handle?"

"Sure, sure," Sheila replied, as she hastily stuffed the schedule into her purse and hurried out the door.

Mitch was sure that document was headed for the nearest trash receptacle.

The waitress came over to the table and asked, "Are you ready to order?"

Feeling a trifle embarrassed, Mitch managed, "Sorry, it doesn't look like I'll be staying for lunch."

He handed the waitress a fiver.

He had no sooner stepped outside when a white Jeep pulled out of the parking lot. What Mitchell Samuels saw eliminated any thought of cooperation from his brother's wife. Sheila Samuels had long ago lost any need for discretion, what with Fred's traveling. At the stop sign, she draped her arm around the driver's shoulders. The kiss she gave him was the kind one usually gives to one's spouse.

That night as they sat down for their evening meal, Brenda asked her husband, "Have you heard anything from Sheila about the visiting schedule?"

Compared to Mitchell's brother's home, he and Brenda lived a simpler lifestyle. The Craftsman style dwelling had three bedrooms, one and a half baths, and a dining area separated from the living room. Brenda had recently convinced Mitchell they should remodel the kitchen with updated appliances and countertops. Having no children, they had converted one of the bedrooms into a His and Hers work area.

Mitchell thanked his lucky stars for marrying Brenda. She was a marvelous cook and never ceased to amaze him with her ingenuity. Tonight, she had created his favorite dish, veal piccata.

"No, nothing."

Even though he knew better than to be disappointed, he was. It was evident in his tone.

"Let me guess," Brenda said, mocking Sheila's southern accent. "Oh, I'm so busy with work. I just don't know when I could find the time."

Though not inclined to sarcasm, it was painfully evident in her remarks. Mitchell almost choked on his bite of veal. His favorite type of meat, he was going to need a digestive aid after this one.

Recovering his composure, he replied, "As a matter of fact, that's pretty much what she told me," he said, as he hastily took a drink of water to clear his throat. He quickly added, "Work isn't the only thing keeping her busy these days."

Years of marriage had clued Brenda into the emphasis Mitchell placed on the last sentence. The quizzical look on his wife's face told Mitchell he needed to say more. He told Brenda about seeing Sheila with an unknown boyfriend.

"That bitch!" Brenda snapped. "Your brother has given her anything she's ever asked for, and then some, and this is how she shows her gratitude!"

Brenda threw her napkin on the table. "I think this calls for a little girl-on-girl time," as the fiery rage inside her enlarged the blood vessels in her temples to the bursting point. The most she had ever done was tolerate this woman, but this bit of news tipped things into a whole new arena.

"Remember, honey, South Carolina is a death penalty state," Mitchell said, hoping humor would calm his wife down.

"And whose cousin runs the largest alligator farm in South Carolina?" came the response—and a smiling one at that.

Brenda never thought much of Sheila as either a wife or a mother. Brenda had bonded with Sandra as if she was her own mother and she detested Sheila's treatment of Sandra. It was all she could stomach just to call Sheila to make a date for lunch, much less carry through with it. Later that week, Brenda called, and the two agreed to meet at the Olive Garden downtown.

The overhead TV finished a news segment on two US senators in a shouting match on the floor of Congress.

"We need more women in politics, don't you agree, Sheila? We could get a lot more done than those bickering Neanderthals we have now," Brenda said, as she started making nice with her husband's sister-in-law.

"I suppose so," replied a totally disinterested Sheila, responding to a text message she had received.

"Mitch said he was going to talk with Fred about spreading out the visits with Sandra between the four of us, but with Fred traveling so much, God only knows when they'd find the time!"

"Fred hadn't said anything to me about it," responded Sheila, who had laid her iPhone on the table.

"See what I mean, maybe we girls should just do it ourselves?"

The depth of Sheila's ability to see she was about to be played matched a shallow half a thimble.

"Okay, sure," Sheila said. Superficial as always, she was happy to portray herself as accommodating.

It took less than half an hour to schedule who would be assigned on what week to visit Dolores for the next three months. Unfortunately, the schedule's success depended on it being followed—something Sheila had no intention of doing.

Following the death of her husband, Clifford, Dolores Samuels had tried living on her own. She had hoped since she lived in the same town as her sons, Fred and Mitchell, that someone would make regular check-ins. It was too bad that responsibility fell mostly on Fred Samuels's older brother, Mitchell, and his wife, Brenda. As so often happens, Mitchell took this responsibility more seriously than did Fred.

In looks as well as temperament, the two boys were as different as night and day. Mitchell inherited his father's good looks and stature. He was slender though not skinny and stood a stately 6' 4". His brown hair and brown eyes complemented a bronze complexion, the result of summers spent on the golf course with his father. Mitchell knew in grammar school that he wanted to follow in his father's footsteps and attend Virginia Military Institute in Lexington, Virginia. The oldest of any military college in America, it was referred to as the "West Point of the South." Clifford Samuels, class of '43, was the cadet commander over the Corps of Cadets in his senior year. Mitchell's dream was to be the second in his family to hold that prestigious position. Following graduation, Mitchell Samuels was drawn to a career in the maritime insurance industry which Fred found as interesting as watching paint dry.

Fred, on the other hand, took after his mother's side of the family. Stretching as much as he could, he never grew taller than 5' 9". Black hair with a noticeable cowlick, reminiscent of Alfalfa in the "Little Rascals" comedy series, and thick glasses needed for reading made him appear to be the bookworm and dreamer he was. He envisioned what could be and then wondered how to make it happen. His flair for electronics led to a degree from Georgia Tech. He had the vision to see the future of fiber optics and what industries would most benefit from the application of this technology. Ultimately, he started his own fiber optics company.

In the years following her husband's death, Dolores Samuels came to agree with her son's recommendation to move into a nearby Del Webb adult development center. At first, she kept busy as a regular in the Women's Bridge Club. She even took up the game of golf again, something she and her husband had played regularly. The Book of the Month Club was another of her favorite activities. In time, however, the occasional missed tee-time with her golfing partners, bridge games forgotten, and lack of focus with the Book of the Month Club became all too frequent—enough so that one of her closest friends, Sarah Owens, had contacted her sons. Soon there would be other signs.

Fred had returned home exhausted after attending a three a.m. conference call. After a power nap, he got up and brewed coffee. With his wife at work, he had a few hours to go over the bills for the last few days. *If there's one thing she doesn't have any problem deciding on, it's putting off paying any bills until I see them*, he thought, as he grabbed several envelopes from the basket next the phone.

A few of the regular bills he expected: Nordstrom's, Chico's and Macy's. However, three bills were a complete surprise. Fred and Mitchell insisted their mother list both as points of contact for her household expenses. It seems Dolores was now three months' delinquent in paying her electric bill, the DirecTV bill and the AT&T bill.

Just then his wife arrived home. "You're home. Good," she said. "Eddie and Pam want us to come over for a barbecue and drinks." As usual, her mind was on anything but the substantial.

"There is an issue with my mother we need to talk about first," Fred said. He tried to mask his frustration, but a furrowed brow, clenched jaw and arms folded across his chest betrayed his true feelings.

"While I was gone last week, did you go see Mom?"

"Honey," Sheila said, "I didn't. Don't you remember? I asked you when you wanted me to go and you never told me what day. So, I didn't go." It was obvious that seeing Dolores was anything but a priority.

"Honestly, Sheila. You took the whole week off. Was I supposed to decide for you what day was best for you? You couldn't make that decision on your own?"

Sensing his frustration, Sheila said, "Okay, so I'll go next week. Just tell me when you want me to go."

Sheila was still not emotionally a part of this issue, but she knew enough to feign interest when Fred displayed this much intensity.

"You know what, never mind. I'll handle it myself," he snapped. Fred picked up his car keys and the three delinquent notices. "I'm going to see Mom about these. You go to Pam and Eddie's. I'll drop by when I'm finished."

Fred Samuels had been out of town the day Sheila received a call from Dolores saying she had lost her checkbook and asking if Sheila could come over and help her look for it.

"I'm sorry, Dolores," Sheila said, "but I'm already late for an engagement. I'll call Mitchell and see if he can come by."

Sheila's engagement was nothing more than trying on several dresses she had bought that day. Mitchell listened to her request, knowing full well that she had unsubstantial reasons for passing the buck. *No sense in asking her why she can't go,* Mitchell thought, *she'll only make things more difficult for Fred.* His inability to rely on his brother would prove fatal.

Mitchell had left work early and had taken the crosstown freeway, which was under extensive construction. Not everyone heeded the caution signs flashing their message to reduce speed. The driver of a flatbed loaded with lengths of steel pipes cut right in front of Mitchell. Realizing he was in the wrong lane, the driver swerved back to his left. The force of the lane change caused the flatbed to overturn into Mitchell's lane. Mitchell had no time to reduce his forward progress. His car smashed into the overturned truck in a frightening crunch of metal. He was DOA.

On his way to his mother's place, Fred mourned more than the loss of his brother. He would need Mitchell's wisdom, now more than ever. Fred would be ill-prepared for what he would discover.

Using his spare key to their mother's house, Fred let himself in.

"Mom, are you home? It's me, Fred," he called out.

Startled out of her afternoon nap, Dolores answered, "I'm in the living room, honey." Her response had a vaguely disconnected ring to it.

Dolores, who had fallen asleep with her TV tray in place, now moved it aside. Remnants of a less than well-rounded meal remained. Some made it to an untidy carpet. Dolores stood up to greet her son with a hug of sincere affection only a mother can express. Fred was dismayed at his mother's appearance. Her always meticulous hair was disheveled. It looked as if she had not applied fresh makeup in days. There was a general unkemptness to the entire room.

"Oh, it's so nice of you to stop by. I really miss seeing you."

"I know Mom. Me too. I've just been so busy at work," Fred replied.

Dolores returned to the couch and patted the cushion next to her. "Sit right here and tell me what's new with you."

Fred described a new project he was working on, and like any good parent who was a couple of generations behind the technology curve, Dolores Samuels listened patiently and smiled as if she understood every word her son said.

"Mom, I really came by to talk to you about these," Fred said, as he handed her the three delinquent notices.

Dolores looked carefully at each one and then in a surprised voice said, "I don't understand. I'm sure I paid these. I'll just get my checkbook."

When Dolores returned with her checkbook, there was a façade of alertness to her. She sat with an erect sense of confidence as she showed her son the checkbook.

"See here's the check I wrote to Direct TV."

Fred looked up from the check journal he held in his hand. There was no entry to Direct TV.

"And here," Sandra continued, pointing to the journal, "here's where I wrote the check to AT&T."

Her son made no response. The pages had a randomness about them, as though his mother was coming in and out of focus when attending to the bills.

"Mom, look a little more closely, would you?"

Her erectness gave way to slumping shoulders and a confused look on her face.

"I was sure," she said, as the uncertainty of her memory overcame her.

"Can I look, Mom?" Fred asked.

Dolores went to hand him the checkbook. Her hand shook noticeably. Her eyes seemed to plead 'What's happening?'

Fred glanced through several pages in his mother's check register. With each page, his concern grew.

"Mom, there are a lot of entries where there's no name to whom the check was written," he said.

Fred saw the look in his mother's eyes. It was distant. Wherever she was at this moment, it wasn't sitting next to her son. No need to tell her the last entry was over three weeks ago, and that the entries before that were full of subtraction mistakes a fifth-grader wouldn't make. He laid the checkbook on the TV tray.

"I'll take care of these," Fred said, picking up the three delinquent notices.

"Take care of what, my baby bumpkin?" she said, as a flickering glaze appeared in her eyes. Whatever anxiety she had experienced a moment before had been replaced by a covering wall of maternal love.

On the way home, Fred wondered to himself how everyone had missed the signs of the onset of dementia. He and his brother had talked regularly when Fred was in town about their mother. There seemed no cause for alarm. The periodic episodes of forgetfulness seemed inconsequential. Even if Sheila had come over to check on Dolores, her lack of attention to detail would have been no help. When Fred talked with Brenda, Mitchell's widow, about Dolores' condition, it was her idea to call Doctor Kahal, Sandra's longtime doctor, to get an appointment.

41

The visit evidenced few surprises. With Fred and Brenda's consent, Doctor Kahal arranged for Dolores to go to Magnolia Gardens.

Chapter 5

MARY HILLMAN'S PATH
TO MAGNOLIA GARDENS

George Hillman charted the latest progression of Bio Rhythmic Inc., a hot commodity one of his old friends had told him about. He pressed click and waited. While he did, he picked up the letter from the Gardens and read it again. How had he become so disconnected from Mary that he had never visited her once? It certainly wasn't due to any feelings for Gilda, he thought. For George Hillman, Gilda Ellis was like any stock or company he bought or sold. Like any merger or acquisition, she was a commodity. Her assets outweighed her liabilities—a commodity with no heart, a commodity that didn't cry when it was sad or laugh when it was happy.

George stared at his computer screen. That insipid little-dotted wheel was still turning. He leaned back in his chair and closed his eyes. He visualized standing in front of the door leading to the balcony. He pushed aside the curtain and stepped out to the most beautiful landscape he had ever seen.

A huge sweeping valley lay before him. Vineyards like an agricultural quilt stretched as far as the eye could see. On many stood centuries old two-story homes with terra-cotta tile roofs and even older brick walls, dating back to the 17th century. From his balcony, George could hear the voices of the locals headed off to pick the grapes. It was that time of year. And there were laughter and smiles.

It was the place of their honeymoon; the wine region of Florina, Italy. Most of all, it was Mary. She brought laughter and smiles wherever she went. She could brighten up a room with just the twinkle of her radiant green eyes. She made a foggy day seem romantic, and a failed business deal seem inconsequential. That was his Mary and right now, God how he missed her.

The ping from his computer caused him to open his eyes. The screen glowed with the latest news that Bio Rhythmic Inc. stock had just split. George Hillman had just made his poker-playing buddies from the country club almost $200,000 each. George stared at the screen showing the wealth he had created; but there was no happiness, no joy, no feeling of accomplishment—just another commodity selection that had done well. He did not want to feel that way anymore.

He knew when and why the change in Mary had occurred. He would go to her and beg her for forgiveness, but there was something he had to do first. He punched his friend's phone number into his cell phone.

"Leo, George. Yeah, I know it's early."

Leo Ainsworth listened patiently on the other end, carefully taking notes as directed. He couldn't believe what he was hearing. He was to activate the financial separation agreement between George and Gilda immediately. See to it that she was gone with all her belongings within the next seven days and give her the vacation home in Florida to sweeten the deal.

As his lifelong friend and personal attorney, Ainsworth had to ask, "Are you sure George? Are you really sure you want to do this?"

"Yes, Leo. I've never been surer of anything in my life."

"As sure as you were over the Harrison merger or the acquisition of Bell Thomas, Inc. Those were two long-detailed and complex transaction, and now suddenly this. May I ask why?" Ainsworth said.

Hillman began rubbing his temple as if to draw out the answer to Ainsworth's question. He got out of his chair and walked into the expansive living room. He stared at paintings by Matisse, Picasso, and Brancusi that hung on the walls. The furniture was original Maloof design, a must-have according to Gilda.

"George, are you still there?" Ainsworth asked.

"I'm still here, Leo."

George spoke carefully. "Leo, you're not poor by any means, so let me ask you this question. What's the one thing in your life you couldn't bear to be without—the one thing that gives your life meaning?"

"That's not so hard to answer, George. It's Lois and the kids. They make my life have purpose," replied Ainsworth.

"Exactly, Leo, and for me it was Mary," George said, strangling on his own words, "and what we might have had." He was surprised at the emotional reaction his words created.

After he ended the call, George thought back to the time where he began to lose his Mary. He was rushing home to deliver exciting news about his work. Mary had her own wonderful news to tell him. Hillman had left his office late that day after closing out the largest acquisition in the history of Pyramid Financial. His commission alone was over $20 million: but more importantly, it was a ticket to managing his own hedge fund at Rothman Brothers. His Mercedes XL set a speed record getting home. He literally ran up the steps to his front door. He practically tore the door off its hinges getting in.

"Mary, it's me," he hollered. "I have some great news."

His enthusiasm brought Mary running from the bedroom.

"Me too, sweetheart," she beamed. "You go first."

That was his Mary, always willing to defer to him. He paced back and forth in front of her as Mary sat on the couch. George had an almost adolescent enthusiasm as he described each stage of the acquisition. He seemed particularly proud that he could drive the asking price down by planting a rumor that the SEC was considering allegations of insider trading by the company's CEO.

"Mary," my commission is just over $20 million, and I'll get that position at Rothman Brothers managing my own fund. Whatever you want, just name it: a new car, diamond necklace, or a vacation home in France, anything!"

His face radiated with excitement. He was practically out of breath.

"I'm so happy for you, George. You've worked so hard, and you deserve everything," Mary said. "You know what I really want?"

The glow on her face should have told George there was more to follow, but the egocentric husband never saw it coming.

"I want this baby. More than anything in this world, more than a new car, diamond necklace or that home in France, I want this baby."

She placed her hands over her womb. "George, I'm pregnant. We are going to have a child."

"You're kidding, right?"

The grimace that appeared on Mary's face told George he had said the wrong thing. He tried to make up for it.

"I mean, you're forty-three years old, Mary. Are you sure it's healthy to have a child at that age?"

Mary patted the Italia Ferrara sectional she was sitting on.

"George, please sit down next to me," Mary said. "All our married life, I've wanted children. You wanted a successful career in the financial world, and I supported you in pursuing that dream. All I'm asking you to do now is to support me in pursuing my dream."

"Mary, if the doctor says there's no problem, of course, I'll support you."

Even as he hugged his wife, George Hillman knew he did not share his wife's dream. His exhilaration for his recent business success vanished with this new development.

"Look, this is what I need you to say, and this is what she needs to see. It's that simple," George said.

"This could cost me my license if it ever gets out," the nervous voice on the other end of the line said.

"No, what would cost you your license is if anyone found out that you had siphoned off $2 million from your medical practice to cover your stock losses; but then I took care of that, didn't I?"

"Yes, you did," came the response with a fatalistic tone.

It was a distant, but still painful memory, as evidenced by the emotion displayed in those three simple words.

Two months later, George Hillman pulled into the parking lot of Zion Medical Center in Los Angeles.

"Are you sure he's the best?" Mary asked.

"Absolutely, darling," George answered. "He's the best obstetrician in the nation, and he flies to LA three times a month from his main office in Manhattan, New York. You have no idea the strings I had to pull to get this appointment."

He was unabashed by this lie he had told.

George and Mary took the elevator to the fifteenth floor. The sign on the door read, "Dr. Edward Lee, Chief of Obstetrics." George held the door open for Mary.

"Mr. Hillman, Dr. Lee is waiting for you. Go on in," the receptionist said.

"How does the doctor know you, George?"

"Honey, I told you I was taking you to the best. I had to see him to check him out," George said, compounding his lie.

The moment she stepped into the doctor's office, Mary Hillman was impressed. Not just with a string of medical degrees adorning one wall, but with the three-sided ceiling to floor glass windows that overlooked the city of Angels.

"Mr. Hillman, Mrs. Hillman, I'm Doctor Lee. Please have a seat."

Mary was immediately at ease in the doctor's presence. He had a firm yet gentle handshake. With his full head of white hair and black horn-rimmed glasses, he looked like a modern-day Marcus Welby and acted the part. Warmth and compassion flowed out his mouth as he spoke.

"Have you had a chance to review the blood test our doctor sent over?" George asked.

"May I call you George, and you Mary?" Lee asked. "Being on a first name basis is like practicing real medicine," he said, with a warm smile on his face.

George and Mary nodded in agreement.

"Mary, do you understand why you're here?" The doctor asked.

"Yes. Our doctor mentioned the importance of a blood test within the first trimester to see if there might be any problems with the pregnancy."

"Very good," Lee said, producing a totally false smile. Unlike George, he was not comfortable in the falsehood.

He pressed his intercom button.

"Helen, would you bring in the results of the Hillman analysis."

Shortly, his nurse came in and handed him two pieces of paper.

"Thank you, Helen," he said. He laid the papers on his desk and turned them around, so George and Mary could see them.

Pointing to the one in front of Mary, Lee said, "Mary, this is what a normal blood test should look like. All indications are this would be a normal pregnancy and produce a healthy baby. Now, look at the one next to it. Do you see where I've marked unusually high levels of Antioch protein?"

Mary looked at the lines checked by the doctor.

"What is this to me, Doctor Lee?" Mary asked as she grabbed George's hand.

"The one in front of you is what we had hoped to see in your results. Unfortunately, the one next to it is yours."

Mary's fingers tightened around George's hand.

"What are you saying, Doctor Lee?"

Lee, who had sworn to uphold the Hippocratic oath, was about to violate it in the worst way. He was not the slightest bit happy about it, but this was survival.

"Mary, George, I'm so sorry to tell you this, but my best medical opinion is that if you, Mary, go to term, this baby will be born with severe mental and physical problems. There is no doubt in my mind that eventually the child would be institutionalized."

It was as if the air had been sucked out of her body. Mary tried to speak, but a barely audible gurgle was all that came out. George put his arms around her and stated, "Dr. Lee, what are our options?"

Lee leaned back in his chair. "Unfortunately, your only other option is to terminate the pregnancy."

If the news wasn't bad enough, the option the doctor presented was like a second kick to Mary's stomach. All she had ever wanted was to have a child, and now this.

"I can't decide right now, I just can't," she said, as a wave of depression swept over her.

"Of course, I understand," Lee said. "Please take your time. I understand what an important decision this is, but be aware that the longer you take, the greater the risk to your health, Mary."

Her face turned ashen. She sat there expressionless.

"We will be in touch," George said, as he helped to Mary to her feet.

After they left his office, Doctor Lee shredded the two pieces of paper he had created for the appointment. He threw his glasses against the wall and slumped back into his chair, sickened at the charade he had perpetrated on the expectant mother.

After the "procedure," as he euphemistically referred to it, life returned to normal, at least for George Hillman. As a hedge fund manager at Rothman Brothers, George had earned quite a reputation in the financial world. None of his clients ever questioned his unethical or unprincipled business practices, least of all the billionaire real estate developer with whom George had recently become involved.

"If there's a rule or law that says we can't do something, do it anyway," the billionaire would often say. "We're here to make money, not be compliant. The rules don't apply to people like you and me."

Normal was a term which would never again apply to Mary Hillman's life. Mary was attractive, but not stunning. She tried to resume her normal activities. She had loved the charitable work the San Diego Women's Club did for children's organizations, and she had personally taken it upon herself to fund several preschool programs. Mary had frequently shown up at story time to read to the children. They filled a void in her heart created by George's unfathomable greed and the decision to destroy the new life they had created.

Her other passion had been serving as a docent at the Botanical Gardens operated by the University of California, San Diego. Mary not only knew the common name for thousands of species, but she also knew their botanical names, which on more than one occasion had embarrassed the paid staff. There was a long list of other civic groups to which Mary had belonged. All of this had changed when her depression had deepened after the procedure.

George was no longer driven to make money, per se. He had more money than he could spend in three lifetimes. He was now addicted to the game. Finding that project everyone said couldn't be done and making it happen was his heroin.

Any addict will tell you they're always searching to re-create that first sweet euphoric sensation that occurred as the drug flowed through their veins. George Hillman was no different. Four months after securing his own hedge fund at Rothman Brothers, he basked in the praise and adulation of his peers. Sid Rothman, the older of the two founding brothers, had taken George to lunch the day of his promotion.

"George, Ethan and I see great things in your future. I was telling him just yesterday I don't think there's a project too big or too complicated for George Hillman. The question is, can we find it? Can we come up with a project so unbelievable only a science-fiction writer would've thought of it and make it a reality?"

George heard his bosses' praise, but his swelling ego had numbed his senses. He fantasized his name being mentioned in the same breath as Buffett and Gates.

With work taking up more and more of his time, George had hired a personal assistant for his wife. Martha Graham was hired to do more than handle Mary's calendar, she was to be Mary's companion, her best friend, the person Mary could talk to about anything. George had hired someone to be what he should have been. By the time he realized it, it would be too late.

George's meeting in Los Angeles had just started when his iPhone started to vibrate. He barely had time to look at it before the mayor walked into the room. It read, Not an emergency, but we need to talk. Martha. George focused his attention on the mayor who had just stepped up to the podium.

"Gentlemen, what I'm about to propose has been called impossible by my critics. Others have referred to it as pure science fiction. Perhaps so," he said, as a smile formed on his face. "But I'm in the business of making the impossible a reality."

The adrenaline started pumping through George's veins. He quickly forgot the message from Martha.

Following the meeting, Hillman headed back to his office. He wanted to start preparing his plan for the mayor's development. *It really was like make-believe, he thought, a twenty-acre commercial development built 30 feet off the ground over a portion of an abandoned refinery storage area which had been condemned by the EPA long ago. No need for an environmental impact report since the ground wouldn't be disturbed. Hundreds of storage tanks had long ago been removed. How to do it? And how to find investors?*

His iPhone vibrated. *Dammit,* he thought when he saw Martha's name, and he immediately texted her, *"I'm on my way home now."* She texted back, *"meet me at Harvey's."* There was an instant urgency in the text.

The parking lot of the swank eatery off La Jolla Dr. was partially full when Hillman pulled into the parking lot. When he walked inside, he spotted Martha Graham sitting at a window table.

"Late meeting, Martha. So, if it's not an emergency, why are we here?"

Martha Graham had carved out a very profitable niche for herself as a personal assistant for hire. She spoke three languages: Spanish, French, and German and had a degree in Political Science from Berkeley. She much preferred clients whose activities included social and political functions, and she had the good looks to move in those circles.

"When I started working with Mary nearly four years ago, she was a delight to be with," Graham began. "She was enthusiastic about her civic projects. Her concern for others less fortunate was as genuine as the air kisses by her friends were insincere. There was only an occasional sign of depression, and that seemed to pass fairly quickly."

"So, what's the issue?" Hillman asked, signaling the bartender to bring him his regular, a double martini up with Tito's vodka.

"George, she's lost the spirit she had. Those brief periods of depression are getting longer and longer. Sometimes I find her muttering about her baby. I didn't think you two had any children," Graham said.

His stomach, or was it his conscience, started to wretch. "We don't. Go on."

"She can't remember the names of people she has known for years without me prompting her. The Woman's Club has asked her to step down as chairwoman of their Children's Education Subcommittee," Graham added.

Hillman sipped his martini. He had seen Mary's decline but used his work to buffer him from dealing with it. Actually, he was annoyed both that he had not taken Mary's condition seriously and that this woman had to bring it to his attention.

"It's no wonder, George," Graham responded. "You're gone to work before she gets up, and she's in bed by the time you get home after a twelve-hour day. No condemnation, just an observation."

"Understood. The problem is," he continued, "my work hours aren't going to get any shorter for a long time, not with this new development I'm starting."

"Look, George, I'll stay on if I can be useful; but when Mary starts needing personal care, you need to think about a live-in nurse."

Six months later, that time had arrived. Hillman had come home around seven p.m. to find Mary sitting on the swing on their porch, wearing a bathrobe over her dress pants. When he called her name, she looked at him as if he were a stranger. Though he had brushed aside Mary's steady mental decline, he couldn't ignore her present condition. A quick call was made to her personal physician. A dedicated healthcare provider, the doctor told him to bring her right in. After an hour with Mary privately, the doctor called George do his office.

"Please have a seat," the neurologist said.

"Let's cut to the chase, Doctor. What's going on with my wife?"

"It's not that simple," the doctor said. "Tell me about any recent health issues your wife has experienced."

George relayed what Martha Graham had told him to the doctor.

"I'm afraid your wife's condition is serious. For starters, I believe she's experienced a stroke, but I'll need to do further tests at the hospital to confirm that. From what you've told me about her recent past, I see the symptoms of advancing dementia."

"What do I need to do, doctor?" George asked.

"First things first. Let's deal with the stroke and assess any damage, be it temporary or permanent. Then we can deal with the dementia issue. I understand how difficult all this is to process, Mr. Hillman, but I assure you we will do everything possible to help your wife."

George nodded in agreement. It felt strange to him to suddenly have to consider what's best for his wife after years of letting Martha Graham handle things. Considering his command position in the other portions of his life, he felt strangely inadequate.

After three days in the hospital and three weeks in a rehabilitation facility, George brought his wife home. Fortunately, the physical effects of the stroke were minimal, and the therapist assured George that with work, there would likely be no lasting side effects. The dementia was another issue. Per the doctor, Mary was going to need twenty-four-hour care.

As he wheeled Mary to the front door, she asked, "Where did we go, George?" Her eyes straining to recognize her own home.

"Oh, we went to see a friend, honey. You get some sleep, and we'll talk in the morning."

Only there would be no talk the next morning. Through the dark of the night, there would be no sleep for George Hillman. He alternated between pacing aimlessly about the living room to sitting at his desk in the den. He thought about all that could have been and all that should have been. His Mary deserved all of it. Instead, all she received was betrayal from the man she had loved with all her heart. It was too late to ask Mary for forgiveness. George doubted God would forgive him, but this time, he would make sure Mary had the best possible care, no matter what the cost. He spent the pre-dawn hours on-line researching long-term care programs, their services, costs, and facilities. There was no denying that Magnolia Gardens, in Charleston, South Carolina, was at the top of the list.

Chapter 6

SANDRA COTTON'S PATH
TO MAGNOLIA GARDENS

*J*im found his mother in the living room. She was standing in front of what she called her "Wall of Fame." Every milestone in the lives of Samantha and her brother, William, was captured in pictures. Sandra was holding Samantha's birth photo against her chest.

"Mom, can I talk to you?" Jim pleaded.

Sandra put Samantha's picture back on the wall and reached for the one of Samantha in a Red Ryder wagon being pulled by her brother. Norman Rockwell couldn't have made a better painting of childhood serenity.

"Why?"

Sandra used her sleeve to wipe the tears falling. At best, it was a temporary fix.

"Really, Mom. You think this doesn't hurt me too?"

She remained focused on the picture. This was her son. She still had faith in him but was deeply disturbed by what had happened.

"Apparently not enough."

Carrie's decision to send Samantha away and her son's feeble acquiescence had taken the very life out of the grandmother. She put the picture back on the wall.

"I'm going to my room."

As weeks grew into months, Sandra Cotton's behavior began to change. Dinner was no longer ready when Jim and Carrie got home. Laundry wasn't being done, and Sandra ceased paying attention to maintaining any sort of orderliness about the home.

If Jim and Carrie thought Sandra was playing some adolescent game of, "I'll show you," they were wrong. It was depression spawned by the absence of her dear grandchild. Sandra was no longer greeted by the excitement in Samantha's voice when she came home from school to tell her grandmother about the events of the day. She longed for the long talks they would have about growing up and making dreams. As the weeks went by, Sandra's depression intensified. Carrie, true to form, was only concerned so far as it affected her. After a takeout dinner of Chinese food, Carrie addressed the issue with her husband.

"Listen, Jim, we both work, and I don't think it's asking too much to expect your mother to start helping out around the house again. I mean, could she make dinner occasionally, do a load of laundry, or even straighten up the living room?"

Hardly interested in a conflict, yet intent on protecting his mother, Jim offered,

"You don't think she's done enough in the years she's lived here and suffered enough with Samantha's leaving?"

Carrie threw the empty container that had held fried rice on the table.

"Don't you dare try to put the blame on me for sending Samantha to live with my sister. You also agreed, remember."

"Unfortunately, I do, Carrie. What you fail to remember is Mom bonded with our kids as though she was their mother."

Displaying unusual insight, he said, "She's depressed. In her mind, she's lost someone she loves, and yes, Carrie, we caused it."

Jim pushed his chair away from the table, got up and put his plate and silverware in the kitchen sink. If he thought his wife had learned anything from the example his mother had set over the years, he was wrong. He had his morning coffee standing in front of the sink still full of dirty dishes.

Jim worried about his mother. She had too much time on her hands to be alone in a large four-bedroom home. He hoped to rekindle his mother's fondness for bridge by having a couple of friends from her bridge club come over to the house once a week for her mother's favorite game. Jim would have to be the fourth player. His mother had taught him how to play the game when Jim was in high school. She claimed it would help his analytical skills. More importantly, weekly games would give him a chance to reconnect in a positive manner with his mother. Carrie offered no objection so long as she wasn't inconvenienced.

At first, the game had its desired effect. Sandra began to shed the more casual cotton capris and sleeveless blouse she wore daily for a more slightly dressy linen pants suit with a colorful pink silk blouse. Occasionally, she would comically chide her son over his not-so-subtle table talk to tell his partner what his strong suits were. The one thing that did not improve was Sandra's ability to stay on point with the bidding. With painful regularity, she had to be prompted as to what had been bid when it came to her turn. Sandra was oblivious to the subtle frustrating nods of those around the table.

It had been nearly six months since Samantha had gone to North Carolina to stay with Carrie's sister, and not a week went by that Sandra didn't write to her. Jim had hoped this ongoing correspondence would help his mother's depression. Unfortunately, it had the opposite effect. For days after mailing each letter, Sandra's depression worsened. Even the rebounding effect of weekly bridge games began to fade.

Sandra sat in front of her "Wall of Fame" as Jim set up the card table for the night's game. Jim walked over to his mother and knelt next to her.

"We're going to be partners tonight, Mom. Florence and Sara better be on their best game."

Sandra looked at her son. Her words frightened him.

"Is Samantha going to be here?"

He took hold of his mother's hands.

"No, Mom." Any more of an answer would be wasted.

With the ringing of the doorbell, Jim stood up.

"It must be Florence and Sara. I'll see to them. Would you mind bringing out the snack tray? It's in the kitchen."

Jim had been forced to tell Florence the truth about Samantha's absence when Florence pressured him for information about his mother's depression.

"Come on in, Florence, Sara. Mom's in the kitchen."

At that moment, his iPhone rang. He recognized Carrie's sister's number.

"I have to take this," he said, as he stepped away.

Florence and Sara went into the kitchen to help Sandra. It would've been impossible for any father not to react to the words coming from the phone.

"The hospital?" He literally shouted into the phone. "Is she okay? Yes, yes, I understand. I'll make arrangements to come up as soon as I can."

Jim ran into the kitchen. His face was ashen. Air filled his lungs in gasps. He studied himself against the kitchen counter.

"Samantha's had a miscarriage. She's lost a lot of blood, and they've taken her to the ER at Durham Memorial."

When he said, "they've called for the chaplain," Sandra screamed. She collapsed into a kitchen chair sobbing incoherently. Between worrying about his mother and wondering if his daughter would live, the next few hours were a blur for Jim. After some discussion, it was decided that Florence and Sara would stay with Sandra while Jim and Carrie went to see about Samantha. The trip to Durham would have significantly different results than what awaited Jim and Carrie when they returned home.

Neither said a word as they sped along the interstate to Durham. Only the sound of passing traffic permeated the silence. Jim would have been perfectly happy to keep things that way, but not Carrie.

"I suppose you blame me for this?"

Her words were both accusatory and a defiant statement of her innocence. Jim said nothing.

Not willing to leave well enough alone, she continued, "Well, you do, don't you?"

"No more than I blame myself."

Nothing more was said until they arrived at the hospital. Jim and Carrie had been waiting for nearly an hour when the doctor called them into his office.

"Mr. and Mrs. Cotton, I apologize for having you wait. Please come in."

After a double shift in the ER, Doctor Marty Miners was exhausted. His appearance did little to instill confidence in Jim or Carrie. His stethoscope hung around his neck at an angle. His unkempt silver hair was damp with perspiration from the bright lights in the operating room. His shoulders were hunched over from hours leaning over a patient. He directed them to a large oblong conference table and pulled up two chairs. There was a raspy tone to his voice.

"Let me start by saying your daughter has lost a lot of blood, but we've taken care of that. Her emotional state is something else. The effects of a miscarriage are devastating, especially for a young person. Frequently, they mistakenly believe they'll never be able to have children or that it's God's way of punishing them for some type of moral transgression. That couldn't be farther from the truth. For the immediate future, she needs to be in a place where she feels loved."

After visiting Samantha, Jim was intent on bringing her home to recuperate. Carrie had a completely different plan.

It was well past midnight when Jim and Carrie pulled into the driveway. The lights on the porch were still on as well as the lights in the kitchen.

"Something's not right," said Jim, to a yawning wife.

He hurried to the house, leaving Carrie to fend for herself.

"Oh, Jim, I'm so glad you're back," cried Florence, as tears began to choke her words. "After you and your wife left, Sandra become more and more agitated. She began to struggle with her breathing. Her rants about Samantha became more and more irrational. Finally, she passed out. We called 911. The ambulance took her to Tampa Memorial. Sarah went with them."

Just then, Carrie walked through the door.

"Don't bother putting anything down. Mom's been taken to the hospital. We're leaving now.

It was nearly four a.m. when the doctor finally called Jim and Carrie into his office. His glasses rested on the very end of his nose allowing him to glance at the papers in his hand and then quickly upward to whomever he was talking to. At least to Jim, the doctor who appeared to be in his mid-sixties, inspired confidence. Carrie could have cared less as she focused on fixing her makeup.

"Mr. and Mrs. Cotton, I'm Doctor Singh, head of neurology. I apologize for having you wait. Please come in."

"I don't understand. What's going on?" Jim said, his words were hurried almost panicked.

"Your mother was brought in with what appeared to be a stroke. After the ER staff evaluated her, it was determined that she had more than likely suffered a panic attack. I'd like to keep her for a few days to do a more thorough evaluation, and I'll need to talk to you about your mother's condition over the past few months."

The doctor's words did nothing to abate Jim's anxiety. Carrie couldn't have shown less concern. All she wanted to do was get some sleep. Jim returned to the hospital the next day to speak with the doctor. Four days later, they returned to get the results of Doctor Singh's evaluation.

Jim thought the doctor would have had a more spacious office. The doctor's certificates hung on one wall. The other wall had several wall lamps used to examine x-rays and other diagnostic pictures. The only furniture was a small desk and a small conference table with chairs.

"Let me start by saying physically, your mother is fine. Her mental functioning, however, is quite different."

"I'm not sure I understand, Doctor Singh," asked a panicked Jim

"Your mother's condition is like the riddle 'which came first the chicken or the egg. From what you told me, Mr. Samuels, she's been depressed for months over her granddaughter's relocation to North Carolina. Some recent studies have indicated depression is a cause of dementia; unfortunately, other studies suggest depression is merely an early indication of already existing dementia. If your daughter were to come home, it just might ease your mother's depression."

Jim sat stunned at the news. A little forgetfulness maybe, but not this.

It was hours before Jim and Carrie could get Sandra released from the hospital and home. The entire trip home from the hospital, Sandra had remained silent, staring out the window. Once they got Sandra settled in her room, Carrie quickly changed into her pajamas, more intent on getting her sleep than discussing Sandra. She walked into the kitchen and informed Jim of her plan.

"I've got to spend some time with my sister and Samantha, Jim, until the school year ends, then we can bring Samantha home without arousing any suspicion among our friends."

Jim glared at his wife. Rage overruled any impulse to appear to be understanding. His hands grabbed the back of the kitchen chair.

"My God, Carrie. Did you pay any attention to what the doctor told us? Bringing Samantha home now might be the catalyst to bringing mom out of her depression."

"Not if she's got dementia, or didn't you hear the Doctor say that!"

Sure I did, Jim thought, *and you couldn't give a damn about it.*

Jim had arranged for a caretaker to be with Sandra when he was at work. Carrie was only home intermittently due to the time she insisted on spending with her sister and Samantha. When she was home, Sandra did not seem to recognize her. One day the caretaker told Jim that Sandra had gotten out of the house. The caretaker found her about two blocks away. Sandra told her she was looking for her granddaughter.

The day Florence came by to see Sandra, she was asleep. Jim offered Florence some sweet tea, and they went out to the patio. The large patio umbrella provided some relief from the rising temperature already approaching ninety degrees.

"I'm out of ideas, Florence, as to what to do about Mom. Carrie is absolutely no help. Samantha's got her own life to live once she gets healthy. My retirement is nine months away and then what."

"It breaks my heart to see my best friend this way," Florence responded. "As difficult as this is to say, you and Carrie should consider an assisted living facility. My daughter-in-law had to place her mother in one, and they think the world of it. It's called Magnolia Gardens. It's in Charleston, South Carolina."

Chapter 7

KILGORE'S FRIENDS

*K*ilgore had finished transcribing his notes for the day. He was exhausted. His friends had been all over the map, emotionally and mentally. He saw the letter on the table from Eddington House, a publishing firm in Chicago. His editor worked there. He read the letter and thought he'd better call. He dialed her cell phone. He was torn between his concern for his "Magnolia friends" and the need to stay on track with his commitment to his publisher.

"Daniel, I'm so glad you called. Did you get my letter?"

"I have it in front of me now," he said. He sounded vaguely distracted.

"Well, what do you think? They loved the first part of your outline, and the $5,000 check is a nice incentive," said Sylvia Mueller. "But there's one question, the ending. What is it?"

Daniel Kilgore had been contacted by Mueller after his first novel, "Secrets," had received a four-star review by the San Francisco Book

Review. Kilgore had seen an advertisement on the review website and thought it safest to send his novel as far away from Charleston as possible, in case it stank. However, success on an initial work was no guarantee that he would sustain it thereafter.

Sylvia Mueller was on the north side of fifty and looked the part of an editor. She wore her hair in a bun, with a number two pencil sticking out on the left side and a red pencil sticking out on the right side. Large eyeglasses trimmed in brown betrayed years of eye strain searching for the next great American novel. After she read Kilgore's rating in the San Francisco book review, she contacted him. As it turned out, Daniel Kilgore, in fact, was working on a new project. Mueller, as well as her chief editor, was intrigued by Kilgore's theme and asked that he send them an outline.

"I don't know how it's going to end, Sylvia. The entire concept is fluid. It changes from day-to-day." He wanted to sound confident, but he failed.

"Daniel, I'm not sure I understand, and I know damn well my boss won't understand." The years of working with eccentric authors were wearing on her.

"Sylvia, do you know how your life will end. The day, the time or the place, huh?"

"Of course not, Daniel," she replied, with no intention of hiding her frustration. She really disliked these flights of fancy.

"Well, these are real people I'm writing about, not some fictional characters I can kill off whenever I want to or make feel whatever I want them to feel. You keep the check. When I'm finished, I'll send you the manuscript, then you and your boss can decide. Bye."

He felt greatly empowered by his assertive behavior. She would love his book, and it would be a good one. The story needed to be told, but only in the proper time frame.

Kilgore's visits with his friends the following week would prove to be revealing. It appeared to Kilgore that for the briefest of moments a connection with the past was reestablished.

From his prior visits with Mary Hillman, Kilgore knew she liked to read. She had a dozen or so books of classic poets like Keats, Frost, and

Elizabeth Barrett Browning in her room. Mary didn't read for any great length of time nor did she retain very much, but she loved to hold the book in her hands. She would have abhorred the thought of using a Kindle. Her hair still retained a trace of its original brown hue now peppered with gray. She was rarely without her favorite powder blue shawl draped over her shoulders. She would occasionally shift its position in an absent-minded manner. The shawl was with her even in times when it was far too balmy for such attire.

Mary's mobility was not an issue, so Kilgore was not surprised to see her sitting on a bench down by the pond despite the unusually cool mid-morning air. She sat with a book in one hand and crumbs of bread in the other. Mary loved feeding the mother duck and her ducklings. The mother hen with her dull brown feather that matched the surrounding reeds at the shoreline watched her ducklings as they swam to crumbs of bread Mary had tossed to them. The ducklings were young as white fuzz dominated their undeveloped feathers. Kilgore walked over to her. The mother duck scurried her ducklings across the pond to the safety of the reeds on the other side.

"Hi, Mary, it's me, your George." He was always cheerful in his opening remarks, yet not overly familiar.

Mary looked at Kilgore with an apparent pensive stare.

"George?"

"Yes, it's me, dear, your husband."

There was a sudden alertness in her eyes as if this was what she had been waiting for. She grabbed Kilgore's arm and pulled him close to her.

"George, I waited so long at the clubhouse. I thought you had left me." Her genuine sense of abandonment was real.

That must be it, Kilgore thought. *The recreational therapists had mentioned years of playing golf kept her in very excellent physical condition. The clubhouse was a remembrance of those days.*

"Never, my love," Kilgore replied. "I went to the Pro Shop to register our scores. You know how important it is for you to keep your handicap updated."

Mary was now staring at the young ducklings as they had returned from the safety of the reeds to compete for the morsels of bread she had tossed onto the water. Under her beauty, the seething bitterness remained. She muttered, "Why couldn't I keep the baby?"

Unsure as to exactly what she had said, Kilgore asked, "What was that, dear?"

Mary looked at him. "I'm sorry, but who are you?" There was an obvious shift in her perception.

"It's me. George, your husband," Kilgore repeated. "Remember we were talking golf."

Mary did not answer. She tossed the few remaining crumbs of bread onto the water as a single tear fell down her cheek, a cheek aged with wrinkles of disappointment. Whatever connection Kilgore had temporarily opened was slammed shut. Kilgore thought about Mary's comment about keeping the baby. What horrific trauma had occurred in her life that dementia had not completely erased from her memory?

"Here to see Sandra?" Ellen asked as she stifled a yawn. She had pulled an all-nighter for her psychology midterm that morning.

"How'd you guess?" Daniel replied.

"I saw a note from Madeline when I checked in to make sure we had Sandra ready when you arrived. She should be out on the veranda."

Midmornings were Daniel's favorite time of the day at the Gardens. Humidity hadn't started to rise, the coolness of the morning still lingered in the air, and the abundance of small birds still felt safe to walk the lawns, pecking at their favorite insects. Sandra was seated at one of the tables with two staff members, Doctor Ashley Dearden and Kayla D. Kayla's last name was a seven-syllable German name most could not pronounce, so she was simply called Kayla D. As he approached, Daniel heard Ashley explain as she dealt the cards.

"Sandra, there's only the three of us so we'll have to play a dummy hand."

Doctor Dearden was a renowned expert in the field of genetics hoping to find some connection between dementia and the DNA makeup of the patient. The expert was not particularly fond of formal clothing, much preferring a casual t-shirt and jeans. Kayla D, wearing a brand-new set of green nurses' scrubs, had recently finished her nursing program and was doing an internship at the Gardens. Both women were accomplished bridge players and often played the game with residents who were capable of the focus required. Sandra paid no attention to the cards lying in front of her. She had on her favorite silk blue blouse, a small turquoise necklace, and matching earrings. Her eyes were fixed on a woman sitting at a nearby table. The woman had striking brown hair. She was wearing a yellow sundress with a necklace of Mother of Ivory pearls.

"Sandra, did you hear me?" Dearden asked gently. Sandra remained silent.

Daniel remembered reading in the intake workup Orsini had made available to him that Sandra's son used to play bridge with Sandra and two friends. He thought it appropriate to interject.

"May I?" he asked, reaching for a chair.

"Please," responded Dearden. "If you play, it might make things easier for her to follow."

"I do," replied Daniel, as he seated himself adjacent to Sandra.

"Sandra, would you like me to sort your cards?" Daniel asked, placing his hand on hers.

That tactile gesture broke Sandra's stare on the woman.

"Cards?" she said. "What are we doing?"

"We're playing bridge and about to start the bidding," replied a smiling Kilgore.

Sandra looked down at her cards, then back to Kilgore. A smile formed on her face. *Was she beginning to remember something?* he thought.

"No table talk, young man," she chided Kilgore, as her frail hands tried to put her cards together.

"Of course not. Let me help."

Daniel deftly picked up her cards, sorting them high to low: spades, hearts, clubs, and diamonds.

"Here," he said, handing the cards to Sandra. "Let the bidding begin."

"One heart," said the cautious Doctor.

"Two diamonds," replied the recent nursing graduate, hoping to make it easy for Sandra who was next in the process.

If Kilgore had any doubts that a connection had been made, Sandra's next remarked convinced him he was right.

"Ace before King, Jim. Have you forgotten?" Sandra replied with a quirky upturned smile as she adjusted her hand to fix Kilgore's mistake.

"Sorry, Mom. It won't happen again," replied her repentant son.

At that moment, the woman sitting at the nearby table who had drawn Sandra's attention earlier stood up. She said to the man sitting next to her, "Honey, stay longer if you want, but I've got to get back to work."

It was an innocent remark, without any intention of sarcasm and innuendo, but to Sandra, it ignited a long-standing hatred. She threw her cards on the table and yelled at the woman.

"Have you ever cared about anyone but yourself, Sheila?"

Sandra struggled to stand as she pushed her chair backward. Arms lined with raised blood vessels and hands marked with deep purple blotches of old age suddenly assumed herculean strength. Sandra was on her feet and headed toward the woman who by now had turned to see who had hollered at her. Kayla stood to block Sandra's path. She placed her hands gently on Sandra's shoulders.

"Sandra, what's happening?"

Sandra stood there, shaking as if a blast of Arctic air had swept across the veranda. Kilgore hurried to her side. If rage had a face, it was Sandra Cotton's.

Her lips quivered as she struggled with unspoken words of hatred.

"I'm so sorry," said Kilgore to the woman to whom Sandra had directed her venom. "She must have had an old memory and obviously not a pleasant one."

Kilgore, along with Dearden and Kayla, took Sandra back to her room.

A young female volunteer guided Dolores Samuels out of the salon where she had just received a haircut and style. The name tag on her red and white striped smock read 'Donna.' In keeping with her buoyant demeanor, her smock displayed various cartoon characters with exaggerated smiles.

"You're looking absolutely beautiful," Donna said. She was eager to make everyone happy.

"Oh, I hope so. I never am really satisfied with the way they cut my hair." She pulled out a compact from the side pocket of her blouse and fiddled with her hair as she gazed into the mirror.

Dolores was quite adept at using her walker. The yellow tennis balls attached to the rear legs allowed her to slide along tile or carpeted surfaces. She was quite confident going over door jambs without looking down. She headed to the outside patio where Kilgore found her. He knew from checking visiting records that no one had come to see her since her admittance in the past year. Dolores had been an elementary school teacher for over thirty years, which accounted for the affinity Kilgore felt for her. Perhaps that would be the connection, he thought. He lined up some issues that would prompt a response from any teacher.

"Hello, Dolores!" Kilgore said cheerfully, as he pulled up a chair next to her.

Still fixating on her hair, she was having difficulty shifting to this new situation.

"Kent, is that you?" she asked.

The anticipation in her voice of seeing an old friend conflicted with the confused look in her eyes. Kilgore sensed this and attempted to keep pace with the ever-changing conversation.

"Yes, Dolores. It's me, Kent," he responded, with sweet affection.

"Why Kent Tipton, it's been years since…" she started to say. Her mind struggled to remember the face. I know you but from where?

"We worked together," Kilgore said, answering for her. "Remember how we used to joke and laugh in the teacher's lounge?"

"Yes, yes, of course," she replied. The confidence in her words was not reflected in the ebbing awareness in her initial response.

Dolores looked at him and placed her hand on his face as if some tactile stimulation would help her remember what her other senses failed to accomplish.

"Kent, Kent Tipton, is that really you?" her voice rose with excitement.

The beginnings of Parkinson's disease caused her hand to tremor slightly. Kilgore immediately took hold of her hand.

"Yes, Dolores, it's me, Kent," Kilgore said, as he gently kissed the back of her hand. "You look absolutely beautiful," he added.

The embarrassment of a compliment she had not heard in years caused her face to eminent a bashful glow.

"And how do I know you?" she asked, as she let his hand slip away.

"We worked together at Jamestown Elementary School," Kilgore said, completely making up the name of the school and hoping it wouldn't matter. It didn't.

"And how about your children?" Kilgore asked.

"My children?" Dolores said. Confusion seemed to have replaced the prior awareness she had displayed.

"Yes, your sons, Fred and Mitchell. Have you seen them?" Kilgore asked.

Dolores looked at him as if she were a student in school and had been asked a difficult question and now had to search for the answer.

"Yes, I think so," Dolores said. "I hope they like my hair."

She fidgeted with the items in the small purse she carried with her, hoping to find the small compact in it. Failing to find it, her hands reached up to her auburn hair and gently fluffed the new coiffure.

Kilgore sensed that any connection he had made was all too brief and was weakening.

"Dolores, I'll come see you again, real soon," Kilgore said.

Dolores looked at him. "Who are you?"

He cradled her hand in his and with an assuring squeeze said, "Kent Tipton, Dolores. I'll call again."

Kilgore began to think of himself as truly connecting with his friends. He picked up bits and pieces of their pasts. He learned names of family members. He was becoming a part of their present and hopefully connecting with their past. But his next visit with Dolores Samuels would change all of that.

The following week he found Dolores sitting out on the patio. It was around ten a.m., and the sun was just breaking through the gray cloud cover of an impending thunderstorm. The beige material hanging over the pergola meant to offer relief from the sun created a shadow that made it seem later than it was. He pulled up a chair next to her.

"Mom, it's me, Fred." This was his time-tested familiar approach to Dolores.

She turned to him. She looked angelic to Kilgore: her hair neatly done, makeup just right. An Italian silk scarf lay across her lap. Its vibrant colors reflected upward, giving Dolores a saint-like aura. A turquoise necklace with matching earrings complemented her long sleeve floral print dress with a white crocheted hankie tucked discretely under one cuff. Everything just so perfect, except for her eyes. They stared off into the distance as if she were in some faraway place. She turned to Kilgore, her eyes now searching for some sign of recognition.

"I'm so sorry, but who are you?" She gently asked. She wanted so much for him to be her son, but she was unconvinced.

Kilgore leaned forward and whispered in her ear, "It's me, Fred, your son," he said, mustering the empathy only a son can express for his mother.

Somewhere in the murkiness that had become her mind, enough synapses fired off to stir her memory.

"Oh Fred," she gasped excitedly, as the corners of her mouth rose upward to form a smile. "You are here!"

Her exuberance caused Kilgore to swallow hard before he could speak.

"I'm sorry I haven't been around more," Kilgore said. The irony was he had said the same thing to his own mother so many times. It only seemed natural to say it now.

"Oh honey, I know you're so busy," she said, as she gave him an apologetic and understanding smile. She spoke in the manner of an affectionate, compassionate mother.

"Your old friends send you their best," Kilgore said.

Perhaps shifting away from the initial greeting too quickly, Kilgore looked for a response, but the silent gaze told him he may be losing the connection. Then it happened. A family was visiting a loved one at a nearby table. A young tow-headed boy, probably about four, dressed in shorts and wearing a Ninja Turtle t-shirt with Michelangelo on the front, played with some toy cars on the ground next to the table. He would take a car in each hand, rub the wheels on the ground and send them crashing into each other. With each collision came a shriek of joy. Periodically, Dolores glanced at the boy. Her increasing level of anxiety was apparent. Then suddenly, after one shriek, she cried out, "No, no. Not my Mitchell."

As protective as if he was a real son, Kilgore placed his hands over her. "Mom it's all right. Everything's all right."

Dolores maintained her level of agitation for a moment and then dropped her head, murmuring mournfully, "My son."

Kilgore ran hurriedly for an aide. Dolores was slumped back in her chair. The aide quickly felt Dolores's wrist for an elevated pulse. There was none.

"I think she's going to be fine, but we should get her to her room," the aide said.

With that assurance, Kilgore led her back to her room. He and the aid helped Dolores onto her bed. He kissed her gently on the forehead and said, "I'll be back, Mom." It wasn't until he got to his car that it hit him. His stomach cramped. His throat muscles contracted. Then Kilgore lost whatever was left of his breakfast. It was just like the day it had happened.

It was Christmas vacation, December 15, 2004, to be precise. Kilgore and his wife, Vivian, had just returned from Sunday services. Vivian had been in the bedroom changing clothes when Kilgore had heard the slamming of car doors. He looked out the kitchen window and had seen two young Marines in their dress blues walking up the steps to the door. He didn't have to hear them speak to know the reason for their visit. His knees had started to buckle, and he grabbed onto the sink for support. There was a knock on the door, and then the doorbell rang. Vivian had called out from the bedroom, "Daniel, can you get that?"

Kilgore didn't respond. He had walked to the front door and opened it.

"Mr. Kilgore, my name is Staff Sergeant Matthews, and this is Corporal Clooney. We have some news about your son, Lance Corporal Gregory Kilgore. May we come in?"

His throat paralyzed, Kilgore had guided the visitors to the living room. As they sat down, Vivian appeared. The two Marines had immediately stood up. Staff Sergeant Matthews introduced himself and the young Corporal. With a sweet smile that made the impending news even more difficult to tell, Vivian had said, "It's almost lunchtime. You two boys must be hungry. Can I get either of you something to eat?" The Staff Sergeant had said no. He had done this so many times before, perhaps too many times. Vivian remained oblivious to the nature of their visit.

"Mr. and Mrs. Kilgore, three days ago your son's squad was on an operation to clear a group of houses in Kabul where insurgents were suspected of hiding. They encountered stiff resistance. It is my unfortunate duty to tell you that your son, Lance Corporal Gregory Kilgore, was killed in that encounter."

Whatever had been said after that, Vivian Kilgore heard nothing. Her screams of emotional agony had startled the young corporal who had instinctively flinched in his chair. The staff sergeant walked over to her and knelt on one knee. Daniel Kilgore had cradled his wife in his arms as the staff sergeant spoke.

"No matter how many times I say this, it doesn't get any easier or less truthful. I am so sorry for your loss, Mrs. Kilgore. Your son gave his life so other Marines might live."

The staff sergeant turned to Daniel. Slowly and deliberately, in his baritone voice, he recounted the series of events that led to the ultimate demise of the younger Kilgore.

"Lance Corporal Kilgore's squad came under heavy automatic weapons fire from insurgents on one of the rooftops. The squad leader directed his team to take cover in an alleyway. They were prepared to turn the corner when your son grabbed the Marine on point and took his place. That young Marine had only been in the country a week, and your son was more experienced. Just as Lance Corporal Kilgore turned the corner, an IED exploded. Your son died from the blast."

Twelve years after his son's death, Kilgore's memory of that day, that moment, every word that was said was as fresh as the day it happened. If that wasn't enough, every time Kilgore passed his son's old high school where he was a starter on the baseball team, every time Kilgore ran into one of Greg's old friends who would politely ask how he was doing, Kilgore's heart was shredded again. Family photos in the living room and on the hallway walls did little to alleviate the agony of their loss. Only in the bottom drawer of Kilgore's desk was there any sign of his son's service.

On rare occasions, such as Greg's birthday or the day of his death, would Kilgore open the desk drawer and take out the small case containing the Purple Heart that had been awarded his son. *Was this the sum of his son's life?* Kilgore thought, *half an ounce of metal and a purple ribbon.* His torture only increased when he thought of what kind of life his son might have lived. It was the particular kind of guilt only a parent could feel who had sacrificed their only son.

Chapter 8

THE NIGHTMARE

*I*n the weeks since their lunch at Sam's Deli where Jane Lincoln agreed to work with Vivian Kilgore, she noticed a disturbing pattern. Periods of awareness had become shorter and shorter. Muscular reaction to physical stimuli was slower and less intense. She had trouble remembering personal history. There were several symptoms which led Lincoln to surmise that the neurological degeneration was not the result of a traumatic brain injury alone. It pained her to see the frustration on Vivian's face when she struggled to remember even the simplest things. Lincoln began to feel more and more guilty at the false hope she had given Vivian that things would get better. Compounding her professional failure with Vivian was the increasing attraction she was developing for Daniel. She found herself clearing her calendar earlier on the days she had a session with Vivian so she could arrive ahead of the appointed time. At first, she had convinced herself the time with Kilgore was necessary to plan the subject matter for Vivian's sessions. In time, the post-session time with Kilgore grew longer as well.

Years of regular attendance at school had shaped Kilgore into a timely punctual being. He arrived home promptly at 12:30 p.m.

"Daniel, can I have a word with you?" Lincoln asked, always striving to maintain a professional demeanor, her attractive features were tense. More so than ever now, Lincoln needed to keep some clinical separation between herself and Kilgore.

The tone of her voice put Kilgore on the defensive.

This sounds a bit formal, Kilgore thought. He set his worn valise down and took a seat on the sofa. The eight-foot-long green plaid sofa was well worn on one end where their son, Greg, routinely sat. The food and liquid stains were remainders of the snacks Greg ate with his father while watching football games on the weekends.

"Certainly," he said. He tried to appear relaxed, but the combination of her facial gestures and the brevity of her remarks put him on edge.

"Daniel, when I first reviewed the medical records, I was fairly certain we were dealing with what is called retrograde amnesia. There were clear indications that the hippocampus of the brain was not processing new information with old information—in other words, turning short-term memories into long-term memories. Now I believe there is something else going on."

On unfamiliar turf, his mind raced. He tried desperately to prepare for what was coming.

"What?" Kilgore asked with enough anxiety in his voice to alert Lincoln he was desperate for good news.

Lincoln's heart writhed with dread for taking Daniel back to yet another of the most painful times of his life. There was no way to cushion the impact of her remarks. She stood up and walked to the fireplace across the room. Lincoln did not want him to see her face, not just yet. She took a deep breath, exhaled slowly and turned around. Kilgore had moved forward, sitting on the edge of the sofa. She had given him the feeling as if he was going to be interrogated. He tried mentally to tell himself to stay calm but to no avail. He found his throat getting dry. An uncomfortable perspiration formed on his forehead.

"You said the accident occurred when you and your wife were returning from a medical appointment."

"That's correct," Kilgore replied. In his mind's eye, he instantly went back to that time, visualizing every detail.

"What was the nature of the appointment? Was it purely medical?"

An uneasiness came over Kilgore. This part of his past he was not comfortable talking about. The stigma associated with the subject heavily influenced him.

"Not exactly," he said, "The doctor's office had called us, wanting Vivian and me to come in for a consultation."

Kilgore leaned back against the sofa. His thoughts began to slow, his emotions stirred. He turned his head toward a small picture, framed in gold, of him and his wife on their wedding day. The days of being less than truthful with Jane Lincoln had finally caught up with him. He would have to be honest with her and himself.

"About a year ago, Vivian began to show signs of short-term memory loss. Certain types of physical activity exhausted her. I thought it wise to get a medical opinion on what was happening. That appointment led to several others. The last one, before the accident occurred, was with Dr. William Forsyth, a supposed expert in the study of dementia."

"I know of his work, Daniel. The man is brilliant," Lincoln added.

"Anyway, what Dr. Forsyth told us was the most difficult news of all. He said Vivian was most likely experiencing the early onset of dementia. Unfortunately, it appeared to him it was a fast-developing form of the disease. I was hoping against hope that her decline had more to do with the trauma to her brain because of the accident, which was why I approached you with my counter-offer. At least then, there might be hope of recovery."

Not realizing it, Kilgore spoke his sentences in a staccato manner, as though releasing them in such a way would mitigate their impact on both.

Kilgore walked across to the fireplace where Lincoln was standing. He said nothing. She knew he was in great pain. She wanted to reach out and hold him, anything to ease his pain. At the same moment, Kilgore wanted nothing more than to be held.

"We had left the doctor's office just after four p.m. and were headed home. Traffic downtown was stop and go at that time of day. We were at the intersection of Lawson and Grant waiting for the light to change. When the light turned green, my mind was still in the doctor's office. Vivian had to tell me the light had changed. As I pulled out into the intersection, a teenage kid ran through the light. He was probably impatient like everyone else and just wanted to get through the intersection without having to wait for another cycle. Anyway, he struck our car on Vivian's side. The impact spun us in circles through the intersection into the light stanchion on the opposite corner. Vivian suffered a broken neck and was paralyzed from the shoulders down. Her mental problems seemed to exacerbate after that."

The urge to put her arms around the grieving Kilgore tore at her heart. Somehow, she was able to keep her professional objectivity.

"Daniel, I think Dr. Forsyth was right. I believe Vivian is suffering from the same type of dementia that led to deaths in several notable cases. Pat Summit, the women's basketball coach at Tennessee, is one such example. I served on the medical research team studying the Pat Summit case. I hate to have to say this, Daniel, but I don't think there's much time left, a year at best. More than likely you can measure her time in months."

Kilgore felt an almost uncontrollable urge to scream. He had to compose himself. Though his answer was direct, almost clinical, it belied the deep pain he endured. His wife was everything to him. He no longer looked 6' 2". The emotional weight of recalling the events caused his shoulders to slump. His face was void of color, and his eyes stared blankly ahead.

"I suppose I always suspected something like that. Does this mean your research with her is finished?"

Lincoln stood up and placed her notebook in her bag.

"My research, yes." *Be professional*, she reminded herself. "But if it's all right with you, I'd like to continue coming. Another aspect of my interest is the effects of dementia on family members."

"So, I become the subject, huh?"

"In a manner of speaking, yes."

"What can it hurt?" Kilgore said, as he denied to himself he was feeling anything other than gratefulness to hear a human voice when he came home.

Madeline Orsini, the Director of Magnolia Gardens, was reviewing the quarterly reports each treatment team had prepared. She set aside the reports written on Dolores Samuels, Sandra Cotton, and Mary Hillman. She wanted the families to know, discreetly, of the time Kilgore was spending with their loved one. She expected them to be gratified by the news. Despite her years of experience, she would be stunned by the response.

Chapter 9

THE FAILURES

Gilda poured herself a second Macallan single-malt scotch and lit the last cigarette from a pack of Virginia Slims. Another argument with the same ending—no, he wasn't going to get a divorce and yes, he loved her. After all, hadn't he taken care of her financial future? Marriage was out of the question, and Gilda fumed. She was the one on George's arm at all the country club functions. It was always her that drew notice at the political fundraisers they attended as a couple. It was her body George loved to explore, and she had let him, whenever and wherever he wanted. The one thing she didn't have, the one thing that would end all the behind-the-back smirks and gossip, was his last name.

She finished her drink far too fast for someone as urbane and sophisticated as she portrayed herself and went to the bar to pour another. George spared nothing when he'd had the custom bar built. It was made of rich mahogany imported from India. It had a silver-plated footrest with a nubuck leather handrail. Each side of the back mirror had four levels to display George's collection of expensive liquors. She didn't care. He was at his monthly poker game and was not due home until late. She got a little sloppy with the pour, spilling some of his favorite scotch on the granite bar. She went to the kitchen for a towel. There on the counter where the maid put the mail was a letter from Magnolia Gardens. It only served to intensify her rage. Gilda grabbed the letter, tore it in half and threw it into the garbage can under the sink. Thinking this act would somehow mollify her anger, it only intensified her ire.

The alarm went off at 4:30 a.m. and George Hillman was instantly awake. It was his normal routine now to rise each day, shower, dress and be at his desk for the opening of the New York Stock Exchange at eight a.m. Eastern Standard Time. He had spent twenty-five years as a hedge fund manager at Rothman Brothers and had retired with a severance package that should have attracted the attention of the IRS, SEC, and any other agency concerned with corporate fraud.

He left Gilda sleeping, her breath still reeking of Scotch, and went to the kitchen to make a cup of coffee and toast a bagel. Her beauty, though apparent, had no effect on him this day. With his last bite of bagel, he wiped his face with his napkin and went to put it in the garbage can. There on the top of the garbage was a letter that had been torn in half. The symbol in the upper right-hand corner of one half of the torn letter caught his eye, "Magnolia Gardens."

Remembering the argument from the night before, he took the two halves of the letter from the garbage can and laid them next to each other on the counter. He began to read. His wife had suffered an emotional outburst that had been handled by her visitor and medical staff. There appeared to be no lasting side effects.

What visitor? he thought; Mary was an only child whose parents had long since passed on. He and Mary had no children, and George's only sister lived in Italy. Who the hell was this visitor?

Why it bothered him, he didn't know. Perhaps it was the way he found out. Anyway, he'd deal with it later. For now, the market was about to open, and though he was retired, George never lost the thrill of the game—the chase to find that perfect company to invest in at the right time and at the right price. His poker-playing buddies had ponied up close to $200,000.00 for George to play with; and so far, they had done quite well by him. As he punched in his account number, the thought of that letter began to haunt him. The years of long hours, time with Gilda, and expensive booze had helped George cope with the guilt of what had happened to Mary. Now his memory of her was flowing back. He would not be able to prevent it.

*N*ever again, Fred Samuels thought, *never two presentations back to back with an installation scheduled in between. After all, he was the founder of the damn company. He ought to have some leeway in his work schedule. To hell with what his CFO said needed to be done for corporate growth.*

The splash of cold water in the men's room at the airport provided momentary relief from his flight. His eyes burned from reading the reports on the installation given him before he left. He had been gone almost five weeks. After a couple of days getting over the jet lag, he'd hoped life would return to normal. The letter from Magnolia Gardens made sure that didn't happen.

Sheila had gone shopping, yet again, leaving Fred with a few hours to catch up on the mail. He looked at the stack of letters which easily could have been reduced to a third of its size, had his wife only decided that anything addressed to "resident" could be thrown away. *Really, Fred thought, as he tossed letter after letter into the trash, all addressed "resident." She couldn't decide whether to throw these away?* He realized he was focusing on a rather trivial matter when there were others that could be of greater concern.

He had set aside the two letters from Magnolia Gardens. He opened the oldest one first. It was the quarterly health summary, sent out by the facility director. Though his mother had no serious issues, the letter stated there was some noted degradation in certain cognitive functions and motor skills. It was the second letter that caused him concern. Apparently, his mother had suffered what was referred to as a memory eruption—called so because of the sudden and intense emotional reaction the memory had evoked. Fortunately, his mother's visitor calmed her down, the letter said.

Who was visiting his mother? he thought. *But more importantly, why had the two letters from the Gardens not been opened by his wife?*

Her inability to share in the responsibility of his mother's care irked him far more than the mail issue. In a moment of cathartic self-analysis, Fred Samuels realized he was as guilty as his wife when it came to making family decisions. There was no reason why he couldn't have decided when to visit his mother. Yes, his work kept him away, but he could have exerted maximum influence on his CFO to schedule less time away from home.

Finding the time for a two-hour plane ride from Dallas to Charleston, South Carolina should never have been a problem. As pitiful as it sounded, in his mind those quarterly health reviews were like a visit to his mother. She was doing okay, no serious health issues, gets along well with others. "I love you, Mom! See you next quarter."

Self-judgement is a horrible thing, and Fred Samuels could no longer tolerate the verdict. With a new-found sense of resolution, he picked up his phone and called work.

"Helen, this is Fred. I need you to do something for me," he said.

His administrative assistant for nearly fifteen years, Helen Wiley had a sense of familiarity Samuels found refreshing among the sycophant office types trying to climb their way to the top.

"Sure boss. What is it?"

"I want you to get hold of Arthur and tell him to clear my calendar after the fifteenth of the month. I'm taking some time off."

"Got it," his assistant said, as she scribbled a note in her day planner. "I'll leave Harry out of the loop?"

"Absolutely, if he knows I'm taking time off, I'll get calls to fix every little nitpicky problem his lazy ass won't try to fix."

The assistant started to laugh. The CFO was one of the few individuals that most everyone at the company thought of as useless. He came to the company with the reputation as some sort of financial troubleshooter. That reputation was shredded the day an assistant analyst had to remind him a number inside parentheses means a loss.

"Consider it done, Fred," Helen said. "Enjoy your time off. You deserve it."

"Enjoy" was hardly the descriptive word Fred Samuels would have used. "Guilt cleansing" was more like it, and to find out who was the mysterious stranger visiting his mother. As he hung up the phone, his wife returned from her shopping trip.

"You're home?" she said, as she set her bags down near the coat tree. "How's the jet lag?"

She intended to feign sincerity, but her husband was well acquainted with her lack of earnestness. There was no need for him to fake the same emotion. For some time, theirs had been a marriage of convenience. For Sheila, their marriage had become a matter of inconvenience. A stack of newspapers laid in the corner by the coat tree in the hallway. Rings on the countertops indicated the absence of a wet sponge being used. Apparently, Sheila no longer used the closet to store her shoes, as several pairs littered the entryway and living room.

When she couldn't wait any longer for him to answer, Sheila asked, "Drink?"

"Sure, make mine a Hennessey on the rocks."

Sheila poured a healthy amount of Hennessey into a glass and dropped in two ice cubes. Then she made herself a Bloody Mary with double the amount of vodka even a professional bartender would pour and sat down next to her husband. Despite their physical proximity, the gap between them was laughable.

"I was going through the mail while you were gone and came across two letters from Magnolia Gardens."

"Yeah, when they came, I couldn't decide whether to open them or not, so I saved them for you."

Her lack of interest was more than obvious. In recent years, the only thing that interested Sheila was her appearance. She had hounded Fred for a breast augmentation. She found every opportunity possible to display as much cleavage as she could. Her makeup counter had every type imaginable of facial cream, wrinkle remover or youth restorer on the market.

Fred decided to take the high road and not instigate an argument. There was no communicating with her, through argument or otherwise.

When Fred had tried in the past, Sheila responded with silence or a sparse, "Whatever you want to do?"

"Well, I read them," he said. "One was the quarterly health summary they normally send. The other one, though, spoke to a small problem mom was having that was handled by her visitor and the staff. I was never aware anyone was visiting her."

His words fell on deaf ears, as she drained half her bloody Mary through the straw. In resignation, he reached for his Hennessey. Fred took a long sip and let it slowly trickle down his throat. *Funny*, he thought, *why did I think I needed Sheila's input. I can do this on my own.* The emptiness of their marriage edged into his mind.

"Anyway, I was thinking; I haven't seen Mom since I placed her in that facility, and it's time for a visit."

He was speaking to himself and saying it out loud was just an afterthought.

"Swell," Sheila said. "I'll check my calendar and see if I can figure out a time when I can go with you."

The tone of her voice expressed annoyance that she would have to take time off for something so petty.

"That won't be necessary, sweetheart. I've already decided to go by myself. You really don't have to figure out how to free yourself."

The affectionate "sweetheart" had a decidedly icy, cynical tone to it.

Sheila was more relieved than feeling any guilt about not going. She had filled five weeks of alone time with someone new. Another absence by her husband was an opportunity for yet another tryst. Fred Samuels had never considered divorce, but he might as well have because emotionally he had abandoned this marriage long ago. There were no shared dreams, only providing for Sheila's dreams when she wanted a new car or to go on a Caribbean vacation. He couldn't remember the last time they had a quiet dinner out. It was usually Sheila who was going out with her friends. Samuels had no one to blame but himself. He had fallen for her looks, not her love of books. The depth of her intellect matched the layers of makeup she wore.

Macdill Air Force Base located outside of Tampa, Florida, had been Jim Cotton's final assignment. In some ways, he was the poster boy for the Air Force in the intense competition with other services to show they were the best. Jim was 6' tall, with a frame toned from years of working out and slender from his daily three-mile runs. His brown hair had not a trace of gray. He was nearing the end of a thirty-year career and had submitted his retirement papers effective the end of the year. Retirement would change nothing for Jim. He'd retire on a Friday and report to work on a Monday at Raytheon for twice what he was making as a full Colonel in the Air Force. *Sweet deal*, he thought.

His wife, Carrie, had maintained an equally healthy appearance, but for completely different reasons. She was the wife of an up and coming young officer and wanted to show herself as his equal, at least in body. Their minds were a different matter. Carrie cared about image and perception. Her competition was the other wives of Jim's peers. Could she be more attractive? More engaging at social gatherings? She viewed joining the Book of the Month Club as a requirement which she met easily by reading reviews from critics rather than the books themselves. She had already begun scouring the real estate market for a suitable home since base housing would no longer be available for retirees. Between real estate brochures, retirement papers and letters from Vanderbilt University about housing, meal programs, parking permits, and preregistration, there was hardly any room on Jim Cotton's desk. Samantha had made an excuse to be with friends and with Carrie on a shopping spree, Jim took the opportunity to go through the mound of mail on his desk.

It wasn't the papers on his desk that caught him by surprise, but rather what fell out from the back of his day-planner when he moved it from its inclined stand—it was a letter addressed to him from Magnolia Gardens. He hadn't put it there; in fact, he had read every single quarterly report they sent, even if privately. Jim would go to almost any length to avoid an argument with his wife. He opened the letter and read it. He laid it on his desk, both angry and confused. He heard the front door open and close.

"Carrie, is that you?" he called out.

"Yes."

"Can you come here for a second?"

She appeared more than a little annoyed at his summons as she hadn't even had time to put the bags with her purchases from Chico's away.

"Really, does it have to be now?"

"Yes, now," he snapped, no longer willing to be patient, "Do you have any idea how this letter from the Gardens got into the back of my day planner?"

Carrie crossed her arms, leaned against the door jam and rolled her eyes upward. Her foot tapped nervously on the floor.

"Well, do you?" He asserted more forcefully this time.

"All right, Jim, yes. I know how it got there," Caroline said, as the rancor in her voice started to grow. "I put it there for you to read later after we got back from taking Sam to Vanderbilt and spending time with Billy before he goes back to Rice. Why are you acting like the Grand Inquisitor? You never paid any attention to them before!"

Cotton literally jumped to his feet and hollered, "Well, I'm damn sure going to pay attention to this one," throwing the letter down on his desk.

Samantha had returned from a day outing with her boyfriend and had overheard the argument with her parents.

"Pay attention to which one?" their daughter said.

Carrie stormed off down the hallway, leaving Jim to explain.

"It's a letter from the Gardens about your grandmother. I get one once a quarter. This one talks about someone who's been visiting her and something about mom talking to a female visitor as if it were you. I think it's time I pay her a visit. It's long overdue."

Samantha stepped into her father's den and shut the door behind her. At twenty, she had her mother's physical appearance: clear complexion, white teeth, gorgeous hazel eyes and a burgeoning model's figure. The apprehension on her face alerted Jim something was up. Her fingers wove nervously through her shoulder-length hair. Her eyes darted left and right, never once looking at her father.

"Honey, what's wrong?"

She pulled up a chair and sat next to her father.

"Daddy, I have to go with you."

"But sweetheart, there's so much to do what with you returning to Vanderbilt. Your mother would have a fit."

"I don't care about what Mom says about returning to Vanderbilt. That's mostly her idea. I want to see Gramma and thank her. You two were the only ones who comforted me, who didn't think of me as some sort of a slut. I need to thank her."

Tears were rolling down both their faces, intensified by their shared experience as well as their strong bond of love.

"It's a little over a seven-hour drive. We can be up and back in three days," Jim said.

Samantha jumped to her feet. "I'll tell Mom." Her tears were instantly gone, and she was exhilarated at the idea.

"No," said her dad, who was now feeling an inner strength he hadn't experienced in years. "I will." It took this brief moment for him to realize how submissive he had become.

Cotton stood up and walked down the hallway to the master bedroom. The door was closed, but he opened it and went inside. His wife was sitting in front of her vanity desk, deftly applying her eyeliner as if she hadn't a care in the world. Jim almost started to chuckle as his wife reminded him of Scarlet O'Hara in Gone with the Wind, and, like Rhett Butler, Jim Cotton had reached a point where frankly, he didn't give a damn either.

"Carrie, I'm taking Samantha. We're going to see my mother."

Caroline Cotton rolled her eyes upward, never looking once at her husband and gently applying another stroke of her eyeliner. "And I care because?"

You have the audacity to say that after all she's done for this family, Jim Cotton thought, as he threw his service hat across the room. His mother had been the glue that held his family together when he had to be deployed to the Middle East, nine deployments over fifteen years. It had been Sandra Cotton, not Caroline Cotton, who was the strength of the family.

His wife, Caroline, was an abject failure when it came to raising their two small children, Samantha and William. That's where his mother came in. Caroline Cotton may have been a genius planning a dinner party, getting just the right caterer and seeing that just the right people sat next to each other, but when it came to her children, helping them with homework, getting them to athletic events, you name it, Caroline was a bust. The nurturing type she was not. Jim's mother, Sandra, was a different story. But Caroline continually sought to minimize her mother-in-law's contribution to the family well-being. This attitude had produced the most serious conflicts in their married life.

Chapter 10

CONFLICTION

There was a time in the beginning when Jane Lincoln and Vivian Kilgore could chat as if they were the best of friends. There would be the repeated prompts from Lincoln to elicit a memory from Vivian. Vivian never took exception to these clinical provocations. She would smile and then thank Lincoln for her help.

Now, months later, in the final stages of the aggressive form of dementia which had invaded Vivian's brain, she was confined to a hospital bed. Most of her memory was gone except for an occasional sudden flash of recognition. Jane and Daniel continued to talk to her, and occasionally they would see a faint smile form on her face or feel the gentle squeeze of her hand.

In some ways, between caring for his wife and visiting his friends, as he called them, Daniel Kilgore was living a double life at home and at the Gardens. The accident had been bad enough, but at least they could converse with each other in the beginning. Then dementia began to take over.

When it was only he taking care of her, he sometimes found himself getting frustrated, even angry, at her mental lapses. Oddly, he never felt that way when visiting his friends. One day he realized why. When he was at the Gardens, he wasn't Daniel Kilgore—he was George, or Jim or Fred or whoever he had to pretend to be. One afternoon, he shared that realization with Jane.

"It's like I'm an actor when I'm there," he said, "but when I'm home, I have to be me. I can't act anymore. I'm ashamed of the frustration I feel about having to care for her."

The sudden verbalization of this truth caused Kilgore to slam his fist on the table.

During her work with Vivian, Jane Lincoln came to think of her as a friend, possibly her best friend? Her feelings for Daniel Kilgore were vastly different and more complex. Though she denied it to herself, there had been an immediate attraction when they had first met at the conference. In the months that followed, the attraction grew, though Jane never allowed herself to admit it, much less act on it. Her professionalism and sense of propriety would not allow it. Still, her emotions continued to be engaged.

When she first started, their interactions had been professional, practically antiseptic in nature. Jane would question Daniel about the data he collected, and she would share hers with him, always with a positive spin, even though that was an assumption on her part.

In time, she became focused on more than just exchanging data. There was a genuine and deep tenderness when he talked about his friends at the Gardens. His laughter was intoxicating as he recounted the truly funny interactions that took place between staff and residents. Like the time Sharon Wilson accused Harold Miller of sneaking into her room one night and then bragged to her therapist the next day how great he was. Apparently, Sharon was quite graphic in her description of Harold's anatomy.

More touching to Jane was his description of his life with Vivian: how they had met in college, their courtship, and the wonder of bringing their son, Gregory, into the world. Tiny forgotten details of a shared lifetime began to emerge: afternoon walks with Vivian and Gregory in a stroller, Saturdays spent watching a six-year-old play soccer, summer vacations on the coast, buying Vivian a kiln for her ever-expanding hobby of ceramics, and their first pet, a dog Gregory named Sparky.

Jane forced herself to be professional—well, not completely professional. She took hold of Daniel's hand and held it. Her face reflected the sincerity of her words.

"Daniel, I don't think you should feel like you're acting when you're talking with Vivian to get some sort of desired response. Forget hoping to be some sort of a bridge to a past memory, as you describe it. Talk to her of falling in love with her all over again. You two built dreams together; talk about them. Tell her of the fears, doubts that you had about your career. Tell her of the confidence you had in her when she told you of her life dreams. She'll hear you. She'll feel your heart all over again. I promise you." *I know, because I do*, she thought.

"I don't know how to thank you for the time you've spent with Vivian and me."

His eyes reflected the sincerity of his statement.

"I'm sorry it didn't turn out the way we expected."

She glanced at her watch and made up some inane excuse that she had to be somewhere. If she didn't get up and leave now, she was afraid she'd throw her arms around him. The feeling was becoming almost beyond her power to control.

"Oh my gosh," she feigned surprise. "I'm supposed to meet some friends from the research center at the school. I really must be going," she gushed.

"I'll see you to the door."

Again, the polite and oh-so-civil hug and she was gone.

Taking Lincoln's advice, Kilgore began to recount their life together. He talked about the first time he saw Vivian standing on the dimly lit steps of her dormitory. She had radiated such beauty that she brightened the entire quad. He talked about the anxiousness he felt on their first date, the hesitancy on his part before their first kiss, and the butterflies he felt the day he told her that he loved her.

Periods of clarity were becoming fewer and fewer. Today, Daniel was lucky. Vivian's bed had been adjusted to a 45° angle, and she seemed to give every indication she was paying attention to the news on the TV. Kilgore reached for the remote control and lowered the volume. She remained focused on the TV. He moved his chair close to the bed and took hold of Vivian's hand with the tenderness and compassion that only comes from nearly thirty years of intimacy and said, "Let me tell you about the day I fell in love with you."

Her eyes turned to the left and then the right, as she tried to locate the vaguely familiar yet somehow unidentifiable voice. With a gentle yet insistent squeeze of her hand, Daniel continued.

"It was the night we went to the concert at the convention center. Glenn Campbell was playing. You were the most beautiful girl in the crowd. I was on cloud nine just from the scent of your perfume. Those freckles that bothered you so; well, they only made you look more vulnerable, and I was going to be your protector. You had your hair done that day, and your makeup was perfect. I couldn't take my eyes off you."

Daniel rested his head on the back of a chair and closed his eyes. He was back in the moment. Although he was not a man given to fantasy, the intensity of that moment had an almost mystical effect on him

"When Glenn Campbell started to sing 'Gentle on my Mind,' my mind was made up. I was going to marry you."

Daniel opened his eyes to see the faintest form of a smile on his wife's face. *Had she heard him?* he thought. *Could Jane have been wrong?* He quickly continued.

"I remember the day I asked your father if I could marry you. Not that I would have listened had he said no, but I thought tradition demanded it. He gave me that 'are you crazy!' look. You were so embarrassed you shouted, 'Daddy, please. He's serious.'"

Kilgore sat silent, watching his wife for any sign of awareness. There was none. He slowly stood up and straightened out the blanket lying across his wife and leaned forward, gently kissing her on the lips. The weight of his emotional remembrance caused his shoulders to slump. A sudden chill came over him, a harbinger of the pain he would soon endure. He walked slowly to his den to make a few notes to tell Lincoln and then make an outline for his next visit to his friends. He had no sooner sat down when the doorbell rang. Damn, he thought, hoping it hadn't disturbed his wife. Kilgore hurried to the front door before the visitor could ring again.

Before him stood a young man about his deceased son's age and his apparent wife, holding a baby. The young man was wearing his green Marine Corps service uniform. He wore sergeant's chevrons with two service stripes about each cuff. Three rows of service ribbons, none of which Kilgore recognized, hung above the Marine's left breast pocket. Below them hung an expert marksmanship medal.

"Yes," Kilgore said to the young man and woman standing in front of him

The young Marine started hesitantly. "Mr. Kilgore, I'm Sergeant Gary Henley. I served with your son, Greg, in Iraq."

Kilgore stared at the young man. His mind raced back to that time he had tried to erase from his memory—of the countless, faceless uniforms that passed before him and his wife offering them their condolences. Slowly, Kilgore remembered. His son, Greg, had written home that the newest member of his fire team was from Columbia, South Carolina, about a two-hour drive from where Greg had grown up. The two young Marines soon became the best of friends. Kilgore's knees weakened slightly as he noticed the resemblance between the young Marine and his son. The dark hair, eyes set wide apart, and a poster-like chiseled jaw with dimples. His blonde-haired wife looked to be in her early twenties.

"I'm sorry for not remembering, Gary. Greg spoke fondly of you in his letters to us."

"No apology necessary, Sir. This is my wife, Sherry."

The young woman extended one hand while she held her baby in the other arm. "Sherry, it's my pleasure," Kilgore replied. "Please come in, won't you?"

Kilgore led them into the living room. The young Marine was immediately drawn to the array of family photos on the wall to his left. He took a moment to look at Greg's high school baseball team picture. The pictures of family camping trips reminded Gary of his own growing up. The focal point of the living room was a large oak entertainment center which housed a 62" HDC television with surround sound, including a blue-ray CD player. To the left of the TV was a collection of Kilgore's favorite books. To the right of the TV, a collection of Vivian's favorite music CDs. At the other end of the living room was a large red brick fireplace. Kilgore adjusted the position of his lazy-boy to face them. The empty plate with silverware on it, a reminder of last night's dinner, begged an explanation.

"Please excuse the mess. I'm not much of a housekeeper," Kilgore said, as he picked up the plate. "Can I get either of you iced tea or water? And what about that young baby? What can I get him?"

He stared at the young baby. Daniel Kilgore loved the children that touched his life as a teacher, and he would have loved nothing more than for his son to have given him a grandchild.

"Water will be just fine, Sir."

Kilgore went to the kitchen. He set the plate in an already crowded sink and returned with two bottles of cold water and iced tea for himself. He had never been comfortable in the kitchen but had forced himself to become somewhat of a cook since Vivian's illness.

"Did you come to talk about Greg?" Kilgore asked, trying to calm his nerves from the last time a Marine came to his door.

Henley reached out to hold his wife's hand. "I was in Greg's unit overseas. I wouldn't be here today if it weren't for him. I have never forgotten what he did for me. After the birth of our son, we knew we had to bring him here for you folks to meet."

The young Marine's voice quivered with emotion as he continued.

"Mr. Kilgore, my wife and I wanted to introduce you and your wife to our son."

"My wife is indisposed," Kilgore said, "But please, let's do the introduction."

Ill at ease with what he wanted to convey, Gary pushed himself to speak. His time in the Marines and subsequent service in Iraq had awarded him with greater self-confidence. Yet, given the emotions at play, he faltered a bit.

"Mr. Kilgore, please meet our son, Gregory Kilgore Handley. We've chosen to honor Greg's memory by naming our son after him. In this small way, Greg will continue to live, though our son."

Kilgore was clearly moved by this tribute to his late son. His glass of iced tea shook uncontrollably, spilling on his lap. He had to set it on the coffee table. His forehead rested on trembling hands. When he looked up, unabashed, tears washed down his face.

"I don't know what to say," Kilgore said, as he tried to absorb the enormity of it all. His son's memory would live on.

"Do you think that we could bring the baby to Mrs. Kilgore?" Henley's wife asked as she cooed to a now restless infant.

The young mother's request compounded Kilgore's agony. For months, he had watched his wife slip deeper and deeper into the Hell of dementia. It was just as Lincoln had predicted. Now he would have to explain it to the young couple.

"I'm afraid that wouldn't do any good," Kilgore said.

The puzzled look on their faces told Daniel Kilgore he'd have to explain. He steadied himself to keep control of his emotions. He began. First, the auto accident. Then the misdiagnosis that Vivian's memory loss was not the result of a traumatic brain injury, but rather the onset of a rapidly progressing case of dementia. Lastly, the failed hope that working with a medical expert in one-on-one sessions might help. When he finished, Sherry Henley was in tears. Her husband sat stunned, wondering how much grief Kilgore was supposed to take—first his son and now his wife.

"I'm so sorry, Mr. Kilgore. Is there anything I can do to help? I owe it to Greg. I was on point the day we were on patrol in Kabul. I hadn't been in the country a month. Just before we started around the corner of an abandoned building, Greg jerked me backward so he could take the point. That's when the IED exploded."

Kilgore thought for a moment, *what harm could it do?* Maybe this would ease whatever painful memory remained. He explained what he wanted Henley to do. The young man did not hesitate. "Where is she, Mr. Kilgore?"

Kilgore led the couple down the dimly lit hallway to the master bedroom. The room was sparsely furnished. Their old king-sized bed had been replaced by an adjustable hospital bed which now dominated most of the room. A single nightstand and a wall mounted TV completed the ensemble. A window box partially shaded, allowed a dim light to enter. The happiness that had once filled the room in the past was now replaced by an overwhelming sense of gloom. The young man took a seat close to the bed. Vivian slept calmly.

He turned back to Kilgore as if to say, are you sure? Kilgore nodded yes. Gary took Vivian's hand in his and leaned forward and whispered her, "Mom, it's me, Greg. I'm home."

Vivian made no response. Gary looked at Kilgore. "What do I do now?" his eyes said.

Kilgore inched closer to the bed.

"Again," whispered Kilgore. "This time squeeze her hand when you talk to her."

Greg nodded obediently.

"Mom, please. It's me, Greg, your son. I'm home. I missed you so."

Still, there was no response from Vivian.

Gary rested his head on the bed's handrail. Craig's wife, Sherry, whispered something to Kilgore. He nodded yes. Sherry whispered to her husband what she wanted him to say, and then she laid her sleeping infant on Vivian's chest. He could not bear the feeling of failure if he let his best friend down. A steel resolve took hold of him as he listened to his wife's words. This time the young man did not whisper.

"Mom, it's me, your baby. I'm home. I love you."

Suddenly, Vivian's chest rose, and she uttered a noticeable sigh. Her hand tightened around the young man's fingers sitting next to her. Kilgore quickly moved to the foot of the bed. The infant made a sucking sound as Vivian's chest rose again. She squeezed the hand holding hers one more time, then let go. Her chest settled for the last time.

Chapter 11

MATERNAL BETRAYAL

Samantha stood in front of her bedroom mirror holding up one outfit after another, trying to decide what to wear on her visit to see her grandmother. Should it be an over-the-shoulder blouse with stylish jeans decorated with bling front and back or her ankle length yoga pants with a long sleeved Orlon shirt with slits exposing her upper arms?

Samantha sat on her bed holding to her chest the sweater her grandmother lovingly and painstakingly knitted for her. A flood of memories now accompanied the tears flowing down her face. Samantha loved the smell of fresh baked cookies her grandmother had ready when Samantha came home from school. She cherished the hugs and kisses after her grandmother's review of Samantha's report card. A dollar for every A was icing on the cake. Most of all, it was the way her grandmother listened to her. No dream was ever impossible, no spat with a friend was worth losing a friendship, but above all, no wrongdoing by Samantha ever brought condemnation. Not that Sandra Cotton believed either of her grandchildren, Samantha or William, were perfect, but when Gramma would say, "Well, I think maybe you didn't make the best decision, now did you?"—you knew you weren't going to be exiled to some island in the Pacific.

Samantha remembered the time when her grandmother really stood by her. It was the second time she gave herself the test, not wanting to believe the results when she missed her first period. The second hand on her wristwatch clicked agonizingly slow until three minutes had passed. She looked at what she had hoped would not be there, but it was—a plus sign. This time there was no denying it, Samantha was pregnant. Nothing tested her grandmother's faith in her like the time Samantha had to tell the family she was pregnant by her eighteen-year-old boyfriend.

S amantha waited for dinner to end; it was the longest meal of her life. Mostly she used her fork to move morsels of food randomly around her plate. Her grandmother had cooked her favorite meal, Swedish meatballs. Samantha hadn't eaten a bit. Normally, she had a healthy interest in food. Samantha's behavior had not gone unnoticed by her grandmother.

"Samantha. You hardly touched your dinner. Is anything wrong?" her grandmother asked.

Samantha put her fork down. Her grandmother looked at her, patiently waiting for an answer. Carrie was absorbed in the latest edition of Women's Health. Her father read the newspaper with one hand while jabbing at his food with a fork in the other.

"Mom, Dad, there's something I have to tell you," she said, as tears began to well up in her eyes.

"Can't this wait until later, Samantha? I'd like to have a chance to relax after dinner," her mother said, never once looking at her daughter. This was not unusual; her mother's priorities were well known to the family.

Anguish turned to anger. *Would you please just look at me*, Samantha thought. *For once, listen and don't shout.* The look on her granddaughter's face told Sandra that Samantha couldn't wait.

"Samantha, why don't you and your mom and dad talk in the living room. I'll clear the table," offered her grandmother.

Sandra began clearing the table as the three headed to the living room. Samantha glanced back at her grandmother. If Samantha wanted anyone next to her when she told her parents, it was her grandmother. Her stomach tightened even more.

Carrie turned the dimmer switch on the living room wall to high. Samantha had hoped to keep the lights dimmed to avoid seeing every detail on her parents' faces. Jim and Carrie took a seat on the couch. Samantha elected to stand, facing them.

Sandra had just finished rinsing the first dish when she heard Samantha's mother scream.

"Good God, Samantha! Do you know what you've done to our reputation in this town? How could you!!!"

It was a little "old school" to think that having a child out of wedlock would be a blemish of the family's reputation, but then that's what Carrie Cotton was, "old school." She had insisted on a coming out Cotillion Ball for her daughter when she was sixteen. Carrie's prideful moment came when Samantha won first runner-up in the "Daughters of the South" pageant. Yes, she was old school to a fault.

Sandra dropped her towel and hurried to the living room. Jim was cradling his daughter in his arms. Carrie was at the wet bar where she poured a healthy dose of Tito's vodka and swallowed it. Then she refilled the glass.

"It's that Mike Callahan boy, isn't it? I told you not to date him!" her mother said, continuing her tirade. "Christ! His father drives a truck for UPS. Samantha, think of the differences between our families."

That was enough for Jim. Apparently, his wife had forgotten she had been pregnant with their son when they got married, and Carrie's mother had been mortified that Jim was an enlisted man who had not yet been accepted into the Air Force's Officer's Candidate Training Program.

"Stop it, Carrie! This isn't about Mike Callahan, his family, or what his father does for a living! It's about our daughter and what's best for her!"

Her husband's unexpected tirade had a negligible effect on her.

With that rebuke, Carrie calmly drained her vodka, then poured another. Sandra took a seat next to her granddaughter. Samantha buried herself in her grandmother's arms and sobbed. Sandra looked at her son. His eyes said, *what can we do for her?* When Sandra looked at Carrie, all she saw was *Me! Me! Me!*

Sandra Cotton knew from her son's own experience that this problem was not about love, but it indeed started with love. It started with how Samantha and her boyfriend felt about each other. What were their plans? From that, there were two sets of parents to consider.

As she did when Sandra found herself in a similar situation when her son brought his girlfriend home, she asked Samantha, "Honey, do you love this boy?"

Between sobs, Samantha nodded yes.

"Does he love you?" Sandra continued.

Again, her granddaughter nodded yes.

"Then what do the two of you want to do?" Sandra asked.

"For Christ's sake Sandra! Apparently, all Samantha and that boy know is how to have sex. She's in no position to decide what to do with the rest of her life!" Carrie roared.

With exploding defiance, Samantha leaped to her feet.

"Yes, I do, Mother! I want it all. I want Mike, and he wants me. We want to go to college. We want a family and to have children. We want to get married. And, I'm sorry if it's not in the order you want."

This was not the answer Carrie Cotton wanted to hear. She rose to meet her defiant daughter.

"So, you think you've got all the answers, don't you? Well, try answering this: what do we tell the members of our church or our friends at the county club? What about the members of the Greater Tampa Women's Association? What am I supposed to tell them? And what about your father, young lady? What's he supposed to tell people at the base?"

Carrie continued to act out the role of a 1950's mother wrapped in social convention. Considering society had moved through the era of Masters and Johnson, open marriages, and couples now routinely living together without being married, the whole scene would have been laughable were it not for the charged emotions now raging.

Now the tiger came out in Sandra. She now assumed the role nature had intended for Carrie, the defiant and protective mother figure.

"No Carrie, you're wrong again, like you've been wrong so many times before. Samantha is a smart young woman who knows her heart. The decision to be made is hers and Mike's alone."

Sandra looked at her granddaughter who had now dried her tears with the handkerchief her father had given her.

"Does your boyfriend know? What does he want to do?" Sandra asked. Her intent was to shift the conversation back to a rational discussion.

"Yes, Gramma. He knows, and he wants just what I told Mom," Samantha said, as she began to regain her composure.

Sandra pulled her granddaughter close to her. "Sweetheart, this is not how I would want your adult life to start. You're in a difficult situation. What matters most is how we respond to these situations."

Having been marginalized by Sandra's rational, caring demeanor, Carrie screamed and ran out of the room.

Never was Sandra Cotton more disappointed in her son than when he announced the decision. Samantha would leave Elgin and spend her senior year studying in Europe. Carrie could maintain the family façade by telling people Samantha was still going to enroll in Vanderbilt when she returned. In truth, she was going to spend the time with Carrie's sister in North Carolina until the baby was born and then put up for adoption. It was all a noble plan by Carrie, but unfortunately, illegal under Florida law as Jim would discover. The most they could do was prevent Samantha and her boyfriend from getting married until they were of legal age. Carrie took some solace in the fact that the pregnancy and birth would be out of town. The rest she would worry about later.

When they told Sandra of their decision, Sandra stood in front of them. No longer able or willing to hide her contempt, she stared down at her son. The venom in her voice was a shock to his system.

"I have never been more disappointed or ashamed of you, James. This is so wrong."

He could not look his mother in the eye nor could he stomach looking at his wife. Sandra turned to Carrie who stood at the wet bar using it for balance and gloating as she stirred her glass of vodka.

"If Satan had a wife, you'd be it."

Carrie responded to Sandra's remark by mockingly raising her glass her, as if to say, "Here's to you, too." Jim remained silent, still recovering from his mother's declaration.

Sandra went off to Samantha's room. Samantha lay prone on her bed, crying uncontrollably. She quietly sat next to the sobbing teenager. Deeply touched by the trauma now in her dear granddaughter's life, she searched for words. For a moment, she was silent as her mind grappled with the problem.

"No matter what you are being forced to do, you are a good person. This decision does not define you. It defines your mother and father, and for that, I will be eternally sorry."

Carrie's rants over Jim's mother's support for the young pregnant teenager compounded the emotional stress on Samantha and Jim as well.

"Good God! Jim. I can't believe your mother," Carrie had exploded. "She's not the one who must face your friends and explain the shotgun wedding of your daughter to the son of a truck driver. I wish to hell she'd keep her mouth shut."

"Honey, this situation is difficult enough without bringing my mother into it."

The calmness in his voice did nothing to ease the tension in the room.

"Really!" Carrie had snapped. "She needs to stay out of our business as far as I'm concerned."

James Cotton, normally the voice of reason when it came to family disputes, had realized his wife didn't need to hear reason—she needed a history lesson. His voice started out firm, which immediately got his wife's attention.

"You need to listen to me, and you need to remember, Carrie," he started out.

Before he could go further, Carrie growled, "Remember what?"

His voice rose. "Don't interrupt me! Remember the years Mom took care of the kids? She was the one, not you, who made their lunches, who made sure homework was done, listened to their problems. As sad as it is to admit, she knows the character of our children as well or better than we do. She is at least as emotionally invested. She believes Samantha can make her own decisions. Maybe we should listen?"

It was mid-morning, and Carrie Cotton was waiting in the car in the driveway, the motor running. The temperature was already in the mid-eighties and with the summer humidity approaching ninety degrees, Carrie had the air conditioning on maximum. She had insisted on driving Samantha to her sister's house in North Carolina by herself. She had wanted some alone time with Samantha. She certainly had not wanted her mother-in-law tagging along after Sandra tried to undermine Carrie's decision. Carrie was more motivated by her sense of place in the community than what was in the best interests of her daughter.

"Would you please tell her to hurry up," Carrie growled at Jim, who was standing next to the passenger's side door.

If the tone of her voice didn't fully convey her anger, Carrie's flared nostrils seemed to breathe fire. Her reddening face belied the volcanic rage inside her. Jim looked at his mother and his daughter. They stood on the front porch. Sandra's arms were wrapped tightly around her granddaughter. A good thing, he thought, as he saw Samantha's legs start to buckle slightly.

Jim called out, "Honey, your mom and you really need to get going."

To give unneeded emphasis, Carrie honked the horn. Samantha looked at her father. Her eyes reflected the enormous sense of betrayal she felt. However, it was the look on his mother's face which tore even deeper into his fractured heart. Sandra called to him.

"No, no. This can't be happening."

Samantha walked to where her father was standing after he had put her luggage in the trunk. It wasn't necessary to say anything; her eyes said it all.

"Please Daddy, don't make me do this!"

Samantha hugged her father as tightly as she could, hoping he would have one last measure of strength and stop this. The only strength her father could muster was to whisper, "I'm sorry," and weakly at that.

When Jim looked back at his mother, she was clutching the wrought iron porch rail for support and weeping uncontrollably.

"Are you going to sit there and not say a word for the next five hours?" Carrie asked.

Samantha said nothing. She had no intention of talking to her mother. She propped her purse against the window, leaned her head against it, and closed her eyes. She folded her arms in defiance as if to say, "Go ahead. Make me talk!"

"Samantha, in time you'll look back on this and thank me. You would have never been happy with that boy."

This was Carrie making a sincere effort to be conciliatory.

Samantha's body recoiled as she pushed herself harder against the passenger door. Without opening her eyes, she said quietly, but with jagged sarcasm, "And you and Daddy are such a perfect example of happy people."

Carrie's fingers dug deeply into the steering wheel as the speedometer rose from 60 to nearly 75. It was going to be a much quieter and speedier trip down the interstate than either could have imagined.

Chapter 12

VIVIAN'S GIFT

Ever since Lincoln informed him she didn't think his wife had much time left, Daniel Kilgore knew this day was coming. He dreaded the thought of it. It interrupted his thoughts during the day and his sleep at night—his wife's funeral. Vivian's sister, Kristin Walters, her husband Brad, and their oldest daughter, Michelle, had been staying with Kilgore since Vivian's death.

In the beginning, it had been both a blessing and a curse. Vivian had been extremely close to her sister and Kilgore had kept Kristin informed of everything the doctors had said regarding the prognosis and the treatment. But most of all, Kristin had always noted Daniel's devotion. Kristin and Brad took care of all the details for the service. *It would be exactly what she would have wanted*, Kilgore thought, as Kristin described the plan for the service.

"What would you prefer? We can have a private graveside service for the immediate family only, or we can extend an open invitation to everyone?"

She was remarkably businesslike, considering the depth of her feelings for her sister.

His depression momentarily jolted by the clinical nature of her question, Kilgore quietly answered, "I want that final moment alone, please."

He just couldn't imagine sharing it with anyone.

"I'll make sure it happens," said Brad.

Kilgore appreciated all his extended family did. Now all he really wanted was to be alone to remember, but that wasn't going to happen. Between neighbors, friends from Magnolia Gardens, and extended family members, Kilgore was genuinely happy that Michelle acted as a receptionist, taking care of all the phone calls and answering every knock at the door. At 5' 8", Michelle was taller than most girls her age. Her short cropped brown hair and black framed glasses gave her the appearance of maturity beyond her sixteen years.

One afternoon when her mother and father went to handle some details for the church service, Michelle quietly and thoughtfully, walked over to her uncle, placing a hand on his shoulder.

"Bet you wish this was all over. I mean the visitors, the phone calls, questions?" It was her best effort at compassion, but she sounded like a kid.

He answered with a shrug and a smile. His handsome features somehow sadder now.

"You know, kiddo, ever since the accident, I knew this day was coming. In her own way, I think your aunt did also."

"Oh, she did, Uncle Dan," Michelle said, as she cuddled next to her favorite uncle. "She told Mom all about it, everything."

Not intending to be blunt, none-the-less, her words jolted her uncle.

"What do you mean all about it?"

Kilgore was somehow slightly offended by this invasion into the intimacy between him and his wife.

"Uncle Dan, please!" Michelle said, as she smiled and gave her uncle that 'don't be so naïve' look. She would never have the looks of a classic beauty, but she still had an innate charm about her.

"Auntie Vivian knew you had volunteered with those dementia patients to see if there was something you could learn to slow the disease down. Even before the accident, at one appointment with the doctor when you weren't there, the doctor told Aunt Vivian how bad off he thought she was. But Auntie was really happy about having Dr. Lincoln here."

Kilgore was mystified by his niece's words. He slowly shook his head side to side. He thought; *I had no idea how well Vivian was taking all of this in.*

"That didn't exactly turn out like I expected."

"But it did for Auntie."

"That's impossible!" Kilgore said. His voice rose, unable to contain his frustration. "I explained to her exactly why I brought Dr. Lincoln here and what I hoped she would accomplish. I was there when Jane, I mean Dr. Lincoln, told Vivian what she thought was going on. How could that have possibly made her happy!"

"Uncle Dan, she wasn't happy about that," said Michelle, who would now display wisdom far beyond her years. "She was happy there was someone you could talk with about normal things you're interested in and stuff that makes you laugh."

The young girl was both clinical and perceptive. Kilgore wondered if her parents appreciated this kid.

At that moment, this was more information than Kilgore needed or wanted to know. Had Vivian really thought about his solitary life after she was gone? Was this some cryptic approval to move on with Lincoln? After all, he had successfully ignored the conflicted feelings that had risen in him in the last six months, or so he had told himself. His niece had now put a crack in that wall of denial. Overwhelmed, he let his head rest against the back of the couch. Michelle got up from the couch and went to another area of the house, leaving Kilgore to his thoughts.

Jane Lincoln sat curled up on the living room sofa. The aroma of freshly brewed coffee rose from the oversized mug resting on the coffee table. The morning paper lay folded open to the obituaries. She had weighed whether to attend the services for Kilgore's wife. The letter she had received from Kristin Walters, Daniel's sister-in-law, made the decision for her. It was a good thing the half-empty box of tissues was next to her as she picked up the letter to read it again.

Dear Jane

"I wanted to thank you personally for the time you spent with my sister. In her more lucid moments, Vivian told me how much Daniel enjoyed your time together. She realized with that final diagnosis there would be less and less quality time for Daniel and her. She knew you would be filling that void, and she was grateful for that. As a matter of fact, she told me she hoped you might continue filling that void after she was gone. Vivian could be very protective of Daniel, don't you know."

Sincerely, Kristin Walters. (Sister of Vivian Kilgore)

Vivian's sister stayed a few more days following the services. With no more visitors to tend to, Kristin had some one-on-one time with her brother-in-law.

"Dan, I think it's time we head back home and give you some space. There's not that much for us to do. If something comes up, you call us, right?"

"I'm eternally grateful to you and Brad and Michelle for everything you've done. Vivian's passing was not a surprise, and I thought I was prepared for it. I was wrong."

Kristin gave her brother-in-law a hug. "You keep as busy as you can. It will help with being alone."

It was the kind of thing people always say to the bereaved out of a lack of anything else to say. They mean it to be encouraging and comforting. Yet, it seldom is. More likely, it falls on ears deafened by sadness.

"Kris, being alone isn't a problem, being lonely is. They're two different things."

He really wasn't trying to sound profound.

"Either way, we're only a few hours away if you need us," she said.

Another platitude, but he knew she meant it.

Kilgore stood in the driveway as Kristin and her family drove away. When he went back inside, he instinctively went to his bedroom. The intensity of the responsibility of caring for Vivian was still there. The feeling of hopelessness had not left him. He carefully opened the door and stepped inside. He was overwhelmed by the vacancy of the room.

Everything was still in place, from the window curtains Vivian had so happily created with the material she found while bargain shopping at the fabric store on the other side of town to the furniture unchanged after many years except for the institutional (and now empty) bed he had brought in to make her more comfortable. The little knickknacks she had collected and so prized. Yet, the room might have been completely barren for all the emptiness it exuded. It was more than he was prepared to endure.

Reverently, he left the room as quietly as he had entered. Desperate for solace, he sought some mindless diversion. Back in the living room, he plopped himself down in his worn lazy-boy recliner, right next to hers. He fingered the remote on the small table between the chairs. The large television bought for their anniversary two years ago popped to life. He surfed channels absently before settling on a National Geographic program focusing on the life of sea turtles.

Part Two

Its color is gone, petals faded and frail,

it lingers on, forgotten with the coming of a new spring.

> —Michael J. Sullivan

Chapter 13

KILGORE'S PROJECT

adeline Orsini had finished her morning tour of the facility's grounds when she noticed Daniel Kilgore drive into the parking lot. She couldn't help but admire how dedicated he was. She should be so lucky to have more volunteers like him. Madeline walked over to his car. She had a meeting planned with her Board of Directors later that day and had dressed accordingly. Her professional pants suit was complemented by a Louis Vuitton handbag hanging off her shoulder. It was her one opulent accessory. Kilgore looked up to see Orsini approaching his car, and he picked up the file, which lay on the passenger seat, and wondered if she would approve his project once she heard it.

"Daniel, how are things going?" she asked. Almost immediately she regretted her choice of words. *You fool,* she thought, *how would you expect things are going. The man just buried his wife barely three weeks ago.*

Like all men, he elected to hide his feelings by offering a bland, almost emotionally void response.

"Every day starts off better than the day before, and every night seems longer and emptier."

She stepped forward as if to offer a compassionate embrace, but his body language stopped her advance. His facial expression was devoid of emotion. Kilgore appreciated the gesture, but he was eager to move on to the project and hopefully receive Orsini's approval.

"Madeline, do you think I could have a few moments of your time?"

"Of course, let's go to my office."

As they made their way down the hallway, half a dozen or more staff stopped. Each offered their condolences for Kilgore's loss and assured him that in time, life would get better. Kilgore shook their hands and thanked them for their kind words. In his mind, he thought, *how can my life get better if everyone keeps reminding me of my loss?* First, he had lost his son and now his loving wife. Was getting better even an option? Human beings were not meant to be alone, without companionship or love, but that's exactly where Kilgore found himself. A sense of relief came over Kilgore when Orsini shut the door to her office behind him.

Kilgore was at ease here. The corner office had windows on two sides looking out to the green expanse of the back property. He was particularly partial to sitting in the large oversized leather chair normally reserved for permanent staff.

"Coffee?"

"Please."

"How do you take it?" as she reached for the coffee pot with one hand and picked up a cup with the other.

"A little cream, half-and-half if you have any."

"You're in luck," as she poured a dash of half-and-half into Kilgore's coffee cup.

"What is it you would like to talk about?" she asked.

Still unclear on the best way to broach his request, Kilgore turned the conversation to the trivial.

He took a sip of his coffee. "Starbucks French Roast, if I had to guess."

"Well, if you had to guess, you'd have guessed right."

Kilgore took another sip of coffee and sat back in his chair. He picked up his brown bag, crinkled from years of holding lesson plans and homework papers. He opened it and took out a folder.

"When Vivian first got the diagnosis of her condition, she insisted I take notes on everything, doctor's appointments, mind games we played, questions I would ask, memories we talked about, everything."

"Did she say why?" a curious Orsini asked.

Kilgore took a noticeable deep breath. Still mired in the depth of the sadness of his loss, words did not come easily. Though his thoughts were disordered, he managed to offer, "She did. A couple of years ago, I tried my hand at writing. I had never done anything like that before. When I ran the idea past Vivian, she thought it was fabulous and that I should try to write the book. To make a long story short, I submitted the story to a company I had found online, the San Francisco Book Review, who provide reviews to authors."

"Why a company on the West Coast when we have plenty of such companies locally?" Orsini asked.

If he lacked confidence in his abilities in the past, the trauma of the recent past had only magnified his insecurity.

"I've never really had a lot of confidence when I tried things out of my comfort zone. I thought if I used a company on the other side of the country there would be less chance that any failing on my part might become public. Anyway, to my great surprise, I got a four out of five-star review."

"Daniel, that's fantastic news, but I don't understand why you're telling me this."

Kilgore shifted uneasily in his chair. He handed Orsini the manila folder he held in his hand.

"I've started a new story, one about Vivian's experiences with dementia and everything we experienced. I'd like to continue that story using my experiences here at Magnolia Gardens," he asked. "If my agent likes the finished product and it's published, I wouldn't want you caught off guard."

"Oh Daniel, What a wonderful idea. I couldn't be more excited for you."

The sincerity of her remarks brightened the smile on his face.

Kilgore went on to explain he would use fictitious names for anyone in the story. The story would take place in a completely different state, and he would use no personal information about any character that might lead a reader to be able to identify them. Lastly, when he was done with the manuscript, he would give it to Orsini for her to review. She would have complete editing authority regarding technical accuracy.

Orsini rose from her chair and walked to the window overlooking the veranda and the grounds surrounding it. She folded her arms and stared out at the view. After several moments, she turned around to face him.

"The story of people like our residents and the thousands of others across the nation in care facilities needs to be told. The value of an antique Chinese vase might be priceless to a collector. Why aren't the lives of our residents valued as such? Not in terms of money, but in terms of how they lived, their accomplishments, the lives they brought into this world. They deserve to be acknowledged for that. People must understand a person's life doesn't stop because they can't remember. They deserve more than to be put away and forgotten. Daniel, please tell their story."

George Hillman knew who the visitor was by the distinctive whine of the high-performance Shelby Cobra sports car. He set aside his freshly poured glass of Merlot. He would want a clear head for the certain failure of a conversation that was about to take place. He opened the front door with a strength of conviction and went out to meet her.

She stood in the middle of the patio. Her hair was disheveled from the open-air ride in the convertible. Her lips, pencil-thin from the rage which roiled inside her, temporarily held back the profanity about to spew out. Her eyes reflected what one could only describe as a satanic glare. In one hand was a crumpled envelope. In the other, an opened bottle of Chardonnay. Apparently, this time Gilda didn't believe in using a glass. A slight stumble betrayed the amount of alcohol she had consumed.

"God damn you, George Hillman! You didn't have the balls to tell me to my face. You had that son-of-a-bitch Leo send me a letter!"

What did I ever see in you? He thought. *Oh well, every deal doesn't work out, so let's get this over with as fast as we can.*

"It's business, Gilda, and in business that's how we do things."

His words were calm, devoid of emotion. "It's what we agreed to, with something extra thrown in, which is not the way I normally do business."

"So, that's what you and I were, business?"

The blood vessels in her neck bulged with rage as she took a swig of wine, not bothering to wipe the drops running down her chin. She swayed a bit, then moved her feet for balance. George took a seat in the Adirondack chair next to the fire pit. He didn't bother to offer one to her.

"Yes, Gilda, it was business, business with benefits, but business just the same."

"And you think going to see your wife is better than what we had? Yes, Leo told me. Don't look so surprised."

The smirk on his face only infuriated her more.

"I told him to tell you if you asked."

"And you think seeing her will get you what?" she screamed.

"Something you wouldn't understand, Gilda, forgiveness."

"You'll get forgiveness in hell, you son-of-a-bitch!"

Her words were filled with so much fury she smashed her wine bottle on the stone patio for added emphasis. The glass shards spewed out over a wide area as the last remaining drops of the expensive beverage flowed across the more expensive Italian tile of the patio floor. George pitied the poor policeman who would undoubtedly encounter her as she sped down the driveway and out on the street. After the inevitable struggle with a woman scorned, Gilda would certainly find herself in jail.

Hillman had been raised a CEO Catholic—mass at Christmas and Easter only. The last time he had thought about mass was during a college physics class where he struggled trying to understand Einstein's theory of relativity, where energy is equal to mass times the speed of light squared. Taking a chance Gilda was wrong, he got in his car and headed to the local Catholic Church. He hoped that God was in a particularly gracious mood.

George Hillman would have never thought of himself as naïve, but the letter from Gilda's attorney came as a complete surprise. It informed George that Gilda was seeking a 50-50 split of community property under the palimony statute of California.

"Are you really surprised, George?" Leo asked.

"Surprised is the wrong term. I'm disappointed I didn't know her better."

Ainsworth started packing the minute he hung up after talking with Hillman on the phone. He had anticipated what Hillman was going to ask and he wasn't disappointed. A couple of hours after they had talked on the phone, George Hillman knocked on Leo's door. After looking at the security screen, Leo pressed the intercom.

"George, come in," Ainsworth said, as he pressed the green light to release the lock on the front door. Ainsworth hurried down the staircase to greet his friend.

"You've got something for me to do, don't you?" Ainsworth asked, as the two men headed to the den.

Leo often worked at home, so his den was a miniature law office. One wall had a ceiling to floor bookcase with the reference books of the latest case law pertaining to taxes and estate planning. A rolling ladder to reach the higher shelves angled out at the base of the wall. An expansive, heavily framed mahogany desk dominated the room. Behind it was a massive leather swivel chair so immense that Leo appeared comically small when seated in it.

"You know me too well, Leo," George said, a surprising smile formed on his face. He sat in a matching high-back metal studded chair directly opposite Leo.

"Well, I have been your friend and attorney for over twenty-five years."

Ainsworth got up and moved to the walnut bar with a marble top and poured three fingers of single-malt Scotch into two Waterford crystal tumblers. He handed one to George and retained one for himself. He slurped a small taste before speaking.

"I've spent the last two hours with Martin Levy," Hillman said.

The fireplace in the corner offered comforting heat.

"Martin Levy as in, Levy, Holloway, and Birch, divorce attorneys to the stars?"

"The one and only."

"And this is funny?" quizzed Ainsworth.

"Yes, it is," Hillman replied. "It seems Gilda's attorney used the same legal argument Melvin Belli did in 1977 when Belli represented Michelle Triola Marvin in her suit against her live-in boyfriend, Lee Marvin."

This time it was Ainsworth's chance to smile.

"Okay, George, what's your ace in the hole?"

"Her putz attorney didn't do his homework. Not only did Belli lose the case, the existence of our prenuptial agreement and the fact that Gilda has maintained a separate residence the whole time we've been together blows her case out of the water according to Levy," Hillman said. "But I still need you to do something."

"Name it."

"I'm going to be stuck here digging up documents, emails, and other evidence for Levy. I need you to go to Charleston and see Mary. Set up a time for me to visit and see if you can find out who's visiting her."

"The one mentioned in that last quarterly report you showed me?"

"That's the one."

"I will catch the first flight I can and call you when I find out anything," Ainsworth said.

"You know, Leo, the thing that really pisses me off isn't Gilda's greed, it's that this delays my getting to see Mary."

For the first time in he couldn't remember when, Leo Ainsworth saw regret on his friend's face. It's ironic, Ainsworth thought. Throughout Hillman's career, he had been driven by greed; greed to make the next best deal, greed to get the next big bonus. It was also greed that motivated George Hillman to rip from his wife's womb the one thing Mary Hillman had cherished—giving birth to a child.

As he looked at his friend now, slumped in that oversized chair, his fingers massaging both temples as if he was suffering from a migraine, Ainsworth wondered what Hillman's life would have been like had he loved Mary as much as he loved money. It was equally ironic that he, the shyster lawyer, was the compassionate one. Hillman would provide Leo with the answer himself.

"You know Leo, in the beginning, I did love Mary. I loved her more than anything in the world. But what fed my ego, what gave me a sense of self-worth wasn't Mary's love; it was greed and self-centeredness even more than the thrill of that next 'Big Deal.'"

Hillman relaxed into his high-backed leather chair.

"You know what I came to realize, Leo? Money doesn't laugh with you. It doesn't hold you. It doesn't caress you. It doesn't dream with you."

Leo Ainsworth sat stunned. This was a side of George Hillman he had not seen since the early years of George and Mary's marriage, and Leo Ainsworth liked what he saw. Hillman took a small sip of his scotch and then set it on the walnut coffee table. Its glass top was etched with the scales of justice. He sat back in his chair and took a trip down memory lane to a time he had forced from his mind years ago.

"Do you know what the priest told me when I went to see him last week?" Hillman asked.

Ainsworth shook his head 'no'.

"He actually said it's never too late to say I'm sorry. Can you believe that! After what I've done to Mary, saying 'I'm sorry' seems incredibly inadequate."

"George, may I ask you a question?"

"Ask away."

The pent-up emotion that Ainsworth felt required the frankest of replies.

"When was the last time you remember saying you were sorry to anyone for anything?" Leo was unsure how this would go over, but he felt the timing and his years of friendship would carry the tide.

Several awkward moments passed as Hillman considered the question.

George thought deeply. *Sorry about what I did, sorry about who I've affected, and the consequences. Sorry can mean many things.* Leo Ainsworth hoped Hillman would realize the word sorry is more than an admission. It is a transitory word that demands a change in behavior. This was definitely not an area of thought where George was comfortable.

"Leo, I don't think I can remember ever saying I'm sorry to anyone for any reason and that's a God-awful cross to bear."

The years of impropriety flooded through his mind. He was both liberated and wretched by the thought.

"Well George, maybe it's about time you lessen that burden."

"I hope you're right, Leo, as God is my judge, I hope you are right."

Chapter 14

THE SET-UP

"Daddy, can I talk with you?" Samantha asked her father.

"Sure, Punkin'. What's up?"

"Could we talk in the den? It's kind of personal."

Jim checked his watch. *His wife won't be home for another hour. It's a good time for a talk.* Jim shut the door to his study. He moved his chair from his custom-made teak wood desk he had ordered when stationed in Thailand and turned to face Samantha, who took a seat in the only other chair in the den. It was a black leather chair on rollers that matched her father's chair. Her father used the wall behind his desk to display his own 'Wall of Fame' with numerous pictures from his deployments overseas.

"Now, what's so personal you don't want your mother to hear?"

"How do you know it's got anything to do with Mom?"

"Honey, I may have been born at night, but it wasn't last night," her dad replied with a smile on his face.

Samantha leaned forward in her chair. Her question shocked her father beyond belief. Like most children, she was acutely aware of the atmosphere in her home. It was blatantly apparent that disharmony reigned.

"Why have you stayed married to Mom all these years?"

It was as if every breath of air rushed from his body. He turned his head away from his daughter's stare. When he turned back to face her, Cotton felt like Adam in the garden of Eden after he had taken a bite of the apple. He was stripped bare. In his nakedness, he had no explanation to give but the truth, no lie could cover his shame, but he would try.

"Samantha, I love your mother. I've always loved her," he stuttered, completely disarmed by his daughter's invasion of his privacy.

The expression on his face said, please believe me so there will be no more questions.

"Maybe in the beginning you did, Daddy, but not after the way she left us all those years to be raised by Gramma. Mom was never a part of our growing up, but Gramma was. I saw your face when Mom would bark at her. Billy saw it also. That wasn't love. I know in my heart Mom's the reason we've never gone to see Gramma."

Jim Cotton had carefully crafted a virtual bottomless pit of self-deception over the years he and Carrie had been married and now, in but a few seconds, his daughter had ripped him from his sanctuary. In the epiphany of that moment, Jim was forced to face the truth. He was not in love with his wife and had not been for several years. Oddly, there was no pain and no shame with this internal admission, and when he admitted it to his daughter, the sense of relief was overwhelming.

"I don't know," Jim said, as he experienced the euphoria of being honest. "Maybe because of you kids, maybe out of habit."

Samantha went to her father and hugged him the way only a loving daughter could. "You deserve to be happy, Daddy, and don't worry about Mom; she'll find someone to take care of her."

Strangely, neither father nor daughter were crying. The clarity of what he was going to do didn't call for tears. Samantha felt equally confident in her decision. When they returned from visiting her grandmother, she would tell her mother she was not returning to Vanderbilt. Samantha had decided to transfer to The College of Charleston to be closer to her grandmother. She owed her at least that much.

Between the time he had spent at the Gardens during the day and working on his manuscript at night, Daniel Kilgore kept busy. It was good to keep his mind busy, but a busy mind could not change the auditory desert within the walls of his home. Kilgore pained to hear Jane's voice again, to share a moment of laughter. He was paralyzed by guilt whenever he thought about calling her. Oddly, it would be Madeleine Orsini who would solve Kilgore's dilemma.

"How is your story coming along?" Madeline had asked, as she and Kilgore shared a morning coffee in the staff lunch room while waiting for the residents to finish the breakfast service.

"It's moving along," Kilgore said. His heart wanted to tell more, but his ego kept the answer brief.

Whenever Orsini questioned him about the story, she got the same ambivalent answer.

"Between continuously checking for spelling and punctuation errors and second-guessing myself on the storyline, I seem to take two steps forward and one step back."

"What you need, Daniel, is someone to edit your work for you. Your brain will always read what you meant to write, but an editor will read what you wrote. I know just the person for you," Orsini said, as she set her coffee cup down. The contents of her favorite blend of imported beans still emanated a wonderful aroma.

"Who might that be?"

"Doctor Lincoln," she said, supremely confident she had thought of the perfect person. "She's worked with Vivian. She knows all about your work here, not to mention her own background, and she's certainly corrected her share of student papers. She's knowledgeable, engaged, emotionally connected, but can maintain her objectivity."

Kilgore did not dare tell Madeline of his growing feelings. Hell, he was not even sure what he felt. Was it attraction with the hope of leading to something serious or just the longing of a lonely man? His lingering silence gave her pause to reconsider her suggestion.

"Well, it's just an idea," Orsini said. In the time she had spent with Kilgore, she did not always find him easy to read.

On the way home, Daniel Kilgore made a mental list of the advantages and disadvantages of employing Lincoln. They would only have to meet when exchanging what he had written or after she had made her corrections. It could be someplace public where the presence of others would lessen the chance Kilgore might inadvertently let slip his longing for her. *Yes*, he thought, *it just might work.*

D aniel's feelings for Lincoln had created an emotional crisis. How does one bridge the gap between being a widower and yet confront the affections for someone new without being crushed by guilt and remorse?

Jane, for all her years as a professional, had maintained a clinical distance from her subjects. Now, through Daniel, she was, for the first time, feeling what he felt.

Jane instantly recognized the number when it appeared on her cell phone. With a tone of controlled enthusiasm, she answered, "Daniel, how have you been?" She tried hard to curb her gleefulness.

"Good days and bad days," he replied. "Even though I knew what was coming, I don't think I was prepared for the finality of her passing."

A wave of suppressed grief swept over him. He was glad they were on the phone as he would not have to conceal the tears welling up in his eyes.

Jane had heard the same sentiment expressed many times by those who had lived through the long and slow passing of a loved one. Somehow the fact that it was Daniel recounting these details had a different effect on her. She allowed herself a bit more empathy for him than was probably safe.

"It's never easy to deal with what you've gone through, Daniel. Surrounding yourself with friends and people who care about you is my advice. Give yourself time to grieve. Find something positive to distract you."

"Speaking of that, I have something, and I believe you can be of help."

"What have you got in mind?"

"Let's talk about it over coffee, say at Starbucks around six tonight?"

"I'll go you one better, Daniel. Let's say six o'clock at my place on 5th and Oak. I'll cook dinner. That way we don't have to worry about anyone eavesdropping on our conversation."

He was both frightened and enthralled by her offer. For a moment, ambivalence reigned. Then a deeper, more basic human need took over.

"Give me directions," said Kilgore haltingly. He could hardly believe his good fortune.

Jane Lincoln lived on three acres just outside of Charleston. Her cedar log home rested on a small knoll at the back of the property. Kilgore was impressed with the raised vegetable garden to the left side of the house. The gravel driveway forced one to drive slowly and appreciate the array of fruit trees on the left. A large granite rock stood on the right with equipment for solar lights and a sprawling fountain in the middle, water gurgling as it passed over descending layers of rock.

"My favorite," she said, taking the bottle of Bogle Chardonnay from Kilgore, as she let him inside. As they headed to the kitchen, she gave the bottle back to Kilgore. "Would you?"

As he followed Jane, Daniel was glad he had not worn his typical end of day attire consisting of jeans and t-shirt. His tan Dockers and royal blue polo shirt maintained a modest decorum of dressiness. Jane had changed into more comfortable shoes, but other than that, she still wore her pants suit.

Kilgore was immediately impressed with the well-lighted kitchen area—granite countertops, stainless steel appliances, a six-burner commercial style stove, and a prep island in the middle, complete with foot-operated hot and cold-water pedals. The kitchen flowed into the dining area with an oak china hutch that matched the oval-shaped oak table for eight. Jane was someone who enjoyed preparing food as completely and tastefully as a professional chef, which she was not.

The living room, with its hardwood floors, was equally as impressive. From the vaulted ceiling, a wagon wheel light was on, providing more brightness than was needed. The leather sectional against one wall curved around to face the wood burning stove in the corner. A large easy chair rested against the far wall. It was country yet chic at the same time.

"If I were a corkscrew, where would I be?" Kilgore asked. Lincoln tried to hide the smile on her face as she turned around.

"I think a cook's tour is in order. Follow me," Lincoln said, taking Kilgore by the elbow.

With a sweeping motion of her arm, she announced, "This is the living room. The pellet stove in the corner is a sign I don't like to cut, split or stack firewood, and the small TV is a sign I don't watch it very much."

Lincoln headed down the hallway with Kilgore in tow. "Guest bathroom on the left. My office to the right," she said, opening the door.

Kilgore glanced inside. He was impressed with the oak bookcases that lined the walls. Jane had an oversized desk with a small oval conference table to one side. Open folders were spread out all over it. A laptop computer rested in the middle. Lincoln stopped at the end of the hallway.

"The door to the left is my room and shall remain private, if you don't mind, and the door to the right leads to a guest bedroom."

Kilgore bowed at the waist and answered in his best Shakespearean voice, "As my lady wishes."

He felt instantly embarrassed by the corny remark, not to mention the fact that he was stepping over some boundaries.

"This door leads to the back porch and my one indulgence."

Kilgore followed her. The back porch was an enormous yet tasteful deck running the length of the house and about twenty feet out. A massive outdoor barbecue sat at one end, equipped with its own refrigerator, sink, and prep area. At the other end, was a redwood hot tub, whose underwater lights gave off a subtle illumination as dusk was setting. The warmth it offered belied the chill of the spring evening.

"Which is your indulgence, the hot tub or that barbecue set up?" Kilgore asked.

"Truthfully, both."

Taking Kilgore by the arm, Lincoln headed to the French doors that opened to the living room.

"I've got vegetables for you to cut, mister."

The smile on her face was infectious and caused Kilgore to smile back and say, "Your wish is my command."

Kilgore enjoyed their bit of comedic repartee. A bit too much, perhaps, but he could not deny the fact that he found Lincoln to be his intellectual equal. There was also a more basic attraction taking place. Kilgore found himself physically drawn to Lincoln's natural beauty. Her smile, her eyes, the sound of her laughter captivated him in ways he could not explain.

Lincoln handed Kilgore a cutting board, a large serrated knife, a couple of red potatoes, one onion, and two large carrots. Kilgore was no different than any other man. He wanted to display his competence at any task, but he was uncertain exactly what to do.

Sensing Kilgore's plight, she came to his rescue.

"Quarter the potatoes and onion and cut the carrots into three-inch pieces. Oh, and here's an apron."

Lincoln got out a large Dutch oven and covered the bottom with a thin layer of olive oil. Once it got to the right temperature, she laid in lamb shanks to brown. Kilgore had finished his part and placed a bowl with the cut vegetables and onions next to the stove.

"I wasn't expecting anything this fancy, Jane," Kilgore said, as he sipped his Chardonnay. He was a man who preferred beer as his adult beverage of choice, but he had to admit he was enjoying this wine.

"Think of it as high-class Southern comfort food."

"That's an oxymoron if I've ever heard one."

There was no need to turn around and reveal her smile as she chortled good-humoredly. Lincoln took the lamb shanks from the Dutch oven, poured in the vegetables and browned them for a few minutes. When they were just right, she put the lamb shanks back in, added two cups of red wine, four cups of beef broth, and set the lid on top.

"That will take a couple of hours; so now we can talk," she said.

Kilgore followed her into the living room. Lincoln curled up in her lazy-boy chair while Kilgore took a seat on the couch.

"Ok, so what's all this mystery? You are not usually shy about what you have to say."

There would be no Reader's Digest version to what Kilgore had to say. He started with his first book and the reaction to a book publisher in Chicago.

"With everything that's happened lately, I mean with Vivian and my work at Magnolia Gardens, I thought there was a powerful story in women suffering from dementia and the dynamics within families that caused them to ignore their loved ones once they've been placed in a care facility. I watched my wife's life degrade from a vibrant, smart person into a person who's only apparent need was to be fed and cleaned. I was frustrated and angry. Is that why some of the residents at the Gardens don't have visitors? Are their loved ones angry at what's become of someone they loved? Were there suppressed childhood memories of abuse or overbearing parents from whom adult children could now be free? As helpless and vulnerable as they've become, can anyone really stay angry or mad at them? Madeline gave permission to use my visits with my friends as material to work from."

Jane was immediately taken with the tenderness in his words and the kindness that radiated from his eyes. She sensed he was reaching out to her in a way that perhaps he did not realize.

"I love your dedication and compassion for these people, but how can I help?"

"Jane, I know you're terribly busy with your research and the classes you teach, but I could really use some help in editing my manuscript. You know, stuff like periods, commas, sentence structure, but most of all the storyline. I've tried to edit some of it myself, but it's useless. My brain reads what I wanted to say, not what I wrote. What with your teaching and research, you could really be a help with the technical parts."

Jane carefully considered his request, mulling over in her mind her sixty-hour work week and the stress involved. Her face could not deny her concern, but in the end, she felt she had to help. This man needed her help and on more than one level.

The relief Kilgore felt caused him to take a healthy taste of his wine. More than he bargained for, it caused him to sputter a bit.

"I brought some of the first few chapters with me to leave with you. That is; if you say yes."

Jane eyed Daniel carefully and then tenderly responded, "Of course, it's a yes. Let me see them."

The genuine nature of her reply cemented the deal and eased his apprehension. Kilgore went out to his car and returned with his bag. He took out a time-worn two-inch three-ring binder and gave it to Lincoln.

"This is the start."

Lincoln picked up her glass and moved to the couch where Kilgore was sitting.

"The lights are better here," she said, as she settled in next to him.

It was a complete fabrication, the kind of gentle, and often harmless deception, a man or woman will employ to accelerate the pace of a budding relationship.

If Kilgore was expecting any positive or negative input predicated on Jane's expression, he was disappointed. She reviewed the document with the practiced eye of a trained professional. When she was done, she closed it, and set it on a glass coffee table supported by a burl from a redwood tree. Its edges were pieces of cedar log stained a dark brown.

"Excuse me for a moment," Lincoln said, as she got up and headed to her bedroom, hoping there would be no need to wipe her tears away before she got out of sight. She returned in a few minutes with a powder blue lace handkerchief in her hand. It had been crocheted by her grandmother. It was already damp from her tears.

"Daniel, I was prepared to read something steeped with compassion and strengthened by the accuracy from your experiences at the Gardens, but I was completely taken back by the way you brought in such raw emotion."

Lincoln had question after question for him. She wanted a list of characters and how Kilgore saw them developing. She asked for an outline of every subplot as well as the main theme as best he saw them evolving. There was a certain excitement in her voice when she spoke. It was as intoxicating as the wine he was drinking.

"How do you see this working?" Jane asked.

"Well, when I get enough pages done, say fifty or so, I could drop them off at your office. When you're done editing, I could meet with you there to go over your remarks. I'll go home, make your corrections, get another fifty pages or so done, and meet you again until the project's finished."

Kilgore hoped he hadn't proposed too much of a workload for her. He was well aware of her devotion to her work.

"I think the pace of your writing needs to be smaller. Let me suggest this, email me whatever you get done each day, and I'll work on each segment. We can meet here on Saturday where I can hone my culinary skills, and you can get a home-cooked meal. I'll have the time to give you a quality critique of your writing."

"Are you sure?"

"I wouldn't have suggested it if I wasn't."

The twinge of guilt he suddenly felt conflicted with the feeling of anticipation he had for their next meeting. He liked the way this was going, but he still experienced a mixed-bag of emotions.

Chapter 15

FRIENDS

*H*is second meal with Lincoln had been every bit the epicurean delight of the previous week. Jane had placed strips of prosciutto layered with basil leaves and sprinkled with asiago cheese inside her sliced chicken breast. Then she rolled the breast in crushed biscotti cookies. He dared not tell her after all the work she went into making the chicken cordon bleu, but his favorite part of the meal was the oven-roasted Brussels sprouts, cubed red potatoes, and slices of red onions that had been drizzled with extra virgin olive oil and balsamic vinegar.

"That dinner was fabulous," Kilgore said, as they stood on the front porch.

Lincoln leaned comfortably against the door jamb. *It really was quite good,* she thought. Her mind was already planning the next meal. *I'm more ready for this than I would have believed.* She began to review recipes in her mind only to remember she needed to address the issue at hand.

"Daniel, I think you have a real gift for writing. I'm looking forward to working with you." *Keep it professional, said her mind's eye. Yes, there is something about this man that tugs on my soul, but for his sake, I need to stay focused.*

"I guess I should be going," he said, unhappy at his inability to express his appreciation in a more satisfactory manner. "I'm sure you have items to prepare for your work at the school." He felt suddenly embarrassed that he had taken up so much of her time.

"Not without a suitable hug," Lincoln said, as she put her arms around Kilgore's shoulders.

The hug was suitable and then some. Professional? Well, maybe just a little more than professional. Both lingered longer than what would have been considered socially acceptable, their hearts inspired by what they felt.

The following day Daniel had planned on arriving at the Gardens by mid-morning, but the lingering thoughts of Lincoln throughout the night deprived him of needed sleep. It was closer to noon when he finally arrived.

"You picked a good day to see Mary, Daniel. She's unusually alert and chatty," Ellen Taggart said.

"Great. It's always easier to judge if you're making progress when she's that way." He wanted to be optimistic, but based on her previous emotional outburst, it was doubtful.

Ellen Taggart was the primary therapist Orsini had assigned to all of Kilgore's friends. It made it much easier for him to gather information when he had only one source. Through Ellen, Kilgore learned each of his friends had their own peculiar and recurring behaviors.

There were times when Mary Hillman would appear to be perpetually depressed, which could go on for days. There were missed meals and scheduled therapy groups because she did not have the energy to get out of bed. Even when she was with other residents, Mary remained to herself. She had been heard uttering disjointed ramblings ranging from, "They took my baby," to Mary's talking to an invisible person she called 'Jane' about the facts of life.

Kilgore also learned Dolores Samuels dealt with a far more volatile memory. The trigger for Dolores's eruption was usually the sound of a man's voice. It didn't matter if it was a young man, middle-aged man or a senior. If that certain tone were there, Dolores would cry out, "Mitchell, is that you? I knew they were wrong."

When Dolores would try to approach the man, staff would have to physically intervene because Dolores would try to grab onto the man, crying aloud, "Mitchell, Mitchell, please!" Once the staff got Dolores sedated, she would mumble, "She killed him. I know she did." Kilgore wondered if this was some rambling of a person deep into dementia or was there some validity to it?

All the women Daniel Kilgore visited had one magnificent and noble trait. Each exhibited tremendous compassion and caring, none perhaps more so than Sandra Cotton. Sandra would often confuse young female staff or the teenage daughter of a visiting family with her own granddaughter.

She was known to approach families with a teenage daughter when they were visiting a loved one. Sandra would gently chide the young female not to interrupt this family's visit and to return with her. "Sweetheart, you need to leave these nice people alone and not interrupt their visit. Come with me. There's something I want to show you."

At times, and with a smiling nod from the young woman's parents, they would allow Sandra to take their daughter and walk around the veranda. Sandra would interrupt other families, and with an angelic smile introduce the young woman to them as her granddaughter. These types of interruptions were always dealt with graciously by the families. Occasionally, they would even ask that Sandra be allowed to stay with them.

Starting with his wife, Vivian, and then with his time as a volunteer at the Gardens, Daniel had become quite the student on dementia. Its cause is the degeneration of the cerebral cortex which is the area of the brain responsible for thought process and memory. The presence of the disease often causes memory distortion when the patient confuses current context with past experiences. This was the world for so many of the residents at Magnolia Gardens.

Kilgore approached the table on the patio where Ellen Taggart was reading to Mary Hillman. Ellen and Mary sat under an umbrella and close to a large oscillating fan there to provide some relief from the heat.

"May I join you two?"

"Please," Ellen Taggart said, as she closed the book she was reading to Mary. "If I read any more of this romance novel, Mary will have emptied an entire box of tissues."

Mary looked at him with a "Do I know you?" look on her face. Her lips parted like she was going to say a name. Knowing a sense of frustration often precedes a backslide into the foggy haze of the past, Kilgore said, "I'm Daniel. I come to see you every week."

A smile formed on Mary's face. She didn't remember him, but the remnants of a deeply ingrained sense of politeness, and a residue of pride would not allow her to admit it.

"Please, Daniel. Please join us," she said.

Mary's eyes followed Daniel as he sat down. She was trying to remember. Mary shifted her weight to adjust her dress which had risen slightly. Propriety was so important to her. Even at her age, Mary had stunning blonde hair and blue eyes.

"Did you like the story?" He asked.

Mary looked at him. It had only been moments ago, but already the memory was fading.

"I think so," she replied, as her eyes stared harder at Kilgore's face.

Her widening smile gave Kilgore hope she had remembered. Now might be the time, Kilgore thought, to try something he had learned in the seminar he had attended. Jane Lincoln called it reminiscence technique. As she had explained it, you share a memory, maybe ask if the resident has a similar memory. You try to match their emotion. He knew of Mary's outbursts about a baby.

"I know you're from California, Mary. Living in South Carolina, what do you miss about California?"

Her smile faded slightly as if she was trying to understand Kilgore's question. Perhaps he had to narrow his question.

"What do you miss most about living here, Mary?" Kilgore asked.

Mary leaned forward and put her hands on his arm. Her frail fingers tightened on Kilgore's forearm, and she whispered, "I miss my baby."

Kilgore seized the moment. "What was her name?"

The chance to talk about her baby brought a sense of joy and happiness to Mary's face. Whether her memories ever really happened was not important. In some fractured sense of reality, Mary Hillman had a chance to talk about what could have been, and it was real in her mind.

"Her name?"

Daniel repeated his question. "Yes, Mary. What was your baby's name?"

Mary became distracted by a hummingbird using a feeder hanging from the edge of the pergola. After several moments, she turned her attention back to Daniel.

"Her name, you say?"

"Yes, her name," Daniel responded.

He was trying to visualize how a woman this age could have an infant when suddenly her demeanor changed. Her hands gripped the armrests of her chair as she leaned forward. The focus in her eyes had shifted from a state of wondering to one of anger.

"They took her," she nearly shouted, attracting the attention of nearby staff, "and she never came back."

Mary's breathing became more rapid. Her head turned back and forth as if she was trying to locate something. Daniel focused his attention on calming her down. He spoke gently and direct.

"I'm right here, Mary. Everything is all right. Look at me, Mary, everything is going to be fine."

He patted her shoulder to reassure her. She leaned back in her chair and rested her head on a cushion. Daniel didn't want to lose her, so he made a stab at the only point of reference that he thought might bridge the gap between them. He was not comfortable with this subject, but he pressed on.

"Mary, I lost my child too. I miss him terribly."

Kilgore tried very hard to maintain control of his emotions, but the pain of his loss cut too deep into the past. He found himself starting to shake. As focused as the staff were who had come over to their table after Mary's outburst, only he noticed his tremors.

Mary Hillman's condition had been deteriorating for some time, but not her innate sense of compassion for others. Once again, her fingers tightened on Kilgore's arm.

"I am so sorry," she whispered. Mary looked directly into Kilgore's eyes and in a miraculous moment of clarity said, "Oh dear, I do hope our pain departs someday, and we can have peace."

Her tense grip on the arms of the chair relaxed. A sense of serenity emanated from the eyes that had just recently appeared filled with anger. She smiled as if content that she had eased Daniel's pain.

L eo Ainsworth's United flight 1241 landed at LaGuardia shortly after one p.m. There were no direct flights from LA to Charleston, so Ainsworth had been forced to take a commuter plane from New York to Charleston. He had hoped to see Mary by late that afternoon. His cross-country flight gave Leo plenty of time to think about his mission—to see how Mary was and find out about the mysterious visitor who had been to see her.

As he smoked his long-anticipated first cigar of the day, he mused, *I have never been satisfied with George Hillman's decision to place Mary in a facility on the East Coast when there were plenty of wonderful such places in California. As if moving her this far away would do any more to bury her memory.*

"George, this makes absolutely no sense. Why South Carolina and not someplace closer? Visiting her would be much less complicated without having to make cross-country flights."

George Hillman was a little annoyed at his friend's judgmental remarks. If he wanted an explanation, George would give him one. *Friend or no friend, this is clearly my business and my decision.*

"The major investor in this new project lives in New York. I can alienate him by insisting he comes to California for updates or I can placate his massive ego and go to him. Leo, when this guy punctuates his threats about what he'll do if anything goes wrong with "trust me," I'd fly to the moon if that's what it would take to keep him happy. It's not a big deal to fly down to Charleston when I'm in New York."

Of course, George had never bothered to make the trip to South Carolina.

It was shortly after four p.m. when Ainsworth arrived at Magnolia Gardens. Most of the visitors had already departed, leaving ample parking space. Leo deftly maneuvered his rental BMW sedan into the end space. The temperature had cooled significantly as Ainsworth walked to the entrance. The sweet aroma of the Magnolia blossoms helped dispel the odor of his discarded unfinished cigar. The automatic doors opened and allowed him to take a few steps inside only to face another set of doors marked "push." He did and entered into the reception area. He walked to the counter with an overhead sign that read "Visitor Information."

"May I help you?" asked a young woman in nursing scrubs. Her name tag identified her as Kristin Andrews. She was uncertain if this well dressed comical little man was a prospective client or a visitor. She couldn't help but notice that he reeked of cigar smoke.

"Yes, Kristin. My name is Leo Ainsworth. I'm here to see Mary Hillman. I'm sure her husband, George, sent word I was coming."

This was the *"all business, I'm the attorney and snap to it!"* delivery Ainsworth was used to expressing.

"Just give me a minute to check," she said, as she entered Leo's information into a computer.

Carefully following the visiting program, she scrolled down the screen to Mary's name. There was Ainsworth as an approved visitor.

"Yes, there you are. Why don't you follow me, Mr. Ainsworth? Mary is out on the veranda."

As they walked through the exit door, Leo thought George had good taste even if he hadn't personally been to the Gardens. The walls were painted a pale ocean green, and crown molding edged the top of the walls which then formed a dome. The art on the walls were originals and not some tacky prints from Walmart. Bouquets of fresh flowers seemed to be everywhere.

Kristin opened the French doors onto the veranda, and she looked around until she saw Mary. Daniel Kilgore was sitting next to her. The first dinner serving had been completed, and several residents were on the veranda taking advantage of a beautiful Charleston sunset.

"There she is."

Kilgore stood up when he saw Kristin approaching.

"My favorite nurse."

Her blush was sincere.

"My favorite volunteer. Daniel, this is Leo Ainsworth. He is a friend of Mary's and her husband, George. He's here to see Mary."

Kilgore extended his hand. Ainsworth extended his short hairy arm and completed the obligatory greeting with little enthusiasm.

"I'll be on my way, Leo. You two can have some privacy, but I'll tell you that Mary may not be too responsive. It's late in the day, and we had a pretty emotional moment earlier."

Leo suddenly adopted a conciliatory tone.

"Please don't hurry off, Daniel. I'd really like to talk to you. Just give me a moment with Mary, if you don't mind."

"Certainly. If she's a little slow in responding or in recognizing you, keep repeating yourself. If she smiles, you've reached her. At least it's a starting point. And don't be taken off guard if Mary displays sudden fits of anger. It's common for people with dementia to connect what's in front of them with the wrong memory."

Daniel was hoping this unexpected visitor would accelerate Mary's associative abilities. His words were not well received by Ainsworth who did not appreciate what he considered to be a lecture by Kilgore.

Ainsworth pulled up a chair next to Mary, who now appeared to be taking a nap. With her head resting against a cushion on the high-back chair, Ainsworth looked at her. No amount of aging had changed Mary's appearance. Her blonde hair was as beautiful as ever. He gently placed his hand on hers. Even asleep, she had the slightest trace of a smile on her face

"Mary, it's me, Leo."

There was no change to her sleeplike state.

A bit more forcefully, he asserted, "Mary, it's me, Leo. Remember me?"

It was as if she were deaf. Ainsworth leaned closer. He patted her hand gently.

"Mary, it's me, Leo. Please remember."

Surprisingly, as his tone modulated, she turned toward Ainsworth.

"That's it, Mary. I'm here," Ainsworth said, hoping to encourage her further, but like so many men, especially attorneys, he was not capable of genuine warmth.

Mary slowly opened her eyes. Her sleepiness could not completely hide their brilliant blue hue. Her lips opened, and hesitantly she uttered, "Leo?"

"Thank God. Yes, Mary. It's me, Leo."

His affection for this long-time acquaintance was suppressing his abusive, lawyer persona.

Mary struggled to right herself in her chair. The physical effort led to a rise in Mary's awareness. Dementia had fogged Mary's mind to any thought of her need for physical activity. Her days had become more and more sedentary, making physical movement slow and deliberate.

"Yes, Leo. Of course, I remember you."

The color returned to her face.

"How have you been?"

Her smile reappeared as her mind caught glimpses of her past.

"We were good friends, weren't we?"

"Yes, we were—you, me and George."

The sound of his name evoked a strange and conflicting emotion in Mary, one of longing and yet at the same time, one of anger. Mary reacted to the former.

"George, my husband?"

Her query gave rise to an erectness in her posture and a sense of anticipation in her eyes.

"Yes, George, your husband. Mary, he's coming to see you. He worries about you, Mary."

His words nearly gagged him. His friend should have been worried about Mary long before his epiphany occurred.

"George is coming? She asked, a tinge of anxiety in her voice.

"Yes," Ainsworth responded.

With this final assurance, Mary blushed, "I've got to get ready. I want to be just perfect for him."

"You've always been perfect, Mary," Ainsworth assured her.

The beam on her face began to ebb. The excitement in her voice subsided. A look of wanting came across her face.

"Please tell him to bring my baby," she whispered.

Her head slipped back against the cushion. There would be no more questions today. Whatever clarity that had been achieved in that moment quickly slid back into the quagmire of a mind controlled by dementia.

$Chapter\ 16$

CONFRONTATION

$\mathcal{A}$insworth found Kilgore waiting in the lobby. Kilgore had taken the time to make notes for his manuscript. He had managed to keep an open mind about Ainsworth visiting Mary and not her husband, George. The same could not be said for Ainsworth.

"Thank you so much for waiting. I was afraid you had left."

"Oh no," Kilgore said. "You are the first of her family I've actually met. I'm anxious to hear about Mary's family."

Despite his years as a barrister, Leo hadn't been able to "read" this guy. He was sure Kilgore had a motive. He certainly had not been visiting Mary out of the goodness of his heart.

Leo looked over the top of his horn-rimmed glasses, "I haven't had a decent meal since I left home. Care to join me?"

Kilgore chuckled. "Then follow me, I know just the place."

Good, Ainsworth thought, once this meal is over, I can drive straight to the airport.

Miss Belle's Inferno was a legendary eatery in Charleston known for its southern seafood dishes. It had long been a favorite of the Kilgore's. He and Vivian had shared many a pleasant meal there. It was a place he had always felt comfortable.

"Mr. K, it's been too long," said Belle Deloume. Wanting to express a note of sympathy, she added, "I miss hearing you and Mrs. K. laugh."

Belle had the caramel complexion of a mulatto, her mother being black and her father white. She was well over 200 pounds and was famous for her large gold hoop earrings and Mardi Gras bead necklaces.

"I appreciate that, Belle."

He was putting on a good face but being reminded of his loss was not always good.

Belle smiled knowingly. "I'll bring you your regular," she said.

Belle made a point of knowing her regular's favorites and serving it just the way they liked it. Her forte was direct contact with her customers, unlike so many of the high-end eateries in Charleston.

"And for your friend?"

Leo's palate had become accustomed to the five-star restaurants in greater San Diego. The thought of anything resembling southern comfort food repulsed him, but he was trapped after scanning the menu.

"Why don't you pick, preferably something not deep fried and spicy."

Ainsworth handed her the menu as if he was holding something contaminated with a deadly virus.

Now that Belle had departed, Leo got down to business. He was direct.

"How exactly did you come to visit Mary?" was his question.

What he really wanted to ask was, why would a guy like you be visiting these people? As an attorney, Ainsworth was accustomed to starting from the negative in considering someone's motives. He naturally assumed that Kilgore had some sort of hidden agenda he was not yet aware of. Rarely would an attorney ask a question they don't already know the answer to, but this was one of those occasions. The unabridged version took about an hour to tell. Add in Kilgore's personal situation and the time stretched to almost two hours.

"What do you know about Mary?" Ainsworth asked, hoping to fulfill George's directive.

"In all my visits with her, when she was reasonably alert, there were only two things Mary talked about, George and her baby, which Mary said had been taken from her. I often wondered if the baby had been kidnapped or met some other horrible outcome. I know in my heart she needs to hold a baby, any baby, just as she would have held her own. Other times, I read to her, and she loves it. If I read a romantic part, she cries. If I read a tragic part, she cries."

Leo spent a few moments reflecting on what Kilgore said and then asked, "Mary spends a lot of time crying, doesn't she?"

His leading question elicited a somewhat evasive answer which put Leo on the defensive.

"I think you know the answer to that, don't you?"

Kilgore's answer reflected both his growing disdain for Ainsworth and the sadness he felt for Mary.

Ainsworth thought to himself, touché. He smiled back and asked, "When Mary read to the children in the after-school programs she visited, the stories always ended with her reaching for her handkerchief. If she watched a news segment on animal abuse, it brought a torrent of tears. Yes, she certainly could cry."

"My Vivian was the same."

Ainsworth pushed his coffee cup aside. The local brew did not compare with the exotic blends he was used to. *That was enough of that crap,* he thought.

"Kilgore, I want you to know that George loved Mary; he truly did."

"Please don't misunderstand me," Kilgore said, almost apologetically. "I've never judged anyone for not visiting. It's just that Mary deserves to have her voice heard, to laugh at happy memories or cry over sad ones. All the residents at the Gardens deserve it. I'm just fortunate to be the one who made that happen to my three friends."

Leo was finally won over. Kilgore was good for Mary. Smiling did not come easily to Leo, but he found himself smiling now. He smiled to himself. He smiled for George Hillman, but mostly he smiled for Mary.

S amantha found her dad in the den.

"Daddy, Judy Beth's family invited me to spend a few days with them at their cabin at Lake Ogallala. What with all the drama around here, it would be nice to get away," Samantha said to her father.

Jim knew his daughter was right. The last two years had been no picnic. The uproar over Samantha's pregnancy, and the decision to send her away to have the baby exacerbated the tension in the family. If Jim's decision to file for divorce hadn't caused enough of an estrangement, the decision to take Samantha and visit his mother added the final layer of explosiveness to the family dynamics. Jim was well acquainted with Beth's family and knew she would be safe. To add fuel to the fire, Carrie had heard a voice message left by an attorney for him to call his office.

"You go and have some fun, kiddo."

Samantha hated herself for lying to her father about where she was really going. She was determined to have her own time with her grandmother, even if it took lying to get it. Only her grandmother would give her the non-judgmental love she so needed now.

Jim had another motive for saying yes to his daughter's request. Samantha had already witnessed enough conflict between him and her mother. When Carrie got home, and the subject of the voicemail would come up, God knows what her reaction would be like. Jim wasn't going to take a chance.

O f late, Carrie had taken to Tito's vodka as her anesthesia of choice as she leaned against the kitchen counter. Though dressed in colorful flower print blouse and tight-fitting exercise pants, Carrie was hardly in a cheerful mood. She pressed "play" on the message machine for the third time.

"Mr. Cotton. This is Myron Webster. Please call my law office at your earliest convenience."

Carrie drained her drink and had just poured a second one when she heard the front door open. She didn't bother to ask who it was, and Jim didn't bother to announce he was home. She walked into the living room and stood at one end of the wet bar.

Before he could even sit down, she icily exclaimed, "Care to explain the message from your attorney?"

The room that had held so many wonderful memories of Christmas mornings and birthday parties when the kids were young, now had the feeling of a courtroom where Jim was about to be cross-examined. Not the family photos on the wall or some of the Father's Day and Mother's Day gifts displayed on the shelf next to the TV could thaw the iciness in the air.

Carrie's confrontational manner used to put Jim into a state of mental gymnastics as he tried to anticipate what hoops he would have to go through to keep the peace between them. Now it was different. Jim Cotton was no longer interested in making peace with his wife. He was more interested in having some peace, his peace.

Should I sit or should I stand when I tell her, he thought. Jim walked to the bar where his wife stood, slowly spinning her tumbler of vodka with her fingers. He chose to stand at the other end of the bar rather than sit on a stool next to her. They were only five feet apart, and Jim wished he had made the bar twice its five-foot length.

"That call was from my attorney, Myron Webster."

"I know who he is, dammit! He left his God Damn name!" Carrie snapped. "Why the hell do you need an attorney?"

Unlike his wife, Jim spoke in slow, measured words.

"Because my dear, when one files for divorce, one usually needs an attorney, and that is exactly what I'm going to do, so I suggest you find an attorney for yourself."

"You wouldn't dare!" she screamed, as she slammed her drink on the bar, showering herself and Jim with the contents.

"Yes, I would dare," he said, as he wiped his face. "I'm going to get some peace and happiness in my life and divorcing you is a small price to pay for it."

Dumbfounded by her inability to rattle her husband, her hand quivered as she tried to pour another drink. An uncontrollable rage filled her every fiber. Spit flew out of her mouth like a snake spewing its venom. Even knowing Carrie as he did, Jim was momentarily taken aback by the ferocity of her attack and defensively moved a bit farther away.

"We'll see just how small a price you pay after I go for child support, alimony, and half your retirement."

Regaining his composure, Jim carefully explained, "That may be somewhat problematic for you." His resolve and confidence rose with each word. "I've filed for divorce in Oklahoma where we have a rental. Oklahoma doesn't award child support once any child reaches the age of eighteen or graduates from high school. Alimony and any part of my retirement will be minimal based on your very successful business selling health supplements, and I have the tax records to prove it."

Now it was her turn to retreat. A look of shock raced across Carrie's features. She was stunned by Jim's rebuttal. Whatever vodka Carrie had been able to pour into her glass was now gone. Jim left his wife standing at the bar filling her glass to the rim. No ice, just plain pain killing vodka. Even then, it was woefully inadequate for the task at hand.

Arriving at the Gardens for his routine visit, Daniel hoped his friend was in a more stable mood.

"How is she doing today?" Kilgore asked as he signed in at the volunteer registry, the therapist on duty evidently distracted by some task at hand and unable to give him the pleasantry of her usual warm greeting.

"Who?" asked Ellen Taggart, the therapist who had counter duty that morning.

"Sandra Cotton," Kilgore answered. "My last visit was a little embarrassing for her and me."

Shifting back into a friendlier, yet professional mind, she stated, "I remember. Too bad the family couldn't have been more understanding. Given the situation with their own loved one, you would have thought that they would have been."

Kilgore remembered the incident in all its unfortunate detail. He had been sitting with Sandra in one of those rare moments of an engaging conversation about bridge. From another table, the sound of a young girl's laughter distracted Sandra. She turned her head in the direction of the voice and then she stood up. She hollered, "Samantha, it's you!" Sandra walked over to the family's table and put her arms around the young girl who struggled to get out of Sandra's grasp.

Frightened, the girl had exclaimed, "I'm sorry, but I don't even know you." Sandra was unfazed by the girl's denial.

"Of course, you do, my dear. I'm your grandmother," she said in a mildly rebuking tone only a grandmother can make.

The girl was completely confused and increasingly frightened.

"My grandmother died a year ago. Whoever you think I am, you need to let go of me now!"

It took Kilgore and another staff member to get Sandra to let go of the young girl. The family said they were going to file a complaint with the director over Sandra's aggressive and unwarranted behavior.

"Don't I know it," sighed Kilgore.

Just then he looked up to see a strange young woman walking down the hallway.

"Looks like you've got a visitor?" he said, nodding toward the young woman.

Ellen turned her attention from her paperwork and quietly complained to Kilgore, "I'll never get this finished with interruptions every ten minutes."

Kilgore remained at the counter.

"Excuse me. I was wondering if you could help me?" asked the young visitor when she got to the counter.

The young girl was pretty, not much older than twenty. *Probably looking for some part-time work to make some extra spending money,* Ellen thought.

"What can I do for you, Miss..." Ellen asked.

"Sorry, my name is Samantha Cotton. I was wondering if I could see my grandmother, Sandra Cotton?"

A quick check of the computer records showed Samantha Cotton as a family member.

"I think we can arrange that," Ellen said. "We encourage visiting with family members, and you have arrived at just the right time.

A smile erupted on the young girl's face. Samantha believed she was prepared for whatever changes time had wrought on her grandmother. She was sure the love between them would transcend all that.

"First, there is someone right here you should meet," Ellen said.

"Daniel, I'd like you to meet Samantha Cotton. She's Sandra's granddaughter. Daniel is a regular visitor of your grandmother, Samantha. He probably has a better understanding of your grandmother than anyone."

The sincerity of her praise caused Daniel to blush slightly.

"Samantha, it's a pleasure to meet you. Are you here by yourself?"

"Yes, but my father is planning on coming up real soon if he can clear up a few things back home."

Although this was not a complete fabrication, she still felt a twinge of guilt.

Kilgore smiled. "I know your grandmother will be glad to see him. Would you like me to take you to her now? She's probably in the atrium." He wondered why someone so young would travel so far without an escort.

"Please," said the excited granddaughter, unable to conceal her anticipation at the prospect of a reunion with her grandmother.

As they walked down the hallway to the atrium that faced the veranda, Samantha turned to Kilgore. She obviously had some doubts about him.

"May I ask you a couple of questions?"

"Fire away, Sam. I can call you, Sam, can't I?"

"Sure. My dad calls me Sam. Gramma too," answered the somewhat embarrassed granddaughter. Her already rosy cheeks glowed a bit redder with that exchange.

"Sam, what's your first question?"

"You are a stranger to my grandmother, yet you visit her. Why would you do that? Is she right in the head? Can she even remember anything about our family?

Realizing she had rambled on, Samantha apologized with adolescent embarrassment, "I guess I asked more than one question."

Kilgore took a seat on the bench outside the atrium entrance in the hallway.

"Your grandmother has her good days and her bad days. She might remember something one day and the next day she's forgotten all about it. She loves to talk about you, Sam. Something happened, though, that I can tell you worries her to this day."

Samantha's throat was suddenly very dry. It was tough enough to talk about the predicament with her family, let along with a complete stranger.

"Has she ever talked about it?" Samantha managed to ask.

"No. The details are something that have become disconnected from her memories, I'm afraid."

A sense of relief come over Samantha as she realized Kilgore did not know all the details of her moving to North Carolina.

"What is your other question?"

"Why do you come to see my grandma? You don't know our family or anything about us."

She sounded a bit like Leo Ainsworth in this exchange.

Kilgore breathed in deeply. His face, already maintaining a day's growth of beard, began to look even more weathered. Sharing his own story was uncomfortable for him, but her naïveté eased his apprehension. He spoke of Vivian and her battle with dementia and how he had been working with the residents hoping to help them reconnect old memories. Working with the residents gave him a sense of satisfaction while providing a greater understanding of his wife's condition.

Still not quite grasping Kilgore's motivation, she exclaimed, "But you don't even know these people, Mr. Kilgore," Samantha said.

"Let me explain it this way, Sam. When you see a homeless person walking the streets, do you ever wonder how he or she got that way? Or what kind of lives they might have had?"

"Honestly, I'm ashamed to say I haven't."

"No need to be ashamed, Sam. Much like the residents who live here, that homeless person is invisible to those who should care. The residents here had a life that mattered. They were parts of families who should have remembered what they did and the sacrifices they made. There were wonderful memories mingled with sorrows and disappointments. I'm just trying to give them the opportunity to remember once more and perhaps feel some of the love and caring missing from their lives."

Kilgore watched as Samantha's eyes were cast downward. Her pretty cheeks began to redden, and shortly she began to shed honest, heartfelt tears. Realizing how his remarks hit home, he attempted to soften them.

"Anyway, I happen to think it's worth every minute I can spend with them to help them remember, to reconnect with the happiness that once filled their lives. I think they've earned it, don't you?"

At that moment, any doubt as to what her future would hold for her disappeared. Her life's path was defined in an instant. Samantha had inherited her grandmother's sense of compassion for family and others.

As she stifled her flowing tears, she managed to utter, "Oh yes! Definitely, yes I do!"

Chapter 17

THE MEETINGS

Sandra sat in a chair near the window, gazing at the veranda scene before her. She was focused on a mother deer and her newborn fawn nibbling on the grass still wet with dew from a late morning rain. The white spots on the fawn seemed to blend together like colors in a kaleidoscope whenever the fawn's undeveloped legs buckled as it tried to nurse from its mother. The mother appeared impervious to the nudging of the fawn, occasionally lifting her head to survey for potential dangers. Kilgore approached and pulled up a chair. He had asked Samantha to wait for his cue before he had her come over. He began softly.

"Good afternoon, Sandra," as he sat next to her.

There was no response. Sandra was smiling as she watched the fawn nuzzle up to its mother's underbelly for a taste of mother's milk. Kilgore tried again.

"Sandra, it's me, your friend Daniel." He stated with a bit more intensity.

Somewhere deep in the recesses of her mind, something clicked. "Daniel?"

He smiled. "Don't you remember yesterday? You killed me in checkers."

That was the bridge Kilgore needed—the connection between something recent and something in the past.

"I did, didn't I." A smile spread across Sandra's face. A moment of clarity in an otherwise muddled appearance.

Kilgore motioned to Samantha. Slowly and deliberately, the girl edged her way to the other two.

"Sandra, there's someone here who wants to see you. I think you know who this is better than I do."

Samantha came around and knelt in front of her grandmother. She gently placed her hands on her grandmother's hands which were folded on her lap and looked upward. Before a word could be said, her eyes welled up, and her lips quivered with emotion.

"Gramma, it's me, Samantha."

Sandra leaned forward in her chair. Her eyesight had worsened recently. Her tender fingers reached out and slowly traced along Samantha's attractive young face. Sandra's eyes strained as she struggled to find something recognizable. Samantha was unnerved by her grandmother's lack of response.

"Gramma, don't you remember? You were the one that taught me how to play checkers."

Sandra's eyes blinked a couple of times, and suddenly tears gushed, "My gracious, Samantha! Is it really you? My darling Samantha, I've missed you so. This is an answer to a prayer. Thank God!""

Samantha rose quickly to her feet. "Yes, oh yes, Gramma, it's me." She turned to Kilgore. Her excitement was like that of a child about to ride on a merry-go-round.

"She knows me!"

Kilgore nodded with a sense of pleasure knowing that this time a connection was rekindled. This was precisely what all his patience and effort was intended to produce.

"Gramma, I've missed you so much!" Samantha said, as she laid her head on her grandmother's lap just like she had done as a small child. Her grandmother's gentle hands soothed her as she had since infancy, providing a sense of relief found nowhere else.

"I've missed you too, child," Sandra said in a voice so tender and caring it could have melted an ice cube. "Tell me, how are your father and mother? Are they coming to visit, at least your father?" The question was almost a plea.

Samantha lifted her head to answer. She saw Kilgore signal with his hands to keep her talking and that he would be waiting outside when she was done.

"Daddy's fine, Gramma. He's finally going to get a chance to be happy." The words hadn't left her mouth when Samantha realized she had said too much. Her dad would probably want to tell his mother himself. If she were lucky, her words would slip through Sandra's mental filter undetected, but luck was not with her. For the moment, Sandra's mental acuity was remarkably sharp.

"Good heavens, child! What do you mean by that?"

Samantha groped for a fabrication but could not bring herself to create it. She had told enough lies already. She waited a moment before continuing.

"Gramma, Mom and Dad are getting a divorce. I know it must be disappointing," Samantha said.

Sandra turned her attention to the mother deer and her fawn as the two headed toward the trees bordering the property. She watched until they disappeared.

"And what about you, darling?" Sandra asked when she turned back to face her granddaughter. "Are you finished with school? And with a twinkle in her eye, Sandra leaned forward. "Have you got a beau?"

Great, Samantha thought, the divorce thing must have slipped by her.

"I've decided not to return to Vanderbilt. I want to be closer to home and you. Mom's not going to be happy about it. But this is my life, not hers. I'm old enough to make my own decisions. I know what's right for me."

Sandra nodded her head that she understood.

She leaned back in her chair and then asked, "How is your friend?"

Thinking her grandmother saw someone next to her, Samantha said, "there's no one here but me, Gramma."

"Oh sweetheart, I don't mean here." Sandra looked left and then right as if someone might be listening. Then she whispered, "I mean your friend back home. I seem to have forgotten his name."

A new smile spread over Samantha's face. "His name is Mike, Gramma."

Even with her poor vision, Sandra could see the happiness in her granddaughter's eyes. Her hazel eyes appeared to twinkle simply by the sound of his name. Clearly amused and pleased by her granddaughter's remarks, she queried, "He must be the reason you want to be closer to home?"

Caught off guard by her grandmother's astuteness, an embarrassed Samantha said, "Yes, it's Mike. Mom does not understand, but he means everything to me."

Sandra smiled, as she rested her head against the back of her chair in an understanding way and not like she had in many months.

"Daddy's coming up to see you in a few days, Gramma," Samantha said, desperately wanting to get the attention off her boyfriend.

"Lordy, he was just here yesterday, I think."

Sensing a shift in her grandmother's perceptual ability, there was no need to correct her grandmother.

"I'll let you get some rest now, Gramma," Samantha said, as she stood up.

Sandra's hand reached out to hold her granddaughter's hand. She pulled Samantha close to her and said with uncharacteristic venom, "I've never liked that woman. I'm glad he's divorcing her."

Sandra closed her eyes. A shocked Samantha went to meet Kilgore who was waiting in the hallway outside the atrium.

"Did your visit go the way you had hoped?" Kilgore asked.

"I think so. At certain points, she seemed to be right there with me and at other times, I think her awareness started to fade."

"Good. I hope your father will have a chance to see her before she's not able to see or remember anything. Samantha, none of us like to think that is going to happen, but the sad fact is it, in all likelihood, it will. With all our advances in the medical field, there is just precious little that can be done to stem the tide of this horrible disease."

"Daddy's coming in a few days, Mr. Kilgore. He realizes he needs to make up for lost time."

"We are all on borrowed time," Kilgore said. "You, your father, all of us."

Much later, after the tragic death of her husband, the memory of that day only fueled Brenda's hatred for Sheila Samuels. The last time Brenda heard her husband's voice was the day Mitchell left a voice message for her. For her, there was only one person responsible, and with all her heart Brenda's deepest desire was that for all eternity Sheila Samuels would reside in a place where her most cherished desire would be for a tall glass of ice water. Brenda read the letter from Magnolia Gardens for the third time when the flight attendant announced they would be landing in Charleston slightly ahead of schedule. Brenda put the letter away and buckled her seatbelt. It shouldn't have turned out this way, she thought. If Mitchell were still alive, everything would be different. As the older brother, Mitchell had a way of explaining things, particularly family matters, that his younger brother could not dismiss. Fred and Sheila, however, were a different story, which was why Brenda had decided to make this trip. Only God knew if those two would ever decide when to visit Fred's mother; and since there had been little communication between Brenda and them since Mitchell's death, Brenda had made the decision.

Kilgore was preoccupied with thoughts of his next meeting with Lincoln the afternoon he arrived at the Gardens and did not recognize the woman checking in with the receptionist. He knew most of the families by face, and many were on a first name basis with Kilgore. Good, he thought, someone's getting a new visitor. The receptionist cheerfully interrupted her work with the visitor to greet Daniel as he put on his official Magnolia Gardens coat. The short sleeved pale blue smock, identifying him as a volunteer, had his name embroidered over the left chest pocket.

"Here to make your usual rounds, Daniel?"

"I'm going to spend some time with Dolores Samuels if she's up to it?"

Ellen Taggart, the physical therapist, was giving the on-duty receptionist a break. She glanced at a status board on the wall that tracked residents' activities.

"She should be in the music room. Sally's getting ready to do her therapy session."

Surprised, the stranger blurted out: "Excuse me, but did you say you were going to see Dolores Samuels?"

"Yes, why?"

"Dolores Samuels is my mother-in-law. My name is Brenda Samuels."

In her later forties, Brenda still maintained a bit of that 'Wow" factor from her days as a model for Olay. With naturally blonde hair, high cheekbones, and a stunning smile, Brenda was a natural as a sales rep for Olay after her modeling days were over.

"Just a moment," Ellen said, as she scanned the computer screen to confirm the stranger was indeed a family member.

"Is your husband Fred?"

"No," Brenda said. Her throat went suddenly dry. She had long ago lost the ability to control her tear ducts at the mention of her husband's name. The weight of emotion at just being at Magnolia Gardens just made it worse. She didn't want to cry. She was here to visit her mother-in-law. She needed to address this man. She quickly composed herself, adjusting her jacket somewhat wrinkled from the flight from Dallas.

"I'm a widow. My husband's name was Mitchell. He was Fred's older brother. I'm sorry," Brenda said, struggling to maintain her composure, "but before I see Dolores, do you think we could talk for a few minutes?"

After an affirmative nod, Brenda followed Kilgore to the staff break room.

"Sorry for the appearance. Some of the younger staff think the cleaning fairy picks up after them," apologized Kilgore, who hastily gathered up several coffee cups and sandwich wrappers left on the table.

Hoping to diffuse her emotionally charged state, Kilgore offered her coffee. Who doesn't like coffee? he thought.

"Would you care for some coffee?"

"Please," Brenda replied, as she tried to repair her eye makeup. It was a valiant but losing effort.

Kilgore gave the woman a few minutes to regain her composure, before setting a coffee cup in front of her with a small bowl of assorted creamers.

"I don't want to appear rude or unappreciative, but the last quarterly review we received from the Gardens indicated you regularly spend time with Dolores. She's an absolute stranger to you. May I ask why?"

Kilgore had become more at ease talking about his personal loss especially after his time at the Gardens and his new-found relationship with Lincoln.

"My wife passed away from the same type of dementia affecting Dolores. For many, many months, I worked with my wife, even utilizing a specialized trainer, trying to get her to recall old memories, and later, things we had talked about in the last few days. I thought by volunteering here at the Gardens I could learn more about the disease and perhaps what it takes to draw out old memories. It was a win-win situation. I got to help my wife and help the residents. At least, in the beginning, that was my motive. In time, I came to realize how many of the residents here at the Gardens seem to have been forgotten by their families. They pass away what time they have left, a forgotten stranger among strangers. I wanted to make a difference in their lives before they pass on. I guess in a way, it's like I still have my wife."

Not wanting to appear too insensitive, Brenda changed the flow of the conversation.

"The last quarterly letter mentioned something about an emotional outburst Dolores had. Can you tell me what happened?"

"We were sitting out on the veranda on a particular Saturday. There were several families visiting that day. Anyway, at a table nearby, a man suddenly broke out in laughter. It started Dolores crying. She got up and walked over to the man,' Mitchell, I knew it wasn't true. You are here.' When I got her back to our table, Dolores's mood changed drastically. She muttered, 'She killed him. I know she did.'"

"My God!" gasped Brenda. "I never thought she understood what had happened."

"Would you mind explaining to me what happened?" Kilgore asked.

Brenda told Kilgore everything—the attempt to make up a visiting schedule, Sheila's failure to keep up her end, Mitchell, covering for the unresponsive Sheila.

"So, Dolores blames Sheila for Mitchell's death?"

"Dolores and I both," Brenda said, as a bit of venomous anger rose in her voice, despite her efforts to contain it.

B renda and Kilgore stood in front of the glass doors to the music room as he described the area.

"The music room is uniquely set up for both individual listening and small therapy groups," he said. "The room is shaped like a horseshoe. Along each side, there are a dozen soft chairs, each with its own headset. The music therapist can pick any genre of music going back eighty years for residents to hear. The color of the room is designed to be both pleasant and stimulating at the same time."

Kilgore pointed to the far end of the music room.

"The rounded end of the room is designed for small therapy groups. Music has a unique ability to draw out memories. Groups of six residents will form a circle with their chairs. Using information from their intake papers, the therapist will play someone's favorite type of music. Hopefully, when the music elicits some type of reaction, like a smile or a head swaying to the rhythm, the therapist can ask what they're thinking about or what they remember about that particular song."

"So, the music serves as a connection to a memory the mind has forgotten?"

"That's the very purpose of everything we do here, Brenda. We try to connect to a memory long forgotten. It's what makes this type of work so rewarding and yet so frustrating. Dementia is like the rabbit hole in Alice in Wonderland. Only unlike in the story, for our residents, there's no getting out. With each passing day, they slip farther and farther into the darkness, so when we can get a smile of remembrance or a laugh when a recollection is brought back to life, words can't describe the feeling we get."

Chapter 18

DOLORES

*D*olores was sitting in the first chair of a group about ready to start their session. Kilgore and Brenda stood several feet behind her. Kilgore motioned to the therapist. He wanted to introduce Brenda to her.

"Sally Brown, Brenda Samuels. Dolores Samuels is her mother-in-law. She's here to see her," Kilgore said.

Sally Brown had been a music major in college and had dreamed of a career as a country western singer. Unfortunately for Sally, short at barely 5' and overweight beyond plump were not characteristics likely to land her on the Grand Ole Opry. However, her photographic memory of lyrics and an unexplained ear for rhythm enabled her to play any song her group requested. This type of work where she could be the star was a tolerable trade-off.

"Always nice to meet a family member," Sally said. "Would you like to take Dolores now?"

"No, please continue. I'd love to see how this works."

"Okay, I'll start with some of Dolores's favorites."

Kilgore and Brenda took seats several feet behind where Dolores was sitting.

"Today we're going to start our session with one of Dolores's favorite groups, the Platters," Sally said. "Let's see where the music takes us."

Sally placed the well-worn CD into the player and pressed play.

Rose Woodall leaned forward as if she were playing "Name That Tune."

"I got this one," she said, with an almost comic determination in her voice.

Dolores had her head turned slightly to the right so that she could look out the window. Despite Sally's best efforts, Dolores was lost in her own thoughts. The words to "Harbor Lights" came softly from the speakers.

Rose blurted out with glee, "I know that song."

"Good, Rose, but let's listen to some more," Sally said, hoping the delay would draw Dolores's attention back to the song.

Rose sat back in her chair, dejected that she wasn't given the chance to name the song.

"But I know it," Rose complained through pursed lips. Her competitive nature had not yet been affected by dementia.

After the second refrain, Dolores's head began to sway back and forth. She turned to face Sally. Her face was aglow, and her eyes had a sudden alertness.

"What is it, Dolores? What are you remembering?" Sally asked.

Dolores did not reply. She folded her arms as if she were cradling a baby. Her head swaying became more pronounced. Sally tried again.

"Dolores, can you tell us the name of this song?" Sally asked.

Dolores looked at the therapist.

"Shush," she whispered. "We don't want to wake him." Dolores continued patting the imaginary infant. "Sleep my sweet Mitchell, sleep."

Brenda gripped the arms of her chair. Dolores cooed to her baby for a minute or so, then suddenly she began to cry.

"No! no! Oh God, no! He can't be gone. Not my Mitchell!"

Sally immediately motioned for Kilgore and Brenda to slide Dolores's chair away from the group.

"You take over, Daniel. You know what to do," Sally said.

"Everyone, Dolores is a little upset so let's try another song, shall we?"

The dejected Rose immediately leaned forward again. This time maybe she would get a chance to name the song.

Dolores rocked back and forth, moaning, "My baby, my baby!" Her head slumped down. Kilgore knelt in front of her.

"Dolores, are you okay?" He gently stroked her arm.

He repeated the question a couple of times before Dolores lifted her head. Her slender hand reached out to his.

"Mitchell?" She asked, as her eyes darted left and right.

Kilgore looked at Brenda and mouthed, "Trust me."

"Yes, Mom. It's me, Mitchell. I've got Brenda here with me."

Dolores straightened herself in her chair. She stared at the woman in the chair facing her. She wanted to recognize her. She tried so hard to recognize her, but she couldn't.

Taking a cue from Kilgore, Brenda knelt in front of Dolores. "Dolores, it's me, Brenda. I'm right here with Mitch."

The woman had an obvious affection for Dolores, and it was evident by her body posture.

"Mitch?" Dolores asked, as if the connection were weakening. In all its muddle state, it was apparent her mind was working hard to grasp the situation.

"Mom, I'm right here with you," Kilgore said, his hand gently squeezing hers. For a moment, Kilgore was her beloved Mitch.

Dolores appeared to focus on him. As she blinked, a smile formed on her face.

"My Mitchell," she sighed with a satisfied realization. "I knew you'd come back. I knew they were wrong."

Dolores looked back to where Brenda, filled with encouragement, was quietly sitting.

"Brenda?" She asked tentatively.

"Oh yes, Mom, oh yes, it's me!" Brenda said. Her voice cracked with emotion as she said, "I love you, Mom."

Her own mother had long been absent from her life, and Brenda was stunned by the realization of the importance of this connection to Dolores.

"I'm so happy," Dolores said, as her head leaned back against her chair. A radiance long absent from her gentle face now appeared. Gradually, she drifted off to a contented slumber, but the glow remained

There was silence in the room for a moment, then Kilgore spoke, "She'll be fine. We should go now."

Sally waved to them as they left the music room. Once outside, Kilgore asked, "Would you like a moment..."

"To relax and sort this out? Yes, I would."

Kilgore took her out to the veranda where they sat at an empty table. The temperature was near ninety and the air sticky from the rising humidity. Fortunately, several oscillating fans, as well as hanging fans from the beams of the pergola, made being outside bearable. Brenda removed a tissue from the hidden recesses of her clutch purse. She dabbed her tear-moistened eyes, aware that her eye makeup was in disarray. The emotional intensity of the previous moment was still present.

"I need help sorting this out. Can you help?" surprised that she was relying on this stranger for help.

Kilgore knew what she was going to ask, but he wasn't sure what he had to offer her.

"Okay."

"You were convincing in there. Do you think she actually believed your performance?"

"Absolutely." The calmness, the certainty in his voice reassured her.

Kilgore pondered this anticipated question for a moment. He was not so pretentious to believe he had the skilled eye of a trained clinician, but he had spent enough time with these people to have an understanding of them.

"In that briefest of moments, her son was alive. The time between their last meeting and his death was erased. Her precious Mitch was as whole and alive as anyone on this earth."

Brenda, her mind racing, now sensed the urgency. Dolores had precious little time left. She needed her family. All bitterness toward Fred vaporized.

"Fred needs to come to Magnolia Gardens and give Dolores the love she craves."

"Brenda, you have seen with your own eyes what love can do. Convince Fred that time is of the essence. These are his mother's last days, for mercy sakes! Until then, I'll be Mitch or Fred or anyone else from her past if it means she can be in that place of familiar contentment that frees her from the tormented hell that is dementia."

Chapter 19

THE STORY

Kilgore found he was more prolific than he had thought. He was writing nearly 800 words a day and emailing them each evening to Lincoln. He was looking forward to hearing her critique, but more than he wanted to admit, he also wanted to hear her voice. Long before Vivian had passed away, her voice had become silent. Kilgore would talk to her, stroke her hair, talk of things that had long since passed, but the excruciating pain was not having a voice to listen to, someone to make plans with or a hand to hold his. He had introduced a new character in his manuscript, and he wondered how long it would take Lincoln to see the connection between reality and fiction.

He drove like a man intoxicated with infatuation, which of course, he was. Once in the driveway, he took a quick burst of mint mouth spray. He was feeling much younger than his fifty-five years. Lincoln had awakened feelings in him he had not felt in years, the elixir of anticipation.

Tonight's dinner was another excuse to see him, besides the editing of his manuscript. Lincoln leaned against the wall and admired the dining room table. She had not spent much time lately adding such touches to her home. Why bother? Up until now, there were precious few people to see them, but now she was again motivated in this area. The bouquet of red and white carnations was a nice touch, she thought. She hoped that the scented Yankee candles would provide a sense of hominess, and perhaps a little romance as well.

She knew that this was the day she wanted their relationship to proceed. Yet, she was not convinced Daniel had the same feelings. Years of devotion to her profession had dulled her to some of the nuances of romance between a man and a woman. She hoped she was not reading him wrong and that he was interested in her as well. The doorbell chimes brought Jane back to reality.

When she answered the door, he said, "Am I too early?"

There was a boyishness to his question that she found very attractive. He held a cold bottle of Prosecco wine in one hand and the finished manuscript in the other. He sensed she was a bit befuddled. After years of marriage, he was more than a little nervous about doing the wrong thing.

Jane quickly regained her composure. "Come on in."

"This is for the refrigerator," he said, handing her the wine, "and this is for you," he added, giving her the manuscript.

"You are sweet," she said, as she gave Daniel a somewhat awkward, yet polite kiss on the cheek.

With the wine chilling in the refrigerator, Jane took him to the living room. Daniel could not help but notice a large new area rug. There were fresh flowers on the end table where a stack of magazines used to be. A shepherd's crook lamp stand replaced the old stained-glass lamp.

She took a seat at the end of the couch to take advantage of the light from the lamp on the end table. She pointed for Daniel to sit next to her.

She hefted the manuscript Daniel had handed her when he arrived. She exclaimed, "Wow! You have really made some progress."

Early on Lincoln realized Kilgore's manuscript paralleled his real life—the main character was widowed, his attraction to a female character so subtly under control. The empathic techniques employed by the protagonist, Sloan, with the residents in the rest home mirrored those used by Kilgore. There were sufficient differences that no one reading it would ever have associated it with Magnolia Gardens or any of its residents, but she knew, and it surprisingly pleased her.

Adam Sloan, the protagonist, had been asked by his sister, Theda, to investigate the mysterious death of her husband, Donald Janes, who died while residing in an assisted living facility in suburban Chicago, Illinois. Sloan had a background as a paramedic and easily convinced the management of Evergreen Manor that he was an ideal hire as a new resident aide.

Sloan was drawn to three residents who had not had any visitors since they had been admitted. Why hadn't anyone come to visit them? What were their families like? As he spent more and more time with them, Sloan learned what things upset them, what things made them happy, and how they were connected to the frail, fading memories that emerged from their diaphanous minds. Clever name for the novel, Lincoln thought, "Diaphanous Minds."

Twenty-five years on the LAPD had taken its toll on Adam Sloan. He was a husband twice over and had no interest in any romantic entanglement. However, he hadn't counted on meeting anyone like Leslie Burns, a leggy 5' 8" brunette who wore her hair pulled back in a bun accentuating her piercing hazel eyes. She was a licensing agent for the Illinois Department of Mental Health. Burns was reviewing the circumstances of Donald Janes' death. In time, she and Adam Sloan began comparing notes on and off the job.

The more she had read, the more she thought she was reading about herself and Kilgore. Was it an accident that Kilgore and Sloan both worked in assisted living facilities, that both men would form an attraction with a woman while working there? Jane had felt it when she started spending time with Kilgore following his wife's death. Yes, she was researching the dynamics of dementia on family members, and yes, if pressed, Jane Lincoln would have to admit she would have made up any excuse to spend time with Daniel.

He was glad she had insisted on casual. Her Levi's fit her perfectly.

Her sleeveless waist length blouse revealed traces of bare midriff when she moved. The translucent material of the blouse teased Kilgore's imagination as he thought about what it covered. Kilgore smiled as Lincoln found her way to the final eighty or so pages.

"Daniel, I'm not a professional like Sylvia, but I read a lot, and I know what moves me. I know what I feel when I read your description of people's emotions, the scenes that take place. This is really good."

"I hope so," he said, hiding the excitement her praise brought to him.

He had a sense that his work had merit, but he was surprised and delighted by her response.

She allowed herself a bit of familiarity or, more correctly, a bit of overfamiliarity. "No, Daniel. It is," she said, as she placed her hand on his leg. "You've written a moving and sensitive story that can't help but touch anyone who reads it."

She gave his leg a little extra squeeze and then leaned over to give him a kiss on the cheek. At the same time, Kilgore turned to face her. Her kiss did not wind up on Kilgore's cheek. It lingered long enough for his hand to reach around her waist and feel her bare skin and for her hand to find the back of his neck when a sense of mutual embarrassment separated them.

Jane rested her head on Daniel's shoulder, too embarrassed to look directly at him. Her hands laid on his chest prepared to gently push him away, but they didn't. *Why am I embarrassed? I wanted that kiss and more.*

"Sorry," she muttered, as she pursed her lips.

"Me too," Daniel stumbled, mortified over his state of arousal.

In those moments away from her, his mind had created just such a set of circumstances for something like this to happen. Now that it had actually transpired, he was stunned by his lack of self-control and clumsiness. There was more silence than either one wanted while they ate, but the embarrassment of that kiss seemed to resonate whenever either tried to speak.

Chicken breasts had been pounded thin, dredged in seasoned flour and browned. Jane added a diced shallot and four sliced Shitake mushrooms to the hot skillet. After a couple of minutes, she put the chicken breasts back in and poured in a cup of marsala wine and demi-glaze sauce. A Greek salad and garlic baked pita slices finished off the meal.

"That dinner was divine," Kilgore said at last, as he dabbed his lips with his napkin.

"Now who's flattering whom?" Jane beamed.

Both giggled a little as he responded, "Touché."

He tapped his wine glass to hers.

Daniel cleaned the table as Jane rinsed the dishes and put them in the dishwasher. As he watched her, Daniel wondered if he had stepped over the line. Did she think he was only interested in her physically?

He must think I'm some sort of a tart, she thought, as she reached for the last dish. She straightened up to face him and apologize once again.

"Can I ask you a rather personal question?" Kilgore said, as the last dish was placed in the dishwasher.

"Okay," Jane said, as she rinsed the last bit of food down the sink drain.

"You're educated, a great conversationalist, someone with tenderness and compassion, why haven't you ever married?"

Jane leaned back against the sink. She found herself annoyed with this overture into her past.

"And what makes you think I haven't?" she replied, more annoyed than flattered by his question.

"I don't know," Kilgore said, oblivious to her feelings. "No pictures anywhere, that kind of thing. In all the time we have been together, you never let anything about a previous guy slip out."

"Come with me."

Jane could feel her emotions slipping out of control. They walked down the hallway to Jane's office. From the bookcase against the far wall, she took out a photo album and opened it. By now, she had regained her composure.

"His name was Bob. We were high school sweethearts and married after we graduated from college. He was in ROTC and was a commissioned officer in the Marine Corps. The Corps and flying meant everything to him."

There was still a tinge of sadness in her voice when she quietly expressed, "He didn't even make it out of flight school. His plane disintegrated on take-off during touch and go training."

Her voice trailed off at the end of the sentence. Jane's sense of loss was still there. Her fingers moved slowly over the face of the man in uniform. Her mother and father were standing next to them in the photo. She was clearly trying to get some tactile sensation from the past.

Trying very hard to sound compassionate, he gently asked, "Ok, but you never remarried?"

Jane closed the album. "No," she said, "and that was a source of considerable consternation for my mother. For years, she saw me bury myself in my work, first grad school, then my teaching career. You can't live in the past with old memories, she would say, or you'll never have a future making new ones."

"Your mother was pretty smart," Daniel said, as he thought back to what his niece had said Vivian told her about Jane. "I'm sorry to have opened old wounds." He was anxious to depart from the sadness her recollections had generated.

"Then let's have dessert, shall we?" she suggested.

"Let's," Daniel answered.

He was smarting from his obvious inexcusable intrusion into Jane's past and was eager to move on. They returned to the living room where Jane had elected to have dessert. She didn't turn on the lights. The glow from the wood stove provided ample light. Yet, it did nothing to dispel the gloom of the earlier conversation.

"Let me ask you a question," Lincoln said, as she set her dessert plate on the coffee table.

"Sure," Kilgore said, uncertain as to where she was heading.

"In your novel, there seems to be this underlying current of attraction between the hero, Adam Sloan, and this Leslie Burns. Is there any chance by story's end these two may be together?"

"Early into the story, I would've said no, but the deeper I got into the story, I knew I wanted them to wind up together."

"I'm glad. I've really come to like that guy, Adam Sloan."

Her smile was particularly sweet after she made that remark. Kilgore found himself smiling as well. Daniel was in no hurry to go home, but propriety ruled the day. Setting aside his baser desires, he gave the gentlemanly excuse that it was getting late and he really should be going.

Jane said goodbye at the door, but not before giving Daniel a more intentional kiss than the one earlier. It was nearly 11 p.m. when he got home, and he was looking forwarding to uninterrupted sleep. Such would not be the case.

Sylvia Mueller took a traditional approach to her duties as a literary agent. She did not look for profound character development or an intriguing and complicated storyline. Sylvia searched for authors who could reach deep inside her and spark that womanly compassion tucked away from her "all business" exterior. So far, Kilgore was succeeding. She reached for tissue number two and punched Daniel Kilgore's number into her cell phone. *Please, please answer,* she thought. *Maybe he's asleep.* She was somewhat embarrassed that she hadn't noticed how late it was in Charleston.

His phone started to go to voicemail when she heard Kilgore's initially faint and slightly confused voice state, "I appreciate your devotion to duty, but jeez, I was down for the count."

She heard the mild annoyance in his voice, yet she continued.

"Forgive me, Daniel, but I just had to call you. I finished reading the last of your outline. I read these sort of things as part of my job, but you have really impressed me with the way you get to the emotional side of the issues."

"What, no urgency to get the project done?" He was well aware of Sylvia's tendency to be a hard-ass.

"No, sweetie. You'll get it done when you get it done, and it will be great."

Kilgore looked at his phone as if he couldn't believe what he had heard. Even with the mild success of his first book, he was unsure how much talent he really possessed.

"I appreciate that very much, Sylvia."

It was gratifying to get that kind of feedback from a professional like Sylvia.

"Hopefully, I can keep the momentum going."

"We both know you will. Now get back to that sleepy time."

Abruptly, her voice was replaced by a dial tone.

Chapter 20

Revelation

"Really?" Jim said.

He was skeptical initially. He could not remember a single time when his daughter was not truthful with him. Walt Haggerty, Judy Beth's father, told Jim that his family had not gone to their cabin on Lake Ogallala as Samantha had told him.

"Thanks, Walt. I'd appreciate it if you could keep this between you and me until I get a chance to talk with Samantha and clear this up. I am not sure why she would mislead me like this, but I would like to believe that there was a good reason."

Walt said he would.

Jim was in the den going over some forms his attorney in Oklahoma had sent him about the divorce when he heard a car door slam. He peeked through the blinds and saw Samantha. *Sheila had to make deliveries to several fitness centers, or so she said. It should take a couple of hours,* he thought. *Plenty of time to talk with Samantha alone.*

"I'm home, Daddy."

There was an unusual bounce in her walk and a renewed freshness on her face that had not been there for some time. She was glad her mother's car was gone. She really wanted to tell her dad the truth about seeing her grandmother. Samantha knew he would be displeased that she had lied to him, but she believed he would be won over with the news.

"I'm in the den, Sam."

He quickly put the divorce papers back in the folder and placed the folder in his desk drawer. Samantha poked her head into the den.

There were papers all over her dad's normally well-organized desktop. *Maybe this was not such a good time to talk with him,* she thought.

"Daddy, if you're busy, we can talk later."

"For you, always."

The excitement on her face as she sat down quickly diffused his anger regarding her untruthfulness.

"There's something I need to tell you, and I don't want you to be mad at me," she said.

"Well, why don't you tell me what you did and then let me decide if I'm going to be mad. We've never kept secrets in the past, have we?"

"I didn't go with Judy Beth's family to their cabin, Daddy. I actually went to see Gramma."

She spoke in a rapid-fire manner. It was as though the speed of her delivery would somehow help her get quickly past her father's disappointment.

Of all the explanations Jim Cotton expected to hear from his daughter, this was not the one. He was relieved, yet his concern continued unabated. A dozen traumatic scenarios ripped through his mind.

"My God! Samantha, that's a sixteen-hour drive round-trip! What were you thinking taking such a trip alone without telling me?"

Seeing that this news was not received as graciously as she had hoped, immediate tears descended from her eyes. There were only two people in the world Samantha hated to disappoint, her gramma and her dad. No doubt she had hurt her grandmother by not visiting. Now she was doing it to her wonderful father.

"I know, Daddy," she sputtered, as her sobs started to increase. "I did have someone go with me to help with the drive. We spent the night in a motel and Daddy, Gramma was wonderful. She was like her old self most of the time."

Jim reached out and took hold of his daughter's hands. Clearly, he was moved by the sincerity and emotions of his cherished daughter's words.

"Going to see your grandmother was a wonderful and thoughtful thing to do. I just don't understand why you didn't tell me. Why did you think you had to lie about it?"

"Daddy, you've been under so much pressure what with everything that's been happening between you and mom, I didn't want to put more on you. I know you were planning to take me to see Gramma soon, but there was something I wanted to tell her, just between her and me. I just felt I couldn't wait to do it."

He leaned back in his chair. He might not mark perceptual ability high on his list of attributes, but he had known for some time that something was amiss with his daughter.

Why does every generation of young people think their mistakes were the first ones ever made, or that their secrets were the first ones to be kept from their parents, he thought?

"Is there more that you haven't told me?" he asked, knowing full well there was.

Samantha did not answer at first, then she slowly nodded her head as she wiped the tears still flowing freely down her youthful cheeks. Jim Cotton took no satisfaction in seeing his daughter dreading to tell him a secret that really wasn't a secret, at least not to him. He stood up and took his daughter into his arms.

"Sweetheart, there's not a mistake you or your brother have ever made that your mother and I didn't make when we were your ages. As for secrets, really! Samantha, the only thing that stays secret between two people is when one of them is dead. Since Mike Callahan isn't dead, yes, I know you two have been seeing each other again."

It was Samantha's turn to be startled. She stepped back from her father and blurted out, "Daddy, you knew and never told me?"

"Yes, I knew and never told you and Mike's father did the same with him. Honey, when you and Mike found out you were pregnant, his dad and I had several conversations. Kyle thought both of you were too young to take on such a responsibility, but he was willing to let you two decide what to do. At first, I agreed, but you know your mother. Need I say more?"

Samantha shook her head. At this point, it was difficult for her to think anything positive in terms of her mother.

"Anyway, as a courtesy to me, when Kyle found out Mike was seeing you again, we decided to stay out of it. After what had been forced on both of you, I wanted you to have a fresh start. I was never comfortable with keeping you apart."

"You never told Mom?"

"Oh, hell no!"

Samantha chuckled at the mild profanity. This was so unlike her proper father, the colonel, but the amusement of it all helped with the tension.

"Is that what you wanted to tell your grandmother?" he asked.

"Yes, and Daddy, Gramma knew what the issue was. Funny thing is, I think she knew before I told her."

Jim Cotton knew his mother. "In the right moment, she probably did, honey."

She had caught him enough times in falsehoods as he remembered.

"There's something else about Mike you should know," Samantha said. "The miscarriage nearly drove him crazy. He thought he had lost me. Anyway, we've been seeing each other all the time I've been back at Vanderbilt, and Daddy, we want to get married."

"Now that I didn't expect."

He remembered the last time he and Carrie had decided for their daughter, and he remembered the look in his mother's eyes. He wouldn't make that mistake again.

"Sweetheart, all I want is for you to be happy. If you've found happiness with Mike, then plan your future accordingly. I'll handle your mother."

"Daddy, I met the man that was visiting her. He's so nice and understanding. You would really like him. He's so patient with Gramma and talks so sweetly to her."

"I'm sure I would, baby. Now tell me about your grandmother."

He was sure that his daughter was describing her as she would like to think of her, not how she actually was.

"You should see her and soon, Daddy. Her health seems okay, but her memory is so fragile that it won't be long before she won't remember anything. At least that's what Mr. Kilgore said."

Somehow his daughter's words managed to penetrate that shield of miscellaneous life details that had previously seemed so significant.

"There's nothing so pressing that it can't wait until after I see your grandmother. I'll need to make arrangements for a rental plane, that's all."

"You're really not mad at me for lying?"

"I don't think it was the best way to handle things, but under the circumstances, no, sweetheart, I'm not mad or disappointed."

They both stood up, and it was Samantha that closed the distance between them. His loving embrace was the approval she needed to feel.

"You are the apple that didn't fall far from the tree, Daddy."

This time I hope you're right, Jim Cotton thought.

Chapter 21

THE EPIPHANY

*B*renda called her brother-in-law on his cell phone. They seldom spoke, but she was fortified by her recent visit and the righteousness of her actions.

"Brenda, long time no see, or should I say, long time no hear?" he said, hoping a tidbit of humor would break the ice between the two. If he thought Brenda was so simplistic that he could easily blunt her efforts by such a move, he was wrong.

"Too much water under the bridge for humor, Fred, but that's not why I called. It's about your mother," Brenda said, immediately sorry she had been so acidic with him.

"What about Mom? Is she okay? Has something happened?" As absent as he had been from his mother's life, he had genuine affection for her.

"No, she's fine," Brenda said, as she took a deep breath. "Fred, I went to see Dolores. I spent some time with her and a man who has been visiting her. His name is Kilgore, Daniel Kilgore."

Fred was relieved to hear his mother was okay, and more than a little ashamed he had to hear it from Brenda, even though this was his own fault.

"I wish I had known you were going. I'm planning a trip to see her myself," he said, sounding way too defensive and not particularly sincere.

"And that was going to happen when?" Brenda snapped, and immediately wished she hadn't. She was disappointed that she had so much trouble fencing in her emotions. She wanted Fred's voluntary participation.

"Sorry Fred, you're not the one who deserves that," she said with a degree of repentance Fred could acknowledge.

"I understand, Brenda, I really do."

Unlike Brenda, he was easily placated by such overtures from women. His voice sounded warmer than she had remembered.

"Tell me about Mom."

Brenda wasn't sure where to start. Was it Dolores fantasizing that her son Mitchell was sitting next to her, or the compassion of the man who allowed her to think so?

"Dolores seems okay physically. There's the normal heart and blood pressure problems for a woman her age, but it's her mind that's fading fast, Fred. Anyway, at one point, Dolores really thought her visitor, Mr. Kilgore, was Mitchell. My God, Fred, you should have seen her face light up! She was euphoric at the thought that the news of Mitchell's death wasn't true because there he was, he was sitting right there next to her."

"No one corrected her?" Fred asked, thinking how cruel a hoax to play on her. The defensiveness he felt for his mother was unavoidable.

"You don't understand, Fred," Brenda replied. "Your mom didn't need to be corrected, she only needed the time to remember the joy and happiness Mitchell and you brought into her life. Believing Mitchell was present brought her closer to the actual world."

"But I thought you said Mom thought this guy Kilgore was Mitchell. How did I get into the conversation?"

"It was brilliant how Kilgore handled it, Fred," Brenda said, as the enthusiasm rose in her voice. "He took hold of Dolores's hands and talked about the years growing up with you, the trouble you two got into, and some of your hairbrained schemes. With each story, her eyes radiated with the joy of remembering. It was no longer Dolores, the near-comatose old woman, but a vibrant, living woman."

"I don't get it, Brenda," he interrupted. "How did this guy know anything about Mitch and me growing up together?" His defensive posture was hardening.

Brenda started to chuckle. Although far too unimportant for her to focus on, she enjoyed having Fred in such an uncomfortable position.

"Fred, work has made you way too analytical. I think Kilgore was telling your mom stories of his own youth and his own growing up. He threw in your name and in your mom's delicate state of mind, she remembered them as really happening. She smiled with each story Kilgore told her."

As he listened to Brenda, the weight of her remarks hit home. Fred Samuels didn't know who he missed more, his brother or his mother. Mitchell Samuels was more than just an older brother. He was Fred's idol. By the time they were in elementary school, it was Mitchell who played catch with Fred and taught him the fundamentals of baseball in the backyard. When Mitchell passed down his bike to his younger brother, Fred acted as though he had been given a brand-new Schwinn of his own.

The two were not without the normal older brother-younger brother spats. Those battles were always tempered by the presence and wisdom of their mother. Never one to chastise, Dolores would calm the turbulent seas between her sons by likening Mitchell to one who should protect and look after his younger sibling. Fred's bruised and tender ego was massaged by Dolores with words that brothers can disagree but never fight with each other. There were so many times Fred wished he could hear his mother's voice again. Since only one was still alive, the decision on who would visit and when was even easier.

"You need to see her as soon as you can, Fred. There's no telling when Dolores won't remember anything, truth or fiction." She pressed this point home the best way she knew how.

"I hear you, Brenda, I really do. Once we hang up, I'm on it."

In a rare moment in his life, Fred had certainty in his heart. He quickly dialed his office.

"Helen, Fred. Listen, schedule me on the first flight from Dallas to Charleston there is. Never mind what else is on the planner. This is priority!"

"Do you want a nonstop flight?" mildly annoyed that she could not read this mind.

"Doesn't matter, Helen, just get me there as fast as possible."

The urgency in his voice had her typing flight information to Charleston, South Carolina into a computer before they finished talking. Her boss was seldom so direct, and the fact that he was now was having the desired effect.

A s soon as he got Leo's text, George called.

"How was she, Leo?" Hillman asked. "Don't sugarcoat the matter, I want the facts!"

He might be showing greater interest in his wife, but he was still the same old George.

Leo Ainsworth had spent a career as George Hillman's personal attorney and financial advisor. He saw his primary responsibility as a presenter of options, options with pros and cons. George would make the final decision. This time it would be different. There were no options, no pros or cons to consider. There was only what George Hillman had to do, and Leo Ainsworth had no problem telling him what that was. It was a relief for both of them, really.

"There's little of the old Mary left, George, and what is, centers on the baby."

"God, Leo, that was so many years ago, does she still suffer over it?" Hillman asked, knowing in his heart the answer to the question. The guilt he had long since buried was now staring right at him.

"Yes, George, she does, and she needs to see you, to hear your voice. Listen, this is a project you need to finish and now. Nothing else should matter, George, not work, not the attorney's stuff. You, my friend, need to get yourself to Charleston and see your wife."

Hillman suddenly remembered the other thing he wanted Leo to research.

"What about this visitor who's been seeing Mary? What did you learn about him?"

"On that subject, my friend, you are about the luckiest son-of-a-bitch I know. In the time you haven't been seeing Mary, this guy, Daniel Kilgore has, as regular as clockwork. When Mary needed to hear your voice, it was Kilgore's she heard. When she cried over the baby or some romantic novel he read to her, he soothed her heart, all the time letting her think it was you. George, you owe this guy a debt of gratitude you could never repay."

"I can't argue that," Hillman said, but still wondering what would motivate a man to visit his Mary in her current condition.

Fear was an emotion George Hillman had rarely experienced. He pursued mergers and acquisitions with a vengeance, crushing anyone and everyone who stood in his way. He was intimidated by no one. He was the one to be feared, not the other way around. After his conversation with Leo however, that was exactly what he felt. In fact, he was suddenly consumed by the thought that the real George Hillman would not measure up to the one who had so tenderly and compassionately looked after his Mary.

Kilgore pulled into the parking lot of the Magnolia Gardens to see his friends as usual. The lawns were covered with wrens pecking the blades of grass searching for the tasty small insects who had surfaced from the light rain during the night. The air was heavy with humidity. He was glad he had chosen a light silk shirt to wear. What greeted him was a sign of the inevitable fate living in a long-term care facility brings. The ambulance had its lights on, as did the accompanying unit from the Charleston Fire Department. Daniel quickened his pace. Had someone been hurt or worse, died?

Once through the entrance doors, Kilgore saw Madeline Orsini talking with one of the paramedics. At that moment, two other paramedics appeared, one pushing a gurney with one of the residents on it and the other one folding up the portable defibrillator kit. Kilgore recognized the person on the gurney immediately—Frank Zapata was one of the longest living residents at the Gardens. He had just celebrated his ninetieth birthday. Kilgore wasn't sure how much celebrating Frank had really enjoyed.

Kilgore had been among a small group of staff and volunteers who had been at Frank's table that day in the dining area. Frank had sat upright in his wheelchair, aided by several pillows stuffed against each side of his body. His once broad shoulders, developed from years of working on a dairy, were now shrunken and sloped forward. Fingers on both hands were permanently pointed inward, the result of arthritis. He had smiled, turning to each person when they spoke, though his eyes indicated he had no idea who was around him or why. The staff made sure Frank was neatly dressed every day.

The smile was what made Frank Zapata so special. Ask Frank anything, and he'd give you a smile. His memory had left him years ago. Frank had been included in several small therapy groups as well as two one-on-one therapy sessions weekly. When asked to participate, Frank would merely smile and sit there. His frail hands lined with dark blood vessels were crossed on his lap. His assigned therapist, Suzan Parks, rarely took any games or activities in which to engage him. Mostly Suzan would sit next to Frank and talk about her plans after she finished college and what life might hold for her. Frank would sit there silently and smile.

Orsini motioned for Kilgore to come over.

"Daniel, this is Joe Greenlee. He heads the paramedic team that responded to our call."

As the team leader, he was younger than Daniel expected. Greenlee looked to be in his late twenties. His hair was cut in a high-and-tight military fashion. He carried himself with a degree of confidence his age did not warrant.

"Joe, under the circumstances I feel awkward saying 'nice to meet you,'" Kilgore said.

The slight grin on Greenlee's face told Kilgore his bit of gallows humor was appreciated. Greenlee watched Kilgore's eyes follow the gurney with Frank's body on it.

"Don't worry, it looks like he passed away peacefully in his sleep."

Kilgore nodded his head. *Jeez! Frank's even happy in death!*

"It seems a shame that his mind went so long before his body finally gave up," the paramedic added.

Kilgore thought about the paramedic's words, then he made the sign of the cross, a rare display of his religious convictions.

"I think something entirely different, Joe," Kilgore replied. "Eventually we will all be faced with bodies that don't respond like they used to or minds that don't work like they once did. There is no shame in that. The real shame, the real tragedy is when we start to slide down that dark and lonely abyss, and there's no one there to listen to us or talk to us. Will anybody be there to try and help us remember? Will anyone care enough to want to see us smile as a faded memory emerges one last time?"

Kilgore quickly knew that his thoughtful words fell on unhearing ears. The paramedic nodded to Orsini and shook Kilgore's hand, then headed outside to his waiting ambulance.

"That was a rather dark prophecy, don't you think, Daniel?" Orsini said.

"Dark, but true nonetheless."

"I think not. Everyone doesn't have to wind up ravaged by dementia and left to spend their last years in some care home forgotten by those who should care. Only one in seven Americans over seventy will suffer from dementia, Daniel, that's only fourteen percent. Think about the other eighty-six percent of the population. Many will live long and productive lives with alert minds. Unfortunately, Daniel, some, like you, will suffer unbearable heartaches like the loss of Vivian. I can't imagine the pain you went through. Daniel, we are not free to choose our fate. But, we are free to choose how we live our lives until that time comes."

Orsini was prepared to go on, but she stopped short, knowing full-well that Kilgore already understood. Daniel Kilgore had chosen to bring moments of immeasurable happiness and tenderness to the forgotten. She was taken with Kilgore from the first day he volunteered at the Gardens. During their orientation talk, she learned of Kilgore's wife's condition and the hours he devoted tending to her care. She was taken with his sense of caring and realized how lucky the residents were to have someone like him, someone who took pleasure in their company and enjoyed making them smile and laugh. Orsini hoped Kilgore would not have to wait that long before he got that lucky.

Chapter 22

A TRIP TO REDEMPTION

illary Braxton had been George Hillman's administrative assistant for nearly twenty-five years. She placed his airline tickets in an envelope; San Diego to LaGuardia and the commuter flight to Charleston was the best she could do. She did nothing to combat her natural homeliness. Lack of orthodontic care left her with a permanent overbite which was exaggerated by her angular jawline. She wore black horn-rimmed glasses rather than move to contacts. The physical fitness craze which affected so many professional women in their drive to look more attractive had no effect on Hillary, who bore enough extra weight to be thought of as plump. However, she had an affinity for equity assessment which made her invaluable to Hillman. In his retirement, he kept her on retainer to act as his administrative assistant. Hillary drove to George's residence.

"Here they are," she said, as she handed George an envelope. "First-class ticket, one way to LaGuardia, LaGuardia to Charleston with the common folks, and a car rental."

Hillman thanked her, as he put the envelope in his coat pocket.

"I'm curious, George," taking advantage of a first name familiarity she enjoyed. "Why only a one-way ticket?"

"I'm not sure when I'm coming back," he replied.

She understood full well her boss's uncertainty. Hillary Braxton was more than Hillman's administrative assistant. For years, she had been his closest confidant. She was the only person George felt secure in discussing not only the backstabbing, winner-take-all politics that festered beneath the façade of the hypocritical motto "Working together, we make our clients successful" of his boss, but also his role in the deterioration of his marriage and Mary's mental health.

"Can I get you something?" he asked, as he headed to the wet bar in his living room. Thanks to the aggressiveness of his attorney, Gilda had vacated the premises earlier than expected.

"Nothing for me, but can I ask you a question?"

"Sure."

The tinkling sound of ice cubes sliding into his glass as he made himself a second Crown Royale on the rocks punctuated his answer.

"What do you think you'll find where you get there?"

"I don't understand?"

"You know, her physical condition, correct? So, what do you think you'll find that you don't already know?"

Hillman took a final swallow of his drink, then slowly poured the contents into the sink. The liquor vanished from sight as had his memory of his wife - until now, that is. His measured words came slowly at first, then gradually built to a crescendo of repressed emotions.

"I'll tell you what I hope to find, Hillary, better yet, what I threw away. I've loved but one person in my entire life and I threw that love away. I followed my dreams, with Mary at my side supporting me all the way, to build a hugely successful financial career, yet when it came to supporting her in pursuing her dream of motherhood, I abandoned her as fast as Peter did Christ."

Stunned by his remarks, Hillary sat there wishing she had taken George up on his offer of a drink. He straightened up and walked from behind the bar like a man about to face his executioner, confident in the righteousness of his cause.

"Hillary, I deserve to spend eternity in hell for what I took from Mary, and probably will. That doesn't matter. I don't care if she doesn't remember me or anything about me. I pray to hear her voice again, maybe even hear her laugh. If that's not to be, I will put my arms around her, and whisper to her how much I love her and how sorry I am for what I did. Hillary, I am never going to abandon Mary again."

Braxton stared at her boss with more admiration and respect than she had ever felt in all the years she worked with him.

"I hope you find what you're looking for, George. Mary deserves it and at last, so do you."

Jim Cotton hadn't spent his entire career in the Air Force focused on contracts and procurements. He had earned his small plane pilot's license and had been the president of the MacDill Aero Club several times over. A former base commander had authorized the formation of an Air Force Aero Club to foster aviation as a career. The club, using authorized Air Force trainers, provided flying lessons to active duty personnel and their children over the age of sixteen. The MacDill Aero Club had a dozen planes ranging in size from single-engine Cessnas to twin-engine Beach Barons, in its inventory. The eight-hour drive from Jim's house near MacDill to Charleston would be cut to about three hours, especially if he could get one of the twin-engine Beech Baron's.

Master Sergeant Woodrow Pearson had drawn the scheduling duties for the Flying Club that month. Any member wanting to use one of the club's planes would have to go through Pearson. Woodrow Pearson had endured a major hiccup early in his career in the Air Force and had to spend some time in promotional purgatory, as the enlisted men call it, until the mention of his name didn't elicit a foul odor to the promotion board. The man who had salvaged Woodrow Pearson's career was James Cotton

"MacDill Aero Club," Pearson said, after running in from the hangar to the club's small office to answer the phone.

"Woody, is that you?" Cotton asked, surprised to hear his old friend's voice.

"Well, if it isn't Cotton Candy! How are you doing, Jimbo."

"Need a favor, Woody."

Knowing the planes were often booked months in advance, Cotton knew finding a plane available at the last minute would be nearly impossible. Cotton explained what he needed and why.

"Give me a minute to check the schedule," Pearson said, as he set the phone down. He was eager to fulfill his friend's request.

Cotton waited anxiously. Pearson picked up the phone.

"What do you know about a Major Carlton Bordeaux?"

"Arrogant, entitled snob from some supposed 'southern gentry' who thinks he's destined to be the next Air Force Chief of Staff. Why?"

"Seems he signed up for the last available Beach Baron. Tough luck for the major," Pearson added, as he scratched a line through Bordeaux's name.

"What do you mean tough luck, Woody?"

"Looks like that particular plane is due for its mandatory six-month maintenance check if I'm reading the record right. Can you be off the ground by 0900 on the twenty-first?"

"You know I can," replied a smiling Cotton, who knew full well what manipulation had just taken place.

"Good."

"I owe you, Woody," Cotton said.

"Not in this world, old buddy."

Fred Samuels had asked his secretary to make his flight plans to Charleston.

"Shit!" Helen muttered under her breath, as she dialed his phone number.

"Fred, Helen. I've got good news and bad news."

"Skip the bad news, Helen. I'm not in the mood for it."

"Okay. You are on a flight from Dallas to LaGuardia and then a commuter hop to Charleston on the twenty-first. There were no flights available from Dallas to Miami international."

"It's okay, Helen. It doesn't matter, just as long as you get me there."

He was irritated by the news but gratified that he would get there.

Fred had no intention of leaving his precious BMW convertible in long-term parking. His iPhone laid on his desk.

"Brenda, it's Fred. Need your help."

"Sure," said Brenda, who was feeling a bit of a renewed spirit after reconnecting with her brother-in-law. They had been on good terms in the past, and she was happy with the initial reconciliation.

"I need a ride to the airport. I'm going to see Mom."

"Fred, that's wonderful. When are you leaving?"

"The twenty-first. I got a flight out of Dallas at seven a.m."

"I'll pick you up about 4:30 a.m., and I'll try not to wake up Sheila when I get there."

Do I tell her now or wait until later? he mused, then acknowledged to himself that waiting wasn't going to bring him any more peace of mind.

"Sheila and I are separated, Brenda. You'd find out sooner or later and I think sooner is better. Anyway, she's moved out so don't worry about waking her up."

Bitch! Brenda thought, thinking back to that day Mitchell saw Sheila and her boyfriend in the parking lot. "How are you doing with that bit of news?"

"To be truthful, I'm not sure I'm unhappy with her leaving. It was the surprise of finding out from her in a four-line note that probably hurts the most. She never was much of a communicator, but I thought after twenty-plus years of marriage even she could have found a way to tell me face to face."

Brenda pondered what to say; some simplistic platitude like, you're better off without her, or there's someone out there who will really love you.

"I'm sorry for the pain you're going through, Fred. Sometimes things have to get worse before they get better."

No need to respond to the obvious, Fred thought. His mother was the focal point of this conversation.

"I'll be ready, and thanks, Brenda," he said.

"That's what families are for," she replied. "And Fred, I can't tell you how happy I am that you're going. Those lucid moments I had with her brought back so many memories. I hope those moments are there for you."

Now that's a novel concept, he thought. *People caring about and looking after their own.*

Three men, perfect strangers, were on their way to Charleston, South Carolina. There they would meet yet another stranger, who wasn't in all reality a stranger at all. He was someone who, in fact, had become each of them, a stranger with whom Mary Hillman shared the greatest tragedy of her life as if he were her husband, someone who gave her the love and support her real husband failed to give. He was the one to whom Dolores Samuels revealed the aching sorrow from which she never recovered. He was a stranger who knew all too well the heartbreaking agony of losing a child. And he shared with Sandra Cotton a family secret that had been kept hidden for years, a secret that had so unnecessarily torn a family apart and two people so much in love. No, this man was not a stranger. He was each of them.

Chapter 23

A NEED TO FINISH

The passing of Frank Zapata had an unexpectedly deep and darkening effect on Kilgore. From the beginning, Madeline had given Daniel access to a computer with visitor information: family members' names and dates they visited. How had he missed the fact that Frank had not had a visitor in over two years? What was worse, how had Kilgore managed to ignore the perpetual smile that was on Frank's face, and never once bothered to spend time with him?

Was the Gardens just a dumping place for the forgotten as he had heard a few staff say, referring to residents who never had visitors? It appeared to Madeline that Kilgore had lost hope, hope that what he was doing made a difference. She knew Kilgore made a difference, but she wasn't sure he realized who was the real beneficiary of his labor. *That may have explained his absence the last two days,* she thought.

When she saw him signing in at the volunteer's desk, she felt better. "Missed you these last couple of days."

"I felt I needed a little break," Kilgore replied, an almost melancholy tone in his voice.

He tried his best to hide his real motives for his absence.

Convinced that Kilgore needed to liven up his spirits, she said, "Come with me, will you? There's something I want you to see."

Orsini took Kilgore down the hall to a reception room used for special events. There was a family there, a husband and wife. The room was arranged with several long tables and chairs easily movable to suit any occasion. A large cork bulletin board was on one wall, decorated with pictures from some of the special celebrations held recently. On the opposite wall, large glass windows hinged with plantation shutters exposed the south garden with large clumps of swamp lilies.

"Daniel, let me introduce you to Peter and Marie Callahan. Frank Zapata was Marie's great-grandfather. They've come to pick up Frank's personal items."

Kilgore shook hands with each of them.

"Were you with my great-grandfather at his last birthday party?" The woman asked.

"Yes, briefly," Kilgore replied. "I really had never spent any time with him, and I apologize for that. It did seem odd at the time that your great-grandfather had such a smile on his face no matter what anyone said to him."

Marie saw the somewhat perplexed look on Kilgore's face.

"My gosh, you didn't know, did you?" Marie said, as she reached out to take hold of Kilgore's hand. "My great-grandfather was deaf, and that's why he had that perpetual smile on his face. In his later years, he was often so embarrassed when he couldn't understand what people were saying to him, he'd just smile. It was his way of saying 'I understand' or 'Thank you' to someone for spending time with him."

"That explains a lot," Kilgore said.

"We'll leave you to your business," Orsini said. "Please ask the staff if there's anything they can do to assist you."

Orsini and Kilgore walked out to the veranda. It was late afternoon. His mood reflected the ominous gray clouds forming in the sky. The absence of sunlight left the normally colorful veranda as drab and gaunt as Kilgore's face.

"Let's sit here," Orsini said, pointing to the table nearest the door. "Frank's passing has affected you, hasn't it?" she said, as she sat down next to him.

"I was thinking of the thousands of missed opportunities the family members of our residents had to show their loved ones the smallest amount of caring. I understand families move. I understand distance and finances can be an impossible stumbling block, but I also believe there's a sense of humanity in people to care."

"And you think, at least with Frank, that you didn't care? Daniel, Frank's last name was Zapata. The visiting files are sorted alphabetically. You just missed going to the last page. It could happen to anybody."

Her attempt to comfort Kilgore had little effect on him. Madeline thought how he's got to see the problem in a broader perspective. It's not getting one person to care. It's about getting many people to care. The graying of America, as it had been referred to, has created a population of elderly who can no longer expect to live with family members until their passing, nor unfortunately do families keep their aging parents with them. It is not just a problem in South Carolina, it's a national problem, or more aptly put, a national disaster.

"Daniel, we don't have enough volunteers to provide every one of our residents with daily or even weekly attention. It's a sad but true story, and I wish I could shout it out from a mountaintop for people to hear.

Kilgore had allowed his mind to drift for a moment. He seemed to hit upon something that inspired him.

"What was that you said?"

"I said, I wish I could shout out our story from a mountaintop, why?"

"I may have a way to do just that," he said, as he got to his feet. His mental load greatly lightened by the thoughts racing through his head.

"I've got to go now. I'll see you Monday."

Friday afternoon traffic from the Gardens toward Lincoln's home was horrible. He had called before he left the Gardens. He held his cell phone to his ear as he slowly pulled out of the parking lot, looking both ways.

"Hi stranger," Jane cheerfully answered.

"Hi, listen. I really need your help with the story."

"Well, I need your help as well. Me first," Jane replied.

What he needed was important to him, and he was annoyed at her insistence to go first, believing for now that it trumped everything else.

"Okay," he replied, his tone less than happy, not wanting to push this too far though, given his affection for her.

"If you're driving, please pull over so we can talk. I can't stand the thought of you being in an accident."

Her concern for him caused his anger meter to start going down. He pulled his aging compact car over to the curb. He was shaded by one of the many trees that lined the street.

"I'm stopped."

"What do you need?" Lincoln said, a broad smile spreading across her face.

"I need you to finish the manuscript this weekend. I thought I could bring my laptop over to write the corrections as you make them."

Lincoln looked at the number of pages left to edit, and she knew she needed to do a final pass of the entire manuscript. She wasn't going to get this done in a few hours. More than likely it would take them the entire weekend if they worked straight through to Monday morning. The smile on her face got broader. She liked challenges.

"Stop at Staples on the way over here. Get a couple of 245XL black ink cartridges and a ream of paper. I'll have dinner ready when you get here, and we can start when we're through eating."

Kilgore first headed home, then to Staples, then to Jane's house. Along with his laptop, Kilgore had packed a change of clothes and a shaving kit. He had caught the implication of working with Jane all through the weekend.

It was six p.m. when he arrived at Lincoln's home. Kilgore left the overnight bag in the car, lest he appear too presumptuous. His knock on the door was answered by a friendly holler from inside.

"Come on in. I'm in the kitchen." A quick check of her face in the reflection of the top double oven door gave her a B+. Kilgore had showered quickly before he left his home. The scent of Irish Spring soap and Musk by Jovan was more than a little intoxicating to Jane.

"Got everything?" she asked.

"Your request was my command, my lady," as he held up the bag from Staples.

"Good. Would you put them in the den?"

Kilgore headed down the short hallway. The overhead lights recessed into log molding, illuminated photographs of Jane and her parents from childhood to her college years. When he returned, Lincoln had opened a bottle of wine, Bogle Chardonnay. He was glad she had. He was really warming up to this wine business.

"To your story," Lincoln said, as she offered up her glass in a toast.

"Why the sense of urgency to finish your manuscript by Monday?" Jane asked Kilgore, as she finished her Cobb salad. Daniel had finished his, and he waited patiently for Jane to finish hers before continuing.

Kilgore had been markedly quiet during dinner, and Lincoln was sure it had to do with this self-imposed deadline of his. She was partially right. He finished his glass of wine while he contemplated his answer.

"One of our oldest residents, Frank Zapata, passed away a few days ago, and it affected me to the point that I took a couple of days off. Anyway, after talking with Madeleine, I knew I had to get the manuscript finished. The story has to get out, sooner than later."

"I'm not sure I follow you."

"Jane, do you know how many of the residents at Magnolia Gardens have regular visitors?"

"Not many, I'm sure."

"Exactly, my story is not just about the bond that is formed between Sloan, and the residents in Evergreen Manor. It's about a bond that should be forming with thousands of volunteers across the country in God knows how many care facilities. It's about people who deserve at least the same attention given to works of art in a museum. These care homes are really museums of living art and their residents ought not to be dismissed and forgotten."

His passion inspired Jane to tempt fate.

"You've been building the bond between Adam and Leslie, the licensing agent, right?"

"Yes, I know. I'm struggling to resolve that issue with something you told me. I'm hoping by weekend's end, I'll figure it out."

"Then let's get at it, Hemingway."

"What about these dishes?"

"They can wait till the morning."

This was uncharacteristic as her home was always neat and orderly. It was a reflection of how her mind operated. Despite all that had happened between them, he was insecure about the obvious her statement implied.

"You shouldn't have to do them alone."

His sweaty hands betrayed his anticipation of her response. He felt like an adolescent.

"I don't intend to, and I hope you brought a change of clothes. I want to get an early start on your manuscript tomorrow."

The tightening in his chest immediately subsided.

Normally, Daniel Kilgore was an early riser, but not so that next morning. The comforter covered his ears and half his head, but nothing could prevent the aroma of fresh coffee reaching his nostrils. With a final stretch of contentment, Kilgore emerged from under the comforter and glanced at the clock on the bed stand.

Damn, he muttered, as the digital dial flipped to 7:45 a.m. He jumped out of bed, grabbed a T-shirt from his bag, and headed to the kitchen. Rubbing the back of his neck, he stammered, "Sorry to have slept so late," as he walked into the kitchen. He was clearly embarrassed.

With her back to him as she poured him a cup of his favorite coffee, he could not see the glow that radiated from her eyes.

"We'll have to work on that," she said, as she tried to control the surge of twitter-pated electricity running through her body.

Except for a quick break for lunch, Lincoln and Kilgore worked nonstop till nearly sunset. She, with a red pen in one hand, would work over every line on every page of Kilgore's story. He would take each corrected page and make the noted corrections or suggestions on his computer. There were many discussions as to how to make this character or that character appear more believable or what emotions they should display. "That's it," he said, as he made the final corrections to the last page, much relieved by this knowledge and showing it.

"Not quite, Daniel," Jane corrected him. "I still need to do one final review before you send it to Sylvia."

His neck and back muscles were knotted from hours hunched over his laptop. He arched his back and rolled his head to get some relief.

"You're not going to do more tonight, are you?"

"No, I doubt your neck and back could take much more on the computer. I'll do it tomorrow."

"Thank God!" Kilgore sighed, as he feigned a miraculous recovery from his ailments.

Jane carefully stacked the pages of the manuscript for tomorrow's work.

"What do you think about dinner?" he asked, knowing full well that they both were famished.

"Yes."

"Why don't you let me make dinner tonight?"

He was a bit annoyed he had not taken this step sooner.

"Spoil me more, my Lord!" came the response, as Jane did a grandiosely exaggerated curtsy.

Chapter 24

DESTINY

ollowing dinner, at Jane's insistence. Daniel slipped into the hot tub on the back deck. For twenty minutes, he let the water from pulsating jets massage his neck and back. His relaxed body seemed to float to the surface. Lincoln appeared with a bottle of Chateau Laffitte Laujac and two glasses. It was a nice change of pace to the Chardonnay she normally served and at thirty dollars a bottle, a bit more expensive. She took an antique kerosene lamp off a shelf above the outside towel rack. She lit it, lowered the wick, and set it on the corner of the hot tub. Kilgore's body was anything but relaxed when Jane let her cabernet satin bathrobe gently fall to the deck. She climbed into the hot tub and handed him his glass.

"I like the way you finally brought Adam and Leslie together," she said, as she took a sip of wine. "But don't you think you plagiarized my mother?"

"Absolutely," Kilgore replied, nearly choking on a hastily taken sip of wine. "You can live with old memories, or you can make new ones."

"Adam decides to make new memories with Leslie?" Lincoln asked.

"It couldn't end any other way."

"What about you, Daniel? Old memories or new memories?"

He reached over and turned off the lamp. The light of a quarter-moon barely reflected through the darkness provided by a cover of wispy clouds.

B y morning, they were back to task.
"More coffee?" he asked, as Jane's editing pencil moved from line to line.

"Please."

Daniel took her cup and headed off to the kitchen. Just as he had filled her cup, he suddenly felt her arms hug him from behind.

"I thought you were bringing me coffee?", she whispered as she rested her head on his shoulders.

"Sorry. I guess I was caught thinking about the past."

Jane suspected sooner or later, Daniel would find himself in that moment when the memory of Vivian would be so alive, so vibrant, they would crash head-on into what was happening between the two of them. She was prepared for it, and she turned to face him.

"Old memories are not fitting so well with new ones, are they?"

The fingers of his right hand slowly turned the wedding band he still wore. He winced as he spoke.

"Believe me when I say this, I wanted what happened last night between us to happen and I want it to continue. Standing here looking out the window, I was overwhelmed with Vivian's memory; the way she looked, the way she smelled after taking a shower, the banter as we did the crossword puzzle from the paper. She permeates every memory of my life."

Jane reached up, placing her hands on his face. They cooled the flush he was sure made him look beet red. She kissed him gently on the lips.

"In that moment, you probably felt maybe either-or, one or the other, but you can't have both?" she asked.

Kilgore's eyes now focused on her. The shame he felt from his memories was vanishing.

"That's exactly how I felt."

"Sweetheart, you can have both. I want you to have both and I want you to remember that the next time you feel conflicted."

"The next time?"

Jane kissed him again.

"Yes, my darling, there will be a next time, maybe many next times until your heart accepts both."

"And that will happen when?"

"Trust me, it will. If I thought differently, you wouldn't be here right now," as she led him back to the bedroom.

By late that afternoon, Jane was done. She tossed her editing pencil on the coffee table.

"I may have missed something, but at least I've made your editor's job a lot easier."

"I know you have. I'm going to make her day," he said.

Mueller's phone rang three times before she answered. Kilgore put her on speaker.

"Daniel, what a surprise!" Sylvia said. "Tell me you've got good news."

"If you call a finished manuscript good news, then yes, this is good news. I'm going to FedEx you a hard copy first thing in the morning, but I'll send you an email later tonight with an attachment. You can burn up your copier this time."

Sylvia and Jane both started to laugh. It was as much out of relief of finishing the job as anything else. Then Sylvia injected.

"Daniel, as a woman, I hope you found a way to unite Adam and Leslie. Their relationship is a story in itself."

Jane spoke. "Yes, he did, Sylvia, and masterfully, if I do say so. I'm Jane Lincoln. I've been doing the editing on Daniel's manuscript."

"Nice to meet you, Jane. I hope Daniel has not been too resistant to your suggestions."

"To the contrary, Sylvia, he hasn't resisted me at all."

Kilgore rolled his eyes as if to say, "Stop."

"Sylvia, I've got a little more to do, including making copies. I'll talk to you soon."

Kilgore looked at Jane. "Very funny."

"I thought so," she replied, as she kissed him.

It took Kilgore about an hour to make the corrections from Jane's final review.

"That about does it," he said, after saving the document to his computer and the flash drive.

"Then I say hot tub and wine." She was uninhibited in her actions in a way Kilgore never could be.

"I second the motion," as his arms encircled Jane.

A wave of satisfaction soothed them both.

The following morning, the roaring thunder with its intermittent lightning bolts that lit up the skies woke them earlier than they had intended. Kilgore showered and shaved while Lincoln got breakfast ready—buttermilk pancakes with country sausage and fried eggs. If not healthy, it was certainly filling. When Kilgore appeared, Jane handed him his coffee and a kiss on the cheek.

"Mind turning on the news?" she said, as she set their plates on the table.

The weather forecast had just begun.

"This is Murray Edwards with your Charleston weather forecast for today, the twenty-first of September. As you can see from this low-pressure system swirling inward from the Atlantic, we are in for some severe lightning and thunderstorms. By late afternoon, we can expect heavy rains through Tuesday morning. The National Weather Service has posted storm warnings from Maryland south to Florida. More details at our noon news segment."

"Tower two, this is whiskey x-ray 101, requesting takeoff clearance."

"Whiskey x-ray 101, this is Tower two, you are cleared for runway four. Be advised of thunder and lightning storm alerts."

"Thanks, whiskey x-ray 101 out."

Fred Samuels eased the throttle forward as he taxied toward to runway four. In a few hours, he would be with his mother.

"Welcome, passengers from California and connecting fliers from Dallas. I'm Capt. Mike Andrews and this is Delta flight 1250 from LaGuardia to Charleston, South Carolina. We've received alerts about possible thunder and lightning storms, which means we may experience some additional turbulence, so please keep your seatbelts on until notified otherwise."

The passenger in first-class A1 had slept through the Captain's entire warning. He was tired from the flight leaving Dallas earlier that morning. All he wanted to do was get to Charleston, and he didn't care what the weather was like.

George looked at the clothing she had laid out on his bed. Hillary had done a marvelous job selecting his clothing, shirts, and trousers made of modal cotton to deal with the humidity at that time of the year, two windbreakers, lightweight walking shoes. He hadn't paid much attention to the color coordination of his clothing for the last few years. That had been one of Gilda's duties, and now one he would have to get used to doing for himself. His Hartmann Faux Alligator luggage set had been another of Hillary's ideas. He packed the clothing selections, then headed downstairs.

Finishing the last half of a toasted sesame bagel, and the remaining Florida orange juice in his glass, George headed to the front door. As he folded his blue blazer on his arm, he could see her through the window curtains, standing next to his car. Gilda Evans was the last person in the world he expected to see, especially after their last explosive meeting. George masked his trepidation with the illusion that Gilda may have wanted to leave him with a more positive last impression. He couldn't have been more wrong. He closed the front door behind him and headed down the cobblestone walkway to the driveway.

"You're the last person I expected to see after our last encounter," he said, setting his luggage down, and taking a moment to make one last assessment of his former paramour.

Hillman studied her. He was good at sizing up his adversaries, spotting that one weakness, a facial tic, raised eyebrows, or a clearing of the throat which signaled Hillman to go for the jugular and crush them.

Three crushed cigarettes on the ground at Gilda's feet indicated she had been waiting for some time. Her hair had been hastily brushed. It didn't appear she had applied any makeup. Her rumpled blouse and wrinkled slacks were signs she had probably slept in them. She was leaning against his car, not standing erect, shifting her weight to adjust her balance, suggesting several Bloody Mary's had been the breakfast fare for the day. Gilda took a last and final drag off her cigarette, flicking it toward George. The homicidal glare in her eyes should have alerted him. It didn't.

"That was childish, Gilda. Now, what the hell do you want?"

Gilda straightened herself and took a few steps toward George.

"You'll never see me again in this life, you bastard!"

"Jesus, Gilda, cut to the chase!!"

"I intend to do just that, George," she said, her words filled with malice. Yet despite her level of intoxication, she was able to execute the act, quickly and effectively.

She reached into her Louie Vuitton handbag and pulled out a chrome plated .22 caliber pistol, yhe very weapon George had insisted she carry for personal protection. The look on his face must have pleased her as she pulled the trigger three times. Gilda walked over to George's crumpled body, his chest heaving as blood gurgled out the side of his mouth. His eyes had a shocked look to them.

"See you in hell, George!"

A single shot rang out.

Jane waited in the car while Daniel ran into the FedEx store. A powerful gust of wind bent his umbrella upward, leaving him drenched by the torrential rains before he got to the door.

"No sense using that to keep dry," said the clerk, referring to Daniel's umbrella, not needing to state the obvious but doing it anyway.

"I'd say you're right. Where's your trash can?" Kilgore said, as he took a package from under his coat.

"I'll take it," said a smiling clerk, taking the umbrella from Kilgore. "What can I do for you this fine southern rainy day?"

"I need to get this to Chicago," Kilgore said, as he placed the manuscript on the counter.

The clerk placed the package on a scale and handed Kilgore an address label.

"Fill this out. Will three-day delivery be okay, considering the storm?"

"Three-day delivery will be fine," Kilgore said.

Between the flooded streets and the traffic lights out due to a power failure, what should've been a twenty-minute drive to Magnolia Gardens took over an hour. Kilgore and Jane took off their coats and shook them as best they could in the foyer. Madeline Orsini came down the hall to greet them.

"Daniel, I told you it wasn't necessary to get it to me today," Orsini said, chiding Daniel as if he were a thoughtless adolescent. "With this storm, you could have waited a few days."

"I know," Kilgore replied," it's just that I wanted it in your hands as soon as possible. After all, it was inspired by this place, you and the residents, and especially my friends."

"Then I can't be mad," Orsini said. "Why don't you and Jane have some coffee with me?"

As they walked down the main hallway, the lights began to flicker.

"Damn," muttered Orsini. "The emergency generator has been acting like that since we turned it on this morning when the power went off."

Once in her office, Orsini poured her guests coffee. She had a couple of battery operated lamps in case they lost all power.

"What do you think of our fledgling author, Jane?" Orsini said, as she handed them their coffee. The only saving grace to the institutional brew was that it was hot.

With a smile that said more than her words, Jane answered, "I'm impressed. I think you'll enjoy the story."

"If it's anything like real life, I know I will."

"I'd say Daniel makes fiction and reality seem interchangeable," added Jane.

Daniel began to fidget in his chair, hoping Jane would stop before she revealed something embarrassing, fictional or otherwise. Her lack of inhibition would take some time for him to get used to.

"I can't wait to read it," Orsini said, as she tapped the manuscript on her desk.

A thunderous roar erupted in the sky, followed by three or four lightning flashes.

"I don't think we'll have much programming today," Orsini said, as she strained her neck to look out the window.

"We've got to be on our way, Madeline," Kilgore said. "This surprise storm caught us a little shorthanded of supplies, like lamps, batteries, and water."

"At least the rain has let up a little. You better get going now," Madeleine said.

Chapter 25

NEW BEGINNINGS

Several hours later, Kilgore and Jane pulled into her driveway. Daniel parked his Honda Civic alongside Jane's Jeep. Lincoln's two-car garage was big enough for a compact and a subcompact, if you were lucky, so the covered breezeway to the house afforded additional protective parking. It had occurred to Kilgore a garage expansion was on the horizon. With the supplies put away, Kilgore and Jane settled on the living room couch.

"Do you think your friends at the Gardens will wind up like the characters in your story?" Jane asked.

"Well, that's the idea. Their families become concerned after hearing how one of the residents was murdered and they started visiting them again."

"I'd like to think something will spark that interest in them," Jane replied.

Jane snuggled a little closer. Kilgore reached for the remote control and turned on the TV. It was set on the local news station. Flames rose skyward, and black smoke filled the sky behind a reporter who was standing on the side of a highway.

"Yes, Harry, this is indeed a tragic scene here today. I'm standing on the side of Interstate 7 just north of the Charleston airport. According to authorities, a Delta commuter flight from LaGuardia was descending through extremely heavy turbulence and lightning when it suddenly plunged thousands of feet and crashed. And Harry, to make this tragedy even more heart wrenching, a twin-engine Beech Baron aircraft from MacDill Air Force Base was struck by the falling Delta commuter flight. Authorities are reporting there are no survivors. The names of the passengers are being withheld until family notifications can be made. This is Michelle Reed for KTVR Channel 5 news."

The first letter Madeline Orsini received arrived about a month after the worst air tragedy in South Carolina history. Forty-three people died in the disaster that day. The letter was from Brenda Samuels, Dolores Samuels' daughter-in-law. According to the letter, Fred Samuels, Dolores' son, was on his way to see his mother when his flight was struck by lightning, causing it to lose power and crash. *Heartbreaking,* Orsini thought, *after finally deciding to see his mother, this happens.*

Brenda Samuels went on to explain she would be taking care of the expenses of Dolores's care until Fred's estate was settled, at which time a trust would be set up for all future expenses. Orsini made a copy of the letter for the accounting office and placed the original in Dolores Samuels' file.

She thought no more of the tragedy until a second letter arrived less than two weeks later. It was from Samantha Cotton, Sandra Cotton's granddaughter. Samantha wrote that her father had been killed in a plane crash while on his way to visit his mother. His small twin-engine plane was struck by a commercial flight that had lost power for some reason. The young girl went on to explain about the unsettled divorce of her parents but promised Orsini she would take care of her grandmother's affairs. She and her soon-to-be husband were enrolling at The College of Charleston. *Quite a load for a young college junior,* Orsini thought.

One resident's loved one killed in a plane crash might be chalked up to "bad things happen to good people." But when two residents' loved ones die in the same crash, well, maybe just a bizarre coincidence. The letter from Leo Ainsworth about George Hillman's death at the hands of a jilted lover completed the trifecta. It caused Orsini to question God's plan, if in fact, God had a plan. Three men on their way to visit loved ones at Magnolia Gardens all die on the same day. *Whose plan could that possibly be?*

Relying on her women's intuition, Orsini called Jane Lincoln's number.

"Hello Madeline," Jane said, as she recognized Orsini's name on caller ID.

"Jane, I'm sorry to bother you at home, but I need to talk with Daniel, and I thought he might be there."

"You thought right. Just a minute," Jane replied.

Orsini smiled as she heard Jane callout, "Honey, it's for you. It's Madeline."

"Madeline, this is Daniel. What can I do for you?" He was surprised that she would call him there.

For the next several minutes, all Jane heard was, "Are you serious?". "What are the odds?". "It can't be."

When Lincoln heard Daniel say, "What's to become of Sandra, Mary, and Dolores?" Her patience gave out. "Daniel, what's going on?"

"Madeline, let me call you later."

Kilgore looked at Lincoln. He shook his head in utter disbelief.

"Sandra Cotton's son, Jim, and Dolores Samuels' son, Fred, were killed when those two planes crashed about six weeks ago and in an even weirder twist of fate, George Hillman was murdered by his estranged girlfriend in California the same day as the plane crash."

"My God, Daniel!" Jane gasped. "Three strangers with a common mission meet their fate on the same day in the same accident. It's the theme from "The Bridge over San Luis Rey."

Kilgore eased himself into a chair. Jane sat next to him.

It's the plan for the universe according to Thornton Wilder."

"I don't understand, Jane. What possible purpose, accidental or otherwise, could possibly be served by this?"

"I may have an answer to that. Wait here."

When she returned, she had a copy of Thornton Wilder's, "The Bridge over San Luis Rey."

The book had been read so many times lines ran down the middle of the spine of the book. Some pages had corners missing because they had been dogeared so often. Lincoln slowly thumbed through the pages.

"Here it is," she said.

"Here what is?"

"The answer to your question, Daniel. The Bridge over San Luis Rey is my favorite novel of all time. I can't tell you how many times I've read it. Listen to this, Daniel. It's a quote from the book."

> If there were any plan in the universe at all, if there were any patterns in human life, surely it could be discovered mysteriously late in these lives so suddenly cut off. Either we live by accident and die by accident, or we live by plan and die by plan.

She closed the book.

"Wilder's saying life and death can be looked at as random events or things that serve a purpose. The purpose of those living at Magnolia Gardens is that someone should care. That's the theme of your book, to impassion readers to care about those forgotten souls warehoused in care facilities, right? That their lives matter?"

Kilgore nodded yes.

"I believe with all my heart this story will inflame that same latent passion in others."

Madeline Orsini's article in the quarterly AARP (American Association of Retired People) magazine about the bizarre and tragic deaths of men coming to visit loved ones at Magnolia Gardens was the match that started the fire. Winds flamed that fire when the editor of the Charleston Times, Helen Stone, read it. She assigned a reporter to do an in-depth article about Magnolia Gardens. This was a human-interest story of the first magnitude!

For the past two years, Courtney Lee had begged her editor to give her a story with real meat to it, not the feel-good Disney type where a lost dog is reunited with its owner. She hadn't gotten a Master's in Journalism from the University of Missouri for nothing. After reading the article about the tragic plane crash given to her by her editor, Lee knew she got her wish. To research her new assignment, Lee called Madeline Orsini and asked if she could interview the staff at Magnolia Gardens. Lee approached the woman at the counter.

"My name is Courtney Lee. I have an appointment to speak with Ms. Orsini."

"She's expecting you. Please follow me," the receptionist said, as she led the young reporter down the hallway to Orsini's office.

"Courtney, it's so nice to meet you," Orsini said. "Please, have a seat."

"The pleasure is all mine," Lee replied, as she took a seat at the conference table in Orsini's office. If she wasn't impressed by the custom-made red maple desk and conference table, Lee was certainly taken by the numerous degrees and certifications that adorned the walls of Orsini's office. Her Bachelor's degree from Old Dominion, Master's and Ph.D. from the University of Georgia, plus a number of certifications from the American Association of Geriatric Medicine were indicators of both her educational and professional expertise.

"So, you want to do an article on Magnolia Gardens?" Orsini asked.

"My editor was really moved by your article in the last AARP magazine. She thinks our readers would be equally moved by the story behind that article. You know, the whole tragic irony sort of thing. Do you mind?" laying a small tape recorder on the table. It was clear she was more excited by the prospect of a good story than buying into the emotion of the events.

Orsini said, "Not at all. I'm not much for tragic irony. The person you should really talk to is our director of volunteer services. Come with me."

Lee picked up her small tape recorder and followed Orsini down the hallway to a door with a brass plate hanging in the middle of it reading, "Director of Volunteer Services." She knocked on the door.

"Come in," a voice from inside the office said.

Orsini opened the door.

"Daniel, there's someone I want you to meet. This is Courtney Lee from the Charleston Times. She's doing an article on Magnolia Gardens for her paper. I think you'll be able to help. I'll leave her to you."

"Please have a seat," Kilgore said, offering Lee a chair.

His office was almost austere compared to that of Orsini's. No custom-made furniture, no degrees or certifications on the walls, just a large, simply made table of Magnolia wood. Several small photographs of Kilgore and residents of the Gardens on the table were the only indicators of any relationships in his life.

"Would you mind if I record our conversation? It helps with my recall."

"Not at all. I suppose accuracy is important in your line of work," Kilgore responded.

Lee smiled, as she took out a pad and pen from her purse to jot down comments on the salient points. She laid her tape recorder on the table.

"Where do you want me to start?" he asked.

"The article by Madeline in the AARP quarterly has drawn a lot of interest in assisted living facilities. Let's start with that and how you were involved?"

For the next hour, without interruption, Lee listened to Kilgore's story of the victims of the plane crash and their relationship to three residents. Thinking there was no harm now, he included the family dynamics as he knew them. He mentioned the staff he worked with and of their devotion to providing the residents some semblance of human dignity. He talked about Mary, Sandra, and Dolores and his relationship with each, a relationship that was both real and theatrical depending on who the women thought Kilgore was at any given time. Her pen moved quickly with her own special form of shorthand when there was something said that she wanted to go back to later.

The interview was going much easier than he expected until Lee asked, "How did you initially come to be here at Magnolia Gardens?"

"May I get you something to drink?" Kilgore asked, as he opened a small refrigerator on a corner table and took out a bottle of water. He was buying time.

"No thank you."

Kilgore twisted off the cap and took a drink. The coolness of the water eased the tightness in his throat caused by Lee's question. Kilgore saw something in the young woman's eyes that convinced him she had a legitimate interest in the Gardens, its residents, and now him. Rather than a bare-bones story, Kilgore took the reporter on an epic emotional story, the likes of which Lee had never heard. He began with the accident that paralyzed his wife and his efforts to reconnect the neuro-pathways to old memories, how he was introduced to Jane Lincoln and her involvement helping Kilgore's wife. Finally, he talked of his relationship with Lincoln, first as someone he was in love with and secondly as his editor. Lee had not noticed the flashing red light on her recorder indicating the tape was full. How could she? She was drawn to the emotional depths of what Kilgore told her. Her tape recorder could capture words, but Lee was captivated by the expression on Kilgore's face, of love lost and love discovered.

"How much room does your tape recorder have to record?" he said, as he noticed the flashing red light.

The question startled Lee, who had become transfixed with Kilgore's story. Embarrassed at her lack of attention to the light, Lee clumsily responded, "Sorry, your story was just more than I expected."

Realizing she had what she had come for, Lee placed her recorder, pen, and pad back in her purse. She stood up and placed the strap of the black leather bag over her shoulder.

"I think I'm done for now, Mr. Kilgore, but I'll be back."

"I look forward to that," Kilgore said. His answer surprised him.

Once outside and in her car, Lee took out her cell phone. Great, she thought, when she heard her editor's voice.

"Helen, this is Courtney. Listen, I've got a great idea. I want this to be a three-part in-depth series on Magnolia Gardens. Not just the residents and the circumstances that brought them here, but about the staff and why they chose to work there, and beyond that, there are the volunteers. They get no money for what they do, hardly any recognition, at least publicly. They deserve to have their story told as well."

Chapter 26

NINE MONTHS LATER IN THE SPRING

Orsini watched from her office window as workers erected two large white tents on the lawns adjacent to the veranda. Each tent was approximately twenty feet wide and forty feet long. Once the guide ropes were secured to stakes which had been driven into the ground, the workers laid out connecting sections of wooden flooring. This would accommodate the movement of those residents using walkers or in wheelchairs. Members of her staff busied themselves wrapping red, white and blue strips of crêpe paper around the railing surrounding the veranda. Others strung long lines of tiny blinking lights along the edge of the pergola. Fresh bouquets of spring flowers had been set on every table along with pitchers of ice water and iced tea. The spring temperature barely reached seventy-five degrees, and the slightest breeze kept everyone more than comfortable. It was hard for Orsini to imagine the idea of this spring festivity came from one of her volunteers, though "volunteer" hardly described the workload assumed by the young college junior.

Even before they reached the left turn off Hickory Lane onto Magnolia Drive, Daniel and Jane could see signs of the impending celebration. Street parking on Hickory Lane was nonexistent. A few entrepreneurial neighbors had signs on their lawns reading, "Parking $5."

"Would you have ever expected this?" Jane said, as she watched lines of people walking up the street to Magnolia way.

"Not in my lifetime," Daniel responded, clearly pleased with what he saw. Turning left onto the driveway marked Magnolia Way, Daniel and Jane were greeted by a volunteer asking if they were staff or visitors.

"Staff," Daniel replied.

The young volunteer traffic director pointed up the driveway to the right. Orsini had the foresight to designate all available staff parking to visitors. As Daniel and Jane moved slowly up the quarter-mile long driveway lined on both sides with red, white and blue balloons, Daniel saw a large area lined with yellow tape and marked, "Staff parking."

As they got out of their car, Jane noticed Madeline waving anxiously to them from the red brick landing in front of the entrance. Next to her was Courtney Lee from the Charleston Times and a photographer. The photographer snapped several pictures, then he and Courtney went inside.

"I think she's glad we're finally here," McCain said.

"I told her a week ago everything was going to be fine, but Madeline was never one to leave anything to chance."

Daniel took Jane's arm as they headed across the driveway to Madeline. The fragrance from every conceivable springtime blossom filled the air, from the sweetness of blossoming honeysuckle vines to the perfume-like odor of the Magnolia trees. Daniel could not help but admire how Jane looked. Her black four-inch heels brought her almost eye to eye with Daniel. A pair of white tapered pants with a peach polyester blouse outlined in suitable Southern good taste Jane's figure. Daniel's tan slacks and a white silk shirt paired beautifully with Jane's attire. They made a handsome couple.

"You made it," said an obviously relieved Orsini.

"You thought we wouldn't?" grinned Daniel.

"Put these on. There's something I want to show you."

Madeline handed them clear plastic nametags with a safety pin backing. Jane did the honors. A steady stream of visitors made their way up to the entrance. Madeline graciously greeted each and directed them down the hallway to the receptionist desk. Fortunately, the new charge nurse came out to help.

"Madeline, you need to be inside. I'll take care of this," the nurse said.

Kay McGinnis had been hired by Madeline back in January. McGinnis brought a wealth of nursing experience with her. With almost ten years in providing home care services, she was a natural with the residents. McGinnis also had made an immediate connection with the younger staff, and why not? Her short spiked blonde hair with streaks of purple and green, several tattoos and numerous body piercings screamed "wild child of the 70s."

"Thanks, Kay."

Together, Orsini, Daniel, and Jane worked their way down the crowded hallway to the receptionist desk. There was a spirit of gaiety and merriment in the air. The visitors had truly gotten into the spirit of the event. Colorful light cotton dresses brightened the atmosphere. Numerous women wore wide-brimmed hats like those worn at Ascot Downs in England. In true Southern style, Magnolia Blossom corsages were the order of the day. Brenda Samuels manned a table near the counter with another volunteer, Jerry Gritz. When the estate of her brother-in-law Fred was finally settled, Brenda moved to Charleston to look after her mother-in-law Dolores. There was nothing holding her in Dallas anymore and looking after Dolores, in some small way, kept the memory of her husband, Mitchell, and his brother, Fred, more alive.

Jerry Gritz's mother had been a resident at Magnolia Gardens for almost two years. She was one of the lucky residents, as Jerry visited her religiously every Friday. He considered himself somewhat of a history buff and had volunteered to write a history of Magnolia Gardens and all its current residents for the celebration. Madeline was able to give him some antidotal information on each resident, such as date and place of birth, names of children and grandchildren, hobbies, and any work history. Gritz had skillfully woven all the information into an artfully designed brochure for staff to use as a reference and for families as a souvenir.

"Quite the day, isn't it!" said a smiling Brenda, as she meticulously entered each visitor's name and the resident they were seeing into a logbook.

"I'm absolutely stunned," answered Daniel.

"May I?" asked Jane, pointing to one of Jerry's brochures.

"Please, it would be my pleasure, Jane," answered Gritz.

"Would you mind signing it, Jerry?"

Blushing as if he were some fifteen-year-old after getting his first kiss, Gritz scribbled his name on the inside cover.

Daniel and Jane then followed Madeleine to her office. Once inside, Madeleine took out a bottle of wine from the small refrigerator near her conference table. She set it on the table next to a tray with several wine glasses and a smaller array of different cheeses and crackers.

"Daniel?" Madeline asked, handing him a wine opener.

An obedient Kilgore took the wine opener and opened the bottle of chilled Bogle Chardonnay.

"This is absolutely beyond anything I could have imagined," sighed Jane in wonderment as she stood in front of the window in Madeleine's office that looked out over the veranda and surrounding grounds.

Under the direction of a Boy Scout leader, a group of a dozen Boy Scouts were assisting families getting their loved ones to their tables. The female residents were dressed to the nines with hairstyles done just so, in outdated dresses still thought to be in style, with the obligatory beaded necklaces. Many of the male residents were dressed in solid colored pants, with wide belts and forty-year-old dress shirts. Nearly twenty young people with nametags reading, "Foster Grandchild," were also assisting in bringing out residents to their families. Out of sight, but not out of smelling range, a group of Marine Corps reservists from C Company, Fourth Landing Support Battalion, were barbecuing an array of southern collectibles, such as ribs, chicken, hamburgers, and hotdogs for those in attendance. If all this wasn't enough, a small Dixieland

Quartet, courtesy of Belle's Inferno, had been set up under a spreading Magnolia tree. Their nostalgic melodies could not help but cause hands to clap and feet to tap. Jane noticed a young woman holding onto the handles of a wheelchair. She was turning the wheelchair left and right in beat to the music and the gleeful delight of the resident in the chair.

Not recognizing the girl from behind, Jane asked, "Who's that young girl?", pointing to the young woman turning the wheelchair in time to the music.

Madeline walked over to the window. A huge smile formed on her face.

"That is the person responsible for all this and who will probably have my job someday. Let me get her."

Orsini walked across the crowded veranda. Daniel walked over to stand next to Jane.

"You're in for quite a surprise."

Jane looked at him. "More surprised than getting this?" As she flashed the three-carat diamond ring Daniel had given her on New Year's Eve.

Moments later, the door to Orsini's office opened, and Madeline walked in with the young woman and Courtney Lee from the Times.

"You look so young," Jane commented. "All this is because of you?"

The young woman blushed at the unexpected but deserved adulation. Samantha Cotton, now Samantha Callahan, had inherited her mother Carrie's good looks; same dark hair, piercing brown eyes, and a number ten figure. Fortunately, she also inherited her grandmother Sandra's heart.

"It wasn't all just me, Jane. A lot of people made this volunteer appreciation day possible."

"That may be true, young lady, but the lion's share of the credit goes to you," interrupted Madeline. "And let me add this, if the joys in our residents' eyes and the smiles on their faces today could be measured in decibels, the roar would be heard all the way across town."

From the smiles on Daniel and Madeline's face, Jane knew there was more to the story.

"Would anyone care to explain?"

"Allow me," Daniel said as he walked over to Samantha, putting his arm around her shoulder.

"When Samantha and her husband, Mike, moved to Charleston to attend The College of Charleston, Samantha came regularly to see her grandmother, Sandra Cotton. In time, she adopted Mary Hillman as well. We would routinely talk about the residents and the importance the visitors played in maintaining positive mental health and possibly delaying the inevitable slide into the retrievable forgotten past. She first came to me with the idea of starting a "Foster Grandchild" program at the College of Charleston. Students who are interested had to commit to a once a month visit with an assigned resident. There was no specific length to the visit, only that the visitor keep the resident engaged in some activity, if only conversation. Within a few months, the program took off like wildfire. We have twenty young people in the foster grandchild program now.

"And the Boy Scouts?" Jane asked.

"Samantha, again. Her brother, William, had been a Boy Scout, so Samantha made a presentation to the greater Charleston Boy Scouts of America Council to develop, as part of their Eagle Scout program, involvement with a designated resident. As you can tell, several chapters have participants here today. Oh, and before you ask, those young Marines doing the barbecuing are from Samantha's husband, Mike's, reserve unit. He's the sergeant directing them."

"There seemed to be even more young people out there," questioned Jane.

"Oh, that's Daniel's doing," Samantha chuckled.

"Now this I have to hear," Jane laughed, as if she were about to hear the secret recipe to Colonel Sanders Kentucky Fried Chicken.

"My professor in my English creative writing class gave us a book for required reading. He uses it in all his classes. Anyway, he said to pay attention to the flow of descriptive language and the depth of character development. It was your book, Daniel, "Diaphanous Minds." When I told my classmates I knew the author, well, the rest is history."

"If he referred to the flow of descriptive language and depth of character development, we can tell you the name of your professor," smiled Madeline and Jane together. In unison, the two women comically chanted, "He, with the vocabulary of William F. Buckley, the one and only Professor Robert Gordon."

When their laughter subsided, Madeline said, "Doctor Gordon was a colleague of ours when we were on the faculty at The College of Charleston."

Retrieving two more wine glasses from her cabinet, Madeline said, "First, let me say this. Courtney, your series of articles in the Times about Magnolia Gardens brought us a million dollars' worth of publicity. Samantha, what could I possibly say about the impact you've had, not only on your grandmother and Mary Hillman, but all the other residents who had received your love and tenderness. And lastly, Daniel; you came here for a very personal reason, a quest to learn from our residents to better help your wife. Though that did not work out as expected, you met Jane, and no words can describe what you two found with each other. That being said, let me make a toast."

The five held out their glasses while Daniel's arm moved smoothly around Jane's waist.

"On behalf of the many who have been forgotten for so long, from the bottom of my heart, thank you for being their friend."

Daniel's arm tightened around Jane's waist. "Time to make new memories, for them and us," he whispered.

"Absolutely."

Dear Reader,

Stay tuned for the enthralling sequel to "Forgotten Flowers."

"Magnolia Gardens will become the Alpha/Omega for Madeline Orsini in the pursuit of an impossible dream after an unspeakable tragedy kept secret for over twenty-five years.

But for the fateful decision to complete the Alpha/Omega for Daniel and Jane Kilgore, Madeline Orsini's dream would never have come true."

—Michael J. Sullivan

The Author

Michael Sullivan resides with his wife, Ginny, in Sonora, California. He is a retired Associate Warden from the California Department of Corrections and Rehabilitation. He began writing fiction in 2012 and soon found himself in a literary evolution to become a better writer. As a member of the Sonora's Writers Group, he has self-published seven books which are all available on Amazon.com. He can be contacted via the publisher, Publish Authority, via www.PublishAuthority.com.

A Note of Thanks

PublishAuthority.com

Thank you for reading

If you enjoyed *Forgotten Flowers*, we invite you to review it online and encourage your friends and family to read it as well.

CPSIA information can be obtained
at www.ICGtesting.com
Printed in the USA
FSHW012155140621
82194FS

9 780996 475594